RYAN MICHELE
CONQUERING
VIPERS CREED MC #2

Conquering (Vipers Creed MC#2)
©Ryan Michele 2016

Copyright ©Ryan Michele 2016

Editing by C&D Editing
Proofreading by Silla Webb at Masque of the Red Pen (http://tinyurl.com/AlphaQueensBookObsessionAS)
Formatting by Pink Ink Designs (http://www.pinkinkdesigns.com/)
Cover Design by Pink Ink Designs (http://www.pinkinkdesigns.com/)
Photography by Shauna Kruse at Kruse Images and Photography (https://www.facebook.com/KIPmodelsandboudoir/)
Model: Matthew Hosea (https://www.facebook.com/MatthewHoseaInkedModel/?fref=ts)

This is a work of fiction. All names, characters, places and events portrayed in this book either are from the authors' imaginations or are used fictitiously. Any similarity to real persons, living or dead, establishments, events, or location is purely coincidental and not intended by the authors. Please do not take offense to the content as it is *fiction*.

Trademarks: This book identifies product names and services known to be trademarks, registered trademarks, or service marks of their respective holders. The authors acknowledge the trademarked status in this work of fiction. The publication and use of these trademarks is not authorized, associated with, or sponsored by the trademark owners.

This book contains mature content not suitable for readers under the age of 18. This book contains content with strong language, violence, and sexual situations. All parties portrayed in sexual situations are over the age of 18.

This is not meant to be a true or exact depiction of a motorcycle club. Rather, it is a work of fiction meant to entertain.

CONQUERING

ONE

CHELSEA

"**C**HELSEA, ORDER UP," CHARLIE CALLED from the back, slapping a plate of grub up on the window ledge of the diner.

I shook off my drowsiness, plastering on a smile and grabbing the food, never feeling the heat from the plate due to the calluses on my hands. They were rock hard, shielding my skin against any amount of heat.

At twenty-nine, I'd worked at Charlie's Diner for thirteen years. Thirteen years of serving people with mediocre tips that had given me feet that, by the end of the night, ached so badly nothing, including soaking them in warm water, helped soothe anymore. Twelve hours a day, five to seven days a week would do that to any woman.

As my grams used to say, "*Can't get anywhere in this world if you don't work hard.*" So, work hard I did, always.

I wasn't complaining. I loved Charlie, the owner. He had taken me under his wing when I was a pitiful sixteen-year-old, and to this day was the only man in my life who had yet to let me down.

I had clean clothes on my back, food in my belly, and a place to crash. I had my sister, my grams, and my mother. What more could a woman ask for? Me, I wasn't asking for anything. I was happy where my life was going. I had a plan. It wasn't some grand extravagant one, but I had it and clung to it because everyone needed to have goals in their lives. Those could be small or large, but people needed something to reach for, work for, and take a hold of. Of course, this all came from my grams, too, but being a really smart woman, I took everything she'd said to heart.

I lived on the cheap and saved as much of my meager earnings as possible. I had a decent savings, but that did not stop me from working at every available opportunity. A dollar was a dollar, and no one knew how far a buck could take you.

My ultimate goal was to own my own home. The American dream, some might say. For me, it was about having my own, doing my own, and it being my way. Hard work and sacrifice would eventually get me there.

Paying rent every month on a beat to hell trailer when I could be making payments on something that would be mine didn't sit right with me. Unfortunately, my credit was shot to hell by a no-good ass of a father.

I shivered with anger at the thought of him and tried shaking it out, but it was impossible when it came to that man.

When I was a teen, he decided to use me for a couple of credit cards. Okay, it was seven of them. No joke. He really did, to the tune of one hundred seventy-nine thousand dollars and forty-seven cents. He swiped and signed for debts he never intended to repay, all of it striking against my credit.

I, of course, did not find this out until I was nineteen and was denied a credit card I had signed up for, which I'd thought was unusual yet passed it off as being young. Grams being Grams, however, immediately set me on a path to checking into it.

When information came back leading to my father, I was crushed. We hadn't been exceptionally close, but he was my dad, the man who was supposed to have my back. He should have protected me, not have done this to me. At least, that was what I had thought a father should do. I'd expected better of him, but I should have known.

Prosecuting my father for the theft still weighed heavily on me to this day. I only had two choices, though: one, not say anything and pay back all the money stolen, or two, I could turn my father in, which had been the only way I could get it expunged from my record and have the debt extinguished. I hated doing it, but really, the choice was made the moment he'd taken out the cards in my name. I couldn't live with that huge weight on my shoulders. I had to bear it for a while when the courts had to do their thing: having creditors call me, looking for their money. And that was enough.

It took me some time, but the courts deemed him guilty, and my credit fell back in line. Thanks to a wise banker, I'd gotten a secured credit card with the little savings I had. Then, like clockwork, I made sure to pay it off.

Never missing a bill, I now had a very decent score to the point that if I saved enough for a down payment, a bank might take a chance on me. And I was almost there. I could almost taste my victory. It was another step in the right direction. "*Eye on the prize, always,*" Grams would say, and my eye was firmly set on loan equals home.

Unfortunately, that had been the end of my relationship with my father. I'd received a few not so nice calls from jail and a very nasty letter that I'd burned, never wanting to read it again. The little girl inside me, though, still yearned for a father, even if mine happened to be a douche.

After everything I'd been through, I took the lesson my father taught me the hard way and kept my name, social security number, and other personal information close to heart. I protected it with everything I had, kept an eye on it, and did routine checks to make sure no credit cards or loans were taken out under my name. Luckily, that hadn't happened beyond the initial time, but I always had that fear it would.

Life was looking up, allowing me to tackle it and reach my goal.

As I walked across the black and white tiled floor of the diner, old man Darren looked up, a wide smile on his wrinkled face. The man had been coming in for years, and we had developed a friendly relationship.

"There's my girl," he cried out, pushing his coffee cup off to the side as I slid his food onto the table, the porcelain hitting the Formica table with a scratching sound. It was a sound I'd come to find comforting over time, though others said it hurt their ears.

"It's nice and hot," I told him, brushing my hands on my apron, feeling like something was on them, which was a job hazard. "Anything else I can get ya?"

He beamed up at me. "That smile of yours sure makes an old man's day," he remarked. Even though he'd told me that hundreds of times over the years, I felt the same heat creep into my cheeks.

"You make mine by coming in here," I responded, trying to shake off the blush. "You good?"

"Some more coffee when you have a chance, sweetie?"

"Of course." I spun on my heel, grabbed the coffee pot, and then topped him off.

The other tables in my section seemed good, so I began my prep for the next shift. I checked and filled the condiments, along with taking two more orders, delivering them, getting more drinks, and cashing out my tables.

Everything at Charlie's was second nature to me, reminding me a lot of home. It did not slip past me that I thought of my job as home, but when you spent so much time in one place, it happened. I counted myself lucky to have this constant in my life.

Charlie's was the hot spot in Dyersburg, Tennessee except for Tuesday through Thursday—those were blah. Hence, why tonight was blah, but a girl could use that every now and then. A rest from the go, go, go, even if it was almost a waste of time because the tips were scarce.

Charlie was into cars and bikes, so the entire place was decorated as such. His old plates off his cars and even handlebars from an old bike hung on the walls. I didn't think some of the stuff actually came from him. Rather, he bought it to go with the theme. Regardless, the walls were covered in a rustic automobile motif, and I loved it.

With the night ticking away at a little past ten, Mitzi and I were the only ones working the floor. I'd worked with Mitzi for a couple of years. Our relationship was purely work-related since a lot of what I'd learned about Mitzi had turned out to be fake. I didn't do fake; hated it. Therefore, working relationship only.

The bell above the door chimed, and instinctively I looked up from wiping down ketchup bottles. My stomach clenched.

Plastering on my wide smile, I greeted them. "Welcome, boys. Go ahead and have a seat anywhere you'd like."

The air in the diner changed—it always did when they came in, which was regularly. The space felt smaller, closed in by their presence alone. They commanded the room just from stepping over the threshold. The farther they stepped in, their boots hitting the tile, the denser the air became.

For most people, waiting on a table full of four large men who were members of an exclusive motorcycle club would come off as a bit intimidating, but they tipped well. As a result, once they sat, I was thankful they were in my section.

When the Vipers Creed MC rode in, my pockets usually went from decent to way off the charts. I'd gladly let my knees tremble for the next hour to have that extra padding in my pocket. Not to mention, they weren't hard on the eyes, either.

I steeled my spine, grabbed my order pad and pen, then strode over to the table.

Since I tended to keep my section steady with the regulars, it was no surprise to find Mitzi giving me the stink eye as I made my way to their table. She hid it quickly, flying under the radar with her perfect smile. She was good at that.

Four men sat at a six-person, speckled, white rectangular table. Each man took a post on the farthest corner. One was a man named Bosco who'd been coming here since I had started and knew nothing about how to wait tables. I even spilled a Coke on him once. I would have thought he'd blow up at me, but he laughed it off, and he'd been kind to me ever since. He had dark hair with some white scattered through it. His beard and mustache were so burly they covered up his mouth almost completely.

Across from him was a man I knew as Ben back in school, but now he went by the name Boner. I mean, really? What kind of name was that? Being a senior, he'd had no idea who my freshman self was, but that was expected considering I didn't socialize much. He had light brown hair that normally was tousled on top like he'd run his fingers through it a million times, but today, he had a dark stocking cap on, covering his locks. He was handsome yet rough looking.

Next to him, one seat over, was a man they called Dawg. Yes, not Dog, but Dawg. My assumption was he played the field a lot. He had been several years older than me in school; therefore, he was unknown to me. He had dark brown hair that curved around his ears. A striking man who turned many a woman's head.

Across from him was Wes, now known in our town as Stiff. With him being three years older than me, we hadn't associated in school, either. That wasn't to say my eyes weren't wide open to him, because they had been ... and still were. Then, he'd had the lightest blond hair imaginable, almost white. Currently, he had nothing. Completely, utterly bald, but it wasn't the freaky bald you saw sometimes on men. No, this worked for him in a major way. Sexy, check. Hot, check. His beard was lightly colored and trimmed. Even as kids, Stiff's eyes were magnetic, and some things never changed. They weren't blue nor green. No, they were both, creating a swirling ocean inside them, sucking you into their depths.

Truth be told, the men were each their own brand of sexy, but not men a person should fuck around with. Stories had been told over the years about the Vipers Creed—hell, Charlie had some doozies. I didn't need any of that in my life. I liked simple, and judging from the stories, they were anything but.

I would be happy to take their tip money, though.

A smile went a long way, so I put it in place as I reached their table.

"Hey, boys. What can I get ya?" I asked, standing behind the empty chair between Bosco and Dawg.

All conversation halted and their eyes turned to me.

My insides shrank a bit from the combination of their penetrative stares, but no way would I show that on the outside. Nope, I was Chelsea Anne Miller, and no matter what was on the inside, it would never show.

"Little Chelsea, how are ya doin'?" Bosco asked.

He *would* consider me little. I was five-feet-six, but anyone next to Bosco would be considered small. Nevertheless, I gave him a genuine smile. I mean, come on! If a man like him forgave you for dumping a pop down his shirt, it was a must.

"I'm good. Hanging in there."

"Good. Can I get a burger with the works, onion rings, and a Coke?"

I wrote all of this down in my usual short script, nodding then turning my attention back to the table.

"Who's next?" I asked, switching my focus between the guys, not allowing myself to linger on Stiff.

"I'll have the tenderloin with onions, fries, and a Dr. Pepper," Dawg answered, and I scribbled then looked up expectantly.

"How long have you worked here?" Boner asked, shocking me a bit. We hadn't ever really conversed casually, but like everything else that life threw at me, I rolled with it.

"Thirteen years," I replied then waited for him to tell me what he wanted. He didn't.

"And you still fill out that uniform so damn well." Boner whistled low.

I felt it coming, and then bam! Cue blushing cheeks. I had never been one to accept compliments easily. I felt a flutter, but it landed more on the shy side, not the hot and wet.

Charlie didn't make us wear a uniform, really. We wore black pants, comfortable shoes, and a white button-down shirt—long for the winter, short in the summer. To me, what I had on was unflattering as all get out, but to each their own.

"Thanks," I responded. "What do you wanna eat?"

Boner chuckled. "I get it, not interested. It was worth a shot."

I kept quiet. Really, though? Not interested? While my interest in Boner was slim, that didn't mean I was dead. I could see how attractive each of them were in their own right. Still, the thought of him even wondering if I was interested was strange.

"I want one of those hamburger horseshoes with a Coke."

"Got it." My eyes lifted to Stiff, and the air left my lungs in a whoosh.

Damn, those eyes were like laser beams cutting into me, swirling like a tornado, sucking me down. My heart picked up, thumping like a jackhammer, and it took everything in my power to stop my hands from trembling. While I might not be interested in Boner, Stiff, well, he just did something to me; had for as long as I could remember.

"What can I get ya?" I asked, hoping to God my voice wouldn't give my rising temperature away.

"You on the menu?" he asked calmly.

I felt the blush slink back but ignored it. Stiff had always been a flirt—a huge flirt to anything in a skirt, that is. Even me. I knew he was just playing around, but over the years, there had been times I'd hoped he wasn't. It was stupid and immature, not to mention utterly ridiculous. As my dad used to say, *"You'll never be anything. No man will ever want you."*

Some things, no matter how hard you tried, you never got over them. This was one. Those words were like brands on my soul, never leaving.

Instead of feeling the embarrassment or heat of the hot man flirting with me, I gave it back to him. As my grams said, *"You have two choices: run away like an afraid, little rabbit or buck up, steel your spine, and hold your head up high."* Me, I held my head high. She also said, *"Fake it till ya make it."* I lived by that motto every day. This situation was no different. My father might have branded me, but that was on the inside. No one could see it if I didn't show them, which would never happen, so I faked it.

Jutting out my hip and putting my hand there, I said, "Nah, Sugar, but thanks for askin'." I gave him a playful wink that took every bit of my strength. "What can I get ya?" I asked, wishing I had some gum in my mouth, as it seemed to taste like cotton.

He scanned my body, the heat from his gaze causing my panties to dampen, something that hadn't happened in a very long time, mind you. And I continued to stare with an expectant look, even raising my brow in impatience.

Instead of answering me, he took his time, and it became difficult to breathe. He caught it and smirked at me.

I looked down, focusing on my order paper. *Breathe in, breathe out,* I reminded myself. *A hot guy checking you out is not a reason for you to pass out on the floor, Chelsea.*

"Burger, tomato, waffle fries, and a Coke." He paused, causing me to look up from my order pad. "Add you on there."

My skin practically burned from arousal, but I once again powered on. "Sugar, you couldn't handle me."

His lip tipped up, and I swore time stopped for a brief moment, allowing me to plug that one movement into my memory bank. Holy shit, it was sexy.

I hadn't had much sexy in my life, but that was by choice, because men sucked. First, there was my no-good father. Then came the asshole who drugged me in high school and took my virginity. Yes, I knew who it was, but it couldn't be proven.

Therefore, nothing had been done. Then there was Steven, who turned out to be way into porn. Barry was next, and at the name, I should have put him in the "no" pile. I learned that one the hard way, too. So, you see, men sucked. I was better off keeping to myself and aiming for my goals.

Stiff scratched his beard while he studied me appraisingly. "Baby, conquering you would be a fucking pleasure."

I couldn't move, couldn't breathe. Did he really just say that? Holy shit, he did.

Somehow, I snapped myself together and ignored his comment. How I did this, I had no idea.

"Anything else?"

"Nah," Bosco replied, and I scooted away from the table right as I heard Bosco say, "Stop that shit, Stiff."

"What? She's pretty."

My step faltered, but I regained it just in the nick of time. He said I was pretty.

I gripped the countertop, needing something to hold on to in order to ground myself. This was surreal. Definitely surreal. Sure, he'd flirted—hell, he flirted with every woman he could when in here—but to have that intense look then to call me pretty, that was just bizarre. Totally unlike the other times.

Regaining my composure, I put their order in and filled their drinks. Then I walked back to their table and began handing the drinks out.

"Coke," I called out, getting a grunt from Bosco.

I continued calling out drinks and passing them around.

"How's that sister of yours?" Boner asked.

This time, I smiled huge, and it wasn't the one I plastered on my face every day. No, this one was genuine because I loved my sister more than anything in this world. Anyone honestly asking about her made me happy.

"She's good. Almost done with college. I'm damn proud of her." My heart swelled with emotion. I'd never been so proud of anything in my life.

Jennifer had always been so damn smart. Mom and I were lucky she had received scholarships, but even if she hadn't, I would have taken on another job to get her through.

Jenn wanted college so badly. It was one of her goals, and she deserved every chance in life. She worked her ass off up there, having a job besides school. I still sent her running money, which she continually returned, becoming our game.

She was only a thirty-minute drive from here, but it seemed like a lifetime away. I missed her. It had been almost a month since I'd seen her last. Though we talked every day, it wasn't the same.

Bosco whistled. "College girl. Always knew she'd do good."

I nodded. "Yep, and she's getting all A's." I knew I was beaming, because my cheeks began to have that twinge in them that bordered on pain from when you smile for too long. But you kept doing it, anyway, since you really felt it.

I looked over at Stiff and saw his eyes dead focused on me.

My smile wobbled a tad, but I held strong.

Stiff had always had that something—call it charisma, charm, badassness, or anything along those lines. Then again, it might just be my hormones considering getting laid was up there with getting a hole in my head. I had no time for either.

"I'll be back with your food in a bit," I told them, striding away.

While filling the mustard containers, my eyes would drift over to their table whenever I heard the barks of laughter between the men. Stiff snagged me once, but I smiled then quickly looked away. I mean, I couldn't have him thinking I was staring at him, right?

The rest of the night went without incident, and as expected, I got a hefty tip from the boys.

TWO

STIFF

"**H**APPY TO HAVE YOUR ASS HERE," I told my baby brother, Xander, slapping him on the shoulder and pulling him in to me tightly.

Xander had served overseas in the Marines, the baddest of the bad motherfuckers, running his own unit. He was honorably discharged from the Corps after being shot in the shoulder a couple of times. He'd had a shit time coming back from that, but after talking to his woman Gabby, I hooked him up with some guys he could talk to, a job at the garage with me, and talked him into becoming a prospect for the club.

I fucking liked having him around every day. Working with him—hell, just having him be in the clubhouse with all my patched brothers—kicked fucking ass. I couldn't ask for any better, and I felt like my family was really together.

"Glad to be here, brother."

I released him then stared at the Chevy Impala on the car lift in the shop. Vipers Creed owned Creed Automotive. With it bringing in the bulk of our income, all the guys worked here, including me. I supervised.

"Gabby having trouble?"

I had mad respect for his woman, sticking with my brother after being gone for so long. I knew she was hurting with him gone, but it was the same for me. Regardless, we both picked up and carried on with our days in hopes we wouldn't get a call that he was dead. The one I did get, telling me that he had been shot, made me lose my shit.

"Just needed to change the oil and wanted to look underneath. She said it was making some tickin' noise. That's woman speak for 'I don't know what the fuck is wrong with the car; just fix it.'" Xander shrugged. "So, we had a break, and I thought I'd see what was goin' on."

My brother's face had changed so much over the years. Not going to sugar coat it. I raised the boy, had to. We had a worthless piece of shit mother who'd been more focused on her next fuck than worrying if her two boys had food. Did that mean I had grown up a lot faster than I should have? Fuck yeah.

I'd had jobs cutting grass, picking up trash at peoples' houses, planting flowers or bushes—whatever people wanted. I had only been eleven, but I'd always found something that brought in some money to keep my brother and me fed.

At thirteen, I'd started working for the rent because our mother couldn't have cared less about moving us from place to place repeatedly. Xander hadn't needed that. What he had needed was some kind of stability.

The guy who'd owned our house had given me odd jobs, and I did each and every one without complaint. The one where I had to re-shingle a house at thirteen was a bitch, but by the end, I'd had it down pat. I'd also learned how to fix plumbing, toilets, flooring, install cabinets—you name it, I did it. It'd been hard as hell, but I did it. One positive from it was it gave me a great skill set.

I'd barely made it through school, but I knew I had to set a good example for Xander, and that was what pushed me through by the skin of my teeth. Even exhausted from working, I still got Xander ready, and we went.

I'd do it all again in a fucking heartbeat, because the man standing in front of me proved that every bit of hard work I'd done helped him become the stand-up man he was today. I was damn proud of that.

"You heard from Mom again?"

Xander's eyes blazed at the mention of the woman, but I wanted to know if she attempted to see him again. She'd tried a month or so after he came home, and then she received a visit from me not long after. No way was I letting her shit fall on my brother again. She had so much coming down on her it wasn't pretty.

I shielded my brother from that shit, but at some point, I knew I needed to tell him. Now wasn't the time for that, though. He was just getting back to his old self, and I wasn't going to fuck it up, at least not yet.

"No," he grunted out. "Nothin.'"

"Brother, this is good," I told him, and he nodded.

When he was a small boy, he'd always tried to be a momma's boy, bringing her cigarettes or fetching her something she wanted. I'd seen it and told him to stop that shit, but he was young and wanted a "mom." When he finally realized we wouldn't get the mom he wanted, it seriously fucked him up. That was another reason I kept information from him now.

"Whatever." He paused. "Oh, hey, man, I need to talk to ya about somethin.'"

I lifted a brow, telling him to go on. He never had to ask that shit with me. I was always and would always be there for him, no matter fucking what.

"Gonna ask Gabby to marry me."

To this, I smiled wide. I wanted him to be happy in any way possible.

"That's good, brother."

"Yeah, it is. I know I've gotta get her a ring, but how the fuck am I supposed to know what the hell she wants?"

That right there was why I loved my brother. He was so damn strong, competent, and had a good head on his shoulders, but for this, he came to me for help. That right there was the sign of a good man—a great man.

"Brother, you know she's gonna like anything you pick." When he raised his brow at me, I knew what he fucking wanted, and dammit, I was going to give it to him. "You want me to come with you?"

He grinned. "Knew I could count on you."

"Fuck me. Goin' ring shoppin'. You owe me a fucking beer. Fuck that, a keg."

He laughed. "Fuck, Stiff, we'll both need that shit before we even go."

I chuckled. Damn, I'd missed this. He'd been gone too long.

"Amen to that. Let me help ya." I nodded to the car.

"Sounds good, man."

"Stiff! Get your ass in here!" Spook called from his office as I sat at the bar, nursing a bottle of Bud.

I hefted my ass up from the barstool and headed into his office, closing the door behind me. The place was pretty well put together except for the stacks of paperwork clouding his desk. I swore he had so much shit going on, and I was happy he'd finally started delegating the work to us brothers.

Spook had a control problem, but I couldn't blame him. He'd been the one to clean up the club years ago after his father tried to run the Vipers into the ground. I was at his damn side during Spook's takeover and clean up. After that, he hadn't wanted anything to get fucked up or out of his control, so Spook had done it all. We could tell it was wearing on him, but he had been stubborn as shit and wouldn't listen.

Thank Christ for Trixie. After reconnecting with her, things changed. She was damn good for him. Hell, she was good for the club.

Now he kept a balance between work and her, and I admired him for it. Boner took on the daily operations of Creed Automotive while I took over supervising it.

"Yeah," I said, standing in front of his desk and swiping my hands on my jeans to rid them of the leftover condensation from the beer bottle.

"I swear to Christ, between your mother and mine, I don't know how the fuck we didn't turn out even more fucked up than we are."

At that, I crossed my arms over my chest, his words grabbing my undivided attention. I hated anything that had to do with the woman who gave birth to me; hence, why I went to lengths to shield my brother from it.

Spook's mother was a gambler and got in deep with a man named Fox who ran tables. Spook pulled her out of that mess, only for her to end up doing it again. Spook had then been forced to cut his mom off from the club completely, which wasn't easy on him. Regardless, a lesson needed to be taught, and as far as I'd heard, she hadn't been back to one of Fox's tables again, but the ban was still on her.

"Yeah?" I prompted when he didn't continue.

His eyes locked with mine. "Ice. She's sellin' now."

My gut clenched as my temperature spiked. "You're fucking shittin' me."

"Nope." He shook his head. "Heard it through Zeke."

Zeke was a dick who knew the streets of Dyersburg, Tennessee. He kept his ears open and fed information for a price. Knowing that, the information was viable and not to be taken lightly.

"Knew if she was using, it was only a matter of time before she'd start selling it," I conceded, rubbing my hand across my bald head.

I thought for sure when she had gone to visit my brother, he would have been able tell she was tweaked, but he'd had shit going on in his head, so she'd evaded him. It was a double-edged sword because, if he would have seen it, I wouldn't have to say shit.

"I don't give a shit about that," Spook declared, placing his hands on his desk then leaning forward on them, his sparking eyes intent on mine. "What I give a shit about is her using your name and this club as protection."

My entire body locked so damn solid I swore I was a statue made of granite. That fucking bitch was using us so she wouldn't get her ass beat on the streets. Probably so she wouldn't get her pussy sold, as well.

Even this was a new low for the woman, one that she'd pay dearly for. I needed to make it perfectly clear that she was not under our protection.

I stared straight ahead as my mind conjured up ways to decimate my mother.

"Brother." Spook brought me to attention, and my focus cleared on him.

I nodded, letting him know I was with him.

"This needs to stop. Now. She's dealing for Gonzo, and that shit will not touch this club."

Fuck, that was even worse. Jamie Gonzales, also known as Gonzo, was a major player here in Tennessee. He didn't even live here in Dyersburg, but he had minions who sold all over for him.

"Fuck, man." I shook my head. "I'll take care of it."

It was Spook's turn to shake his head. "No, brother, *we* will take care of this shit. This is serious, and we all go in together. Not only are we gonna need to talk to Gonzo, but your mother will need to be dealt with, and the news of this needs to spread wide." He rose to his full height. "I know she was shit to you growing up, but she's still your mom, man. You sure you can do this shit?"

My body unlocked. "Fuck yeah. I've been cleaning up her garbage for too long. It's time to get it sorted and over."

"I want us to go together, but if you need us to, we can go in without you."

That pissed me right the fuck off.

"Fuck no, brother. I'm in this. Xander doesn't know anything, though, so I've gotta take care of that. He's gonna want in on this, too."

"Done," Spook said. "Talk to your brother and get it sorted. Then we'll take this shit to church and get it done. The sooner, the fucking better."

"So, what the fuck is this?" Xander asked, sitting on the couch in my house.

We all lived on the compound, which I loved. I'd brought him here because he hadn't been the same since getting back from overseas. Sure, he'd made progress, but he still had things to work through. As a result, I wanted to give him a safe place to hear what I had to say, away from anyone. Not that the club brothers would have anything negative to say, but I wanted to respect my brother and give him the privacy to let it out.

I walked to the fridge, grabbed two beers, and handed him one.

"Fuck, it's that bad?" he asked, twisting the top off then taking a hefty pull.

"Yeah." I fell into the reclining chair that faced the television. My place was a man cave, no other way to put it: huge TV, places to sit, beer in the fridge, and shit a bit everywhere. I did clean it up, but as long as it was livable, it didn't matter to me.

"Give it to me," he said as I turned toward him.

"Mom's been doing ice."

His face stayed the same, but the small tick in his jaw told me he'd heard.

"Not that I give a shit, but the problem is she's using the club and me for protection while selling the shit."

"That fucking bitch," Xander growled out. "How long's she been doing this shit?"

"Coupla years, the ice. Using me and the club, just recently."

His intense eyes hit me. "And you didn't bother to fucking tell me?" he snapped, the tick getting worse.

"Nope," I replied, pulling my beer thirstily. "You didn't need to know that shit until now."

"So that's how this is gonna be, brother? You keepin' important stuff from me?" Xander slammed his beer down on the side table, the loud *thunk* echoing. "Bullshit! Don't fucking lie to me, Stiff. I'm a grown ass man."

"You don't think I fucking know that shit?" I asked. "You don't think I know you fought, got fucking shot, and I could have lost you out there? I fucking know all that shit too well. You damn sure know when you came home, your mind wasn't in a good place. You think I was gonna add more to that pile for you? Fuck no."

Xander reclined, resting his head on the back to look up at the ceiling, clenching his hands at his sides as I continued.

"You need to know this shit now, so I'm tellin' ya now. It is what it is, brother. Now we make it clear to everyone out there that she's not under our protection."

"They'll fucking destroy her," he said.

"Probably. Not that I like that shit, but she chose this path, not you or me or our club. *She* chose to put herself out there. She chose to start ice. She chose to sell it. She chose to use my name and the club's as a way of thinking she's hot shit and untouchable. Those are all *her* choices."

"Just like she made the fucking choice to be a shitty mother," he grumbled.

I knew that shit still ate at him, and I wished I knew what to tell him so he could let it go.

"Yeah, brother. Fucking sucks, but this shit has to be done. Time to clean up."

He popped his head up. "How exactly are we gonna do that?"

"Vipers' style."

THREE

CHELSEA

"Grams, seriously."

I loved her—I swear I did—but she was off her rocker … again. This time, I didn't have time to argue with her, though.

"I have to get to work. Just take the money." I held out twenty-five dollars as my grams just shook her head at me, keeping her eyes glued to the television.

"Just go. My money will come in a few days, and I can get my medicine then," she replied, not giving me a damn inch. Instead, she smiled up at me from the recliner.

While I loved it when she smiled, this didn't make me happy.

Grams' living room was all her. Small reddish-pink roses were on every inch of fabric, like a flower shop had puked, dispersing itself throughout her home. Her couch: roses. Chair: roses. Curtains: roses. Bathroom toilet cover: roses. Throw over her bed: roses. I was sure, if she could have found carpet with the darned things, her floors would be covered, too.

"Grams, you need to take it tomorrow to keep on schedule. I have to work late tonight and won't be able to stop by and pick it up before they close. I wish you would've told me about this yesterday so I could have picked it up on the way here."

"There's no need to bother yourself," she insisted.

Was it correct to want to strangle an eighty-five-year-old woman? No, it wasn't, but in that frustrating moment, I kinda-sorta wanted to.

"Why isn't Mom here?" I groaned.

My mother lived with my grams so she could take care of her. But Mom also worked, which was where she was now; hence, my question was rhetorical. If she were here, she'd just take the damn money, and I would be on my way. Sure, the money would magically appear a few days later, ending up back in my hand, but at least she took it at the time she needed it, unlike Grams.

"Because she works, which is where you need to get to. Now go and let me watch my stories." Grams pointed a boney finger at the television screen where some soap opera was playing.

I rolled my eyes, turning back to the woman. "I'm leaving this on the kitchen table and calling Mom. That way, if she doesn't have the cash for your meds, it's there. At least she can pick them up after work if she has it." I hastily walked into the kitchen and plopped the money on a rose-covered table cloth.

As I walked back into the living room, I saw Grams' eyes were fixated on the television, and my eyes drifted to it.

Good Lord, was this a soap opera or porn?

A man and woman were rolling around under the sheets, kissing like ravenous teenagers. And fake. The woman's face wasn't into the scenario at all.

Whatever. I'd never had time to watch before and didn't care to start now.

I turned back to her. "I've gotta go. Make sure you get your medicine."

She batted at the air like she was swatting a pesky bug. "Don't you worry about your grams. I'll be just fine."

I leaned down and kissed her soft, wrinkly cheek. "You will be if you take your medicine."

Grams let out a huge huff. "Proud of you," she said quietly, making my heart swell.

I bent down to her ear. "Love you, Grams. Now get your medicine," I demanded, which made her chuckle.

I gave her another peck and was off.

I called Mom and Jennifer on the way. While Mom answered, Jenn didn't. That wasn't unusual. With my sister's workload at school then actual work as a waitress in a coffee shop, she was busy most of the time. I left a message for her to call me back, confident she would when she had a moment.

Today was a 'crazy on your feet,' 'not sitting down,' 'squeezing in the fastest pee break I possibly could' kind of a day. Even after the sun fell, we stayed busy. That was both good and bad. Good because more tips. Bad because of screaming, aching feet, and a stomach that growled from not having time to eat.

I snuck in a few peanuts from my apron, but my stomach still grumbled, and I felt my energy waning.

By nine-thirty, things were beginning to slow enough that I ate a quick sandwich and began all my prep for the next day, sitting down while doing it. While it was nice to take a load off, I thought it might have been better to stay on my feet and keep them numb. Then at least I could get through the rest of the night. The way they felt now, it would hurt to get back on them.

The bell over the door chimed, and I looked up with a smile on my face as Bosco, Boner, Stiff, and Stiff's brother Xander walked in. Same as before, the room started closing in from all their … bulk or aura or something.

It had only been a couple of days since the last time the guys came in. I couldn't lie and say I never thought of Stiff during that time. Of course I did. It was hard not to. But thinking about him was the closest I'd ever get. It was a fact, one that I was perfectly fine with because a man wasn't part of my goal, and I needed to keep that in sight.

"Have a seat wherever, boys," I told them before going back to rolling up silverware in napkins. I hated those stupid paper things that went around them with the self-adhesive that never worked. I ended up throwing more away than using them.

I finished up my stack, glancing over to where they sat. Even with the busy as hell day and the fact that I had racked up tips, I was happy to see they sat in my section.

Mitzi came up to me and shoulder bumped me. Not hard, but enough to get my attention.

I looked at her, but she was staring at the guys.

"No fair. You had them last time." She mock-pouted.

I smiled then shrugged. "It is what it is."

I moved to their table, my feet groaning from their small reprieve, but a smile was plastered to my lips.

"Little Chelsea, how we doin' today?" Bosco asked.

It was a strange feeling to have uneasiness yet comfort run through you at the same time in the presence of these men. I never thought for a moment they would hurt me, but I also knew if I toed a line, they'd have no trouble putting my ass back over it. Even with that, I still didn't fear them.

"Good," I assured him, giving my mega smile. "What can I get you boys?" I eyed them, waiting for the first to order.

The menus were on the table, but most people already knew what they wanted when they stepped foot inside Charlie's. Everyone seemed to have a favorite something.

As they placed their orders, I wrote quickly. When I looked up, Stiff's eyes were on me, the same as the last time he'd been in here.

Unnerved a bit, I kept my smile on and finished up.

"Chelsea, you remember my brother?" Stiff asked as I was just finishing up writing their orders.

"Of course." I looked at Xander. He had the same good looks as his brother, although he had hair. "Hi, Xander. Welcome home."

Everyone in town knew that Xander had been a Marine. We also knew he'd been hurt and sent home. Word traveled quickly in a small town, and Charlie knew everything. Moreover, he liked to pass on tidbits of information at every available opportunity. I swore, at times, he was worse than a teenager.

"Thanks for everything you did," I finished with a smile.

He nodded, looking a bit uncomfortable, which confused me. I'd had no intention of offending him. I was honored that he'd fought for us. Charlie had fought in the service, and every now and again he told us stories of that time. Some weren't pretty. Xander could just be in a bad mood. Lord knew I'd had enough of those throughout the years.

I said no more, just lifted my head and moved away.

I heard a slap of flesh then Stiff said, "Don't be a dick."

"What the fuck do you care?" That had to have come from his brother.

Stiff kept quiet, but I felt heat race up my neck as if he were penetrating me with a stare. I rounded the counter, keeping my eyes focused on anything but the table, not wanting to know the answer.

"Oh, fuck," I heard then tuned them out, not wanting to hear any of it.

I placed the order card on the wheel, spinning it toward the cook, Rickie, in the back. Charlie had the night off.

"Order up!" I called out, and Rickie turned around then waved, acknowledging me.

I filled their drinks and made my way back to the guys' table, nodding at a call out from another one of my tables to let them know I would be there in a few.

"Here ya go, boys," I announced when I arrived at their table.

All eyes focused on me, which I ignored as I handed out their drinks.

"You seein' anybody?" Boner asked in his deep tenor that sent chills through me. He might not really do it for me, but his voice was sexy as hell. Any woman would melt from it.

I arched a hip, putting on my fake-it, cocky face. "Hell no."

His eyes widened. "Why 'hell no'?" he questioned in a goofy voice, as if he found this hilarious.

With the tray in one hand, the other on my hip, I said, "Don't need the shit that comes along with a guy. Y'all need anything else?"

"So, you think women don't have a lot of shit they carry around?" Boner asked, ignoring my attempt to cut off the discussion. The man was like a dog with a bone.

I steeled my spine, not really ready for this type of personal conversation, but so be it.

"Didn't say that. Bottom line is, I have enough of my own to deal with, so I don't have time for anything else."

I noticed Stiff's smart-ass comments and come-on lines were absent for once. Nothing. He simply sat there quietly as his brother chuckled. I was pretty sure I had entered an alternate universe.

"Anything else?" I asked.

"I—" Boner started.

Bosco reached out and squeezed his shoulder. "Leave the girl alone," he ordered, and Boner laughed. "We're good, doll," Bosco said, lifting his chin to me.

I nodded to the table and went to the other that needed me to check on them.

A little while later, as I finished up the sugar refill, my feet burned, muscles ached, and I was ready for the day to be over.

I looked up as Mitzi sashayed her way over to the boys' table.

"Hey, there," Stiff said in what I liked to call his 'yes, I'm flirting with you; come to my bed' voice.

The twinge of jealousy hit me square in the chest. While he'd barely spoken two words to me tonight, there he was, acknowledging Mitzi in a way that made my hands want to shake.

Sure, she was pretty with dark brown hair instead of my blonde. She was tall and slender rather than my semi-tall, all ass and boob body. She had a clear face, while I had just a sprout of freckles that went over the bridge of my nose. Mitzi had green eyes compared to my blue. Her makeup was perfect as opposed to my barely noticeable natural look. So, yeah, she was hot, and any man would be taken aback by her.

I tried to shake my feelings off and ignore the rest of their conversation. It wasn't my place, and really, why did I care? I couldn't lay claim, not that I even wanted to.

"Order up," Rickie yelled from the back, thankfully pulling me out of my thoughts.

I took a tray, piled on the guys' food, and made my way to their table.

Mitzi had moved away, and I was relieved by that. Most everyone was gone in the diner except the guys and two other tables, each with two people at them. All of them were in my section and not Mitzi's. They must have caught on to her attitude, too.

"Here we go, boys," I said, placing their food in front of them, the sound of the porcelain sliding across the table like music to my ears. Sad, I know, but very much true.

I slid Stiff's in front of him and got a, "Thanks, doll."

A thrill raced up my spine. Sure, I'd been called doll before by customers. We were in the South, so everyone had hospitality, but the deep, sexy way Stiff had practically growled it made regions in my body wake up that I'd thought for sure were dead by now. I pushed that down and kept my smile in place, though.

"Sure," I managed to get out without it sounding like a breathy exhale. Stupid hormones.

The first order of business when I got home was to get out my vibrator—if I didn't pass out from exhaustion, which was a high probability.

I skated away, needing a bit of distance between me and the guys. Who was I kidding? I needed room from Stiff.

I turned to the counter just as the bell overhead the door chimed. I lifted my gaze and was about to welcome the next guest when my world stopped. My heart fell, stomach knotted, and anger bubbled in my veins when my sister fell into the door, crashing to the floor, a bruised and bloody mess.

I tossed the tray in my hands to the floor where it clattered loudly, and then I darted for her. The bell chimed again, and two large men stepped through, their eyes fiery, angry.

Instantly altering my direction, I ran behind the counter and grabbed Charlie's Louisville Slugger. If these assholes took one step near my sister, I was going to start swinging.

Too bad Charlie had the night off. Now would have been a good time for his gun.

"Get out!" I yelled in a bark of anger so loud I shocked myself, the bat weighing heavily in my hand. I wanted to swing it. I'd had practice—Charlie had made sure of it, especially working later at night.

"You Chelsea?" a man asked casually like my sister wasn't whimpering in pain on the ground. I also heard chairs scraping across the tile, but no way was I taking my eyes off the two buffoons in front of me.

"What's it to you?" I wasn't stupid enough to confirm who I was to some thugs. I wasn't given much growing up, but I was given love and street smarts. Survival had always been key. My momma had done the best she could with us girls, and my grams had helped out, and along the way, she had taught me. I swore, most days, street smarts were better than the book kind.

"Got a message for Gary."

My father, my fucking piece of shit father, was responsible for this. He hadn't been around in years, and now this!

My veins burned with lava from the anger I felt toward him. I would fucking kill him. With my own goddamned hands, I'd annihilate him. He'd fucked up my life so damn badly, and I refused to let it happen to my sister.

"Tell him, if he doesn't get his shit together quick, next time, we take little cherry here." He pointed to my sister, and I moved in front of her as a guard. No way was he getting any closer to her. He'd have to get through me first. "And you." He pointed at me. "But next time, we won't be so nice." He grabbed his very small junk, making me want to puke. "I would've loved to fuck her." His eyes slithered down my body. "And you."

"You—"

"What did you just say?" Stiff quipped from my side.

"Who the fuck are you?" guy one in a blue shirt and navy dress slacks demanded in a cocky as hell voice, which I didn't think would go over well with Stiff and his boys.

"I'm your fuckin' nightmare, motherfucker." Stiff pointed at my sister. "You do that shit to her?" he asked as Bosco, Boner, Xander, and Dawg came up, forming a line between my sister, me, and the assholes.

Five against two, this was good. Really good.

"What's it fuckin' to ya? This shit ain't got nothin' to do with any of you," the second man in a white dress shirt and black pants said, which wasn't smart. He had splatters of blood on his shirt— my sister's blood.

I sucked in deeply through my nose, and my grip on the bat became so tight the pain felt nice.

My sister whimpered.

Not taking my eyes away from the men, I reassured, "It's alright, Jennifer. I've got you."

"Chels," she cried, sniffling.

"I know, baby girl, I know. Just sit tight." I moved so my feet were touching Jenn's body enough for her to know I was there with her, but also keeping my focus on the assholes ahead.

"Motherfucker, answer his fucking question." This came from Bosco, and while I thought Stiff's tone had been damn near volcanic levels of anger, Bosco's reminded me of a grizzly bear. It was almost like Charlie when I'd seen him get pissed—fatherly. Too bad my fucked up father got us into this shit.

The assholes standing by the door showed no fear, which I couldn't understand since the vibes coming off them weren't good. Either they didn't take the men standing next to me seriously, or they were completely stupid. I couldn't decide which yet.

"Fuck yeah," the asshole in white with my sister's blood on him finally answered.

"What did my father do?" I asked, though I had a feeling I knew what it was about. My father had always had a drug problem. Ice, coke—you name it, he took it. It was also his excuse for everything.

Stiff looked at me from the corner of his eye, but I didn't acknowledge it, keeping my focus on the man in front of me.

"He owes Gonzo. It's payment time. Either he pays or you do," the stupid asshole with the dark slacks vowed, sneering at me.

"Motherfucker," Stiff said with a grunt, tilting his head to his brother. I had no clue what any of that meant.

"Take it out of his ass. We have nothing to do with him," I stated firmly. Not for the past ten years as a matter of fact. After he'd put my credit in the shitter, he went to jail. Then he'd gotten out and disappeared, and I'd thought, *Good riddance.*

"Can't find him." The asshole laced his fingers, flipped them inside out, then cracked them, trying to be some badass. I mean, come on; he beat up a college student who wouldn't hurt a damn fly. Me? I would burn the motherfucker.

"Not her fucking problem," Stiff chimed in.

While I secretly liked his help, I could stand on my own two feet. Considering these were two big guys and I only had a bat, though, I let Stiff take the lead.

"Gonzo says—"

Stiff took a step closer, and one of the men reached into the back of his pants. Bosco held up a gun, aiming it at the man. "Don't fucking think so."

Any sane person would be nervous that a gun had been pulled in the middle of a diner, but not me. Nope, I was fucking ecstatic. I would do anything to keep my sister protected.

FOUR

STIFF

YOU'VE GOTTA BE SHITTING ME.

Gonzo. There was that fucking name again. First my mother and now Chelsea's fucking father. Add this shit in front of me going down, and I was ready to fucking destroy the man. My mother had a fucking choice about getting hooked on the shit and starting to deal, while Chelsea and her fucking pint-sized sister had shit to do with any of it.

The reason we'd stopped at the diner tonight was because we had been casing the warehouse down the road. Since Gonzo wouldn't return Spook's calls and didn't live here, the only way to get to him was through his people, and the warehouse was a known hideout for them.

This would end. We would get to him.

"Dawg."

He grunted in response.

"Need you to clear the four people out of here. Make sure they understand," I told him.

"You've got it." Dawg had been around forever, so he knew I meant no cops were to be called on this. They needed to walk away and keep their mouths shut.

"Xander, help Chelsea get her sister out of here." Hearing Chelsea about to protest, I cut in, "Chels, not now. Get your sister out of here and get her cleaned up."

"Now, Chelsea," Boner said when the damn woman wanted to refuse.

She put her hands on her hips, and her expression turned defiant. Shit, she was a spitfire, and truthfully, it was hotter than hell, but I couldn't focus on that right now.

"Fine," she huffed out as Xander walked behind me and lifted Chelsea's sister.

She cried out in pain, which only pissed me off more. I'd be surprised if the little one even weighed more than a hundred pounds, and these two assholes were quadruple that shit. Totally un-fucking called for.

I waited until everyone had cleared out before addressing the men.

"First, motherfucker, we're lookin' for Gonzo. Where the fuck is he?" I asked while Bosco trained his gun on the men.

Boner just stood back, keeping his menacing eyes on them. With Boner being our vice president, I was a bit surprised he was letting me continue to take the lead.

The two men still looked too fucking cocky for their own good. While I'd love to shoot them in their legs just to prove a point, Charlie's was still open, which meant this needed be taken outside soon.

"He don't wanna be found," one of the assholes sneered, infuriating me further.

Searching for Gonzo's whereabouts was pissing us off. Now, with Chelsea in the mix, pissed didn't cut it.

I shook my head, getting back in the game. Then I stepped closer, moving so damn fast the asshole who'd spoken didn't see it coming when I jabbed him hard in the throat, using the web between my index finger and thumb.

He clutched his neck as he fell to the ground, gasping.

The other guy moved, but Boner was on him, and I heard the grunts from the man, though I didn't take my eyes off the asshole choking.

"Outside," Boner called out.

Fuck yeah, outside.

"Need you to call Spook to get someone here to get Chelsea and her sister back to the clubhouse. Can't take her to the ER unless it's dire," Boner continued.

I reached in my leather, bringing out my phone, and clicked Spook's name.

"Yeah," he answered.

"Boss man, got a problem." I laid it out for him in detail, including Chelsea and her sister.

He listened, taking everything in.

"Hooch is around. I'll have him come and get the women. Trixie will deal with them here while we get ahold of Needles. I'm joining you."

"No way to transport them, boss. All on rides." No way in hell was I riding my bike with one of these fuckers unless he was chained to the back and I was dragging him.

"Hooch and I'll bring the vans. We'll be there in ten." He clicked off as Boner kicked the shit out of the man I chopped in the throat.

"Brother," I called out, catching his attention. "Ten out and we move."

Boner nodded, and Bosco grinned. It wasn't his happy, 'I'm getting laid' one; this one was the devilish one that no man wanted to be on the receiving end of.

This was going to be fun.

CHELSEA

"Be careful," I told Xander, who rolled his eyes at me.

"She's fucking beat to shit. Any way I touch her, she's gonna hurt."

Duh, I knew that; I just didn't want her to hurt any more than she had to. Nevertheless, I shut up and led him into the employee break room.

I pushed three chairs together, forming a makeshift bed, and Xander laid a groaning Jennifer down. Tears and blood streaked her face as I bent down to her.

"Jenn, look at me," I told her. Inside, I wanted to cry, wanted to bawl at the sight of my sister's eyes so swollen she could barely open them to look at me. This was the worst pain imaginable, and I wished it were me lying there, battered and bruised, instead of her. I would do anything to make her pain go away.

"Can you talk?" I asked, and unknown grumbles came from her throat.

Shit, did they break her jaw?

I felt the tears begin to sting, but no way in hell were they going to break through. My sister needed me, and I would damn well help her.

"Oh, my God!" Mitzi came into the room, a sobbing mess and being all dramatic, which there was no time for.

"Either get me the first-aid kit or go, Mitzi," I barked, and her jaw practically fell to the floor. No, I had never talked to her like that before, but my kid gloves had come off when my sister had landed on the floor.

"Where is it?" Xander asked as I looked over at a stock-still, pale-faced Mitzi. At least I knew who not to call in an emergency. That woman couldn't handle shit.

"Far top cabinet." I pointed. "There should be some towels in there, too. Next to the sink is a bowl; can you put warm water in it?"

He was already on the move before I even got the last words out. He had the bowl in hand and was getting the water. Damn, he was quick.

Feeling Mitzi's eyes on me, I said, "Go, Mitzi." I wasn't trying to be a bitch, but if she was just going to stand there like a fucking mannequin and not help, she had no business being back here.

I heard a huff then a door opening and closing.

"Few bricks shy of a full load?" Xander joked, and I felt the cord of tension in my chest relax a small bit.

Xander seemed to have an easy-going nature about him. And even though this situation didn't call for any kind of joke whatsoever, his ease made it seem okay. It made me feel a sense of calm, enabling me to do what needed to be done and to fight back the anger and tears.

He must have seen my reaction, because no other words were spoken as he knelt down beside me. Then he put the cloths into the water before he handed me one at a time. It hit me at that moment that he more than likely had training in this and should probably be the one working on my sister, but he'd given this to me. He didn't step on my toes and take over.

I worked, each stroke of the rag scraping against my sister's once flawless skin, making her cringe. I hated that, hated that someone thought it was okay to hurt my baby sister. I hated that the assholes that did it were so close, yet I was in here with her and not out there, rearranging someone's balls.

"They'll take care of him," Xander said, and I turned to him, my brow raised.

How in the hell had he read my mind?

He quirked his lip, and in that moment, I saw Stiff. I liked that and let it roll through me.

"Stiff isn't gonna let those assholes just walk out of here," he told me. "Let him and the boys take care of it. You worry about your girl here."

"She's bad," I whispered, wiping the last of the blood from her face and revealing large gashes. "The way she's holding her ribs." I nodded to them.

"You mind if I take a look?" Xander asked, and I liked that he'd given me that sliver of control.

"No." I turned to Jenn's swollen face. "Baby girl, Xander here is gonna take a look and see what's going on with your ribs." When she groaned, trying to pull away, I looked at him and explained to her, "He was trained in the military. He knows what he's lookin' for." I had no idea for sure if he did, but she didn't need to know that, and I was trusting Xander to do what needed to be done.

"Hey, there." His deep voice sounded soothing, but Jenn still flinched when Xander came close to her. Then, when he touched her ribs through her thin shirt, she cried out. He looked glumly at me. "Pretty sure she's cracked a couple of ribs. She's not wheezing, so nothing's poking her lung."

Anger bubbled, so much so I started to shake.

Xander touched my hand. "Let Stiff deal with this. I get you're pissed. I would be, too. But Stiff'll handle it."

Eyes glaring, I barked, "*I'll* handle it."

He rose to his full height. "Just take care of your sister. The rest will work out."

Before I could respond further, the door to the room opened, and my eyes focused on it as I rose, ready to protect my sister if I needed to.

Stiff walked in, followed by another man. I believed his name was Hooch. He'd spent limited time in the diner; therefore, my knowledge of him was at a minimum.

Stiff walked right up to me, and I felt the need to step back, so I did. He followed, putting his arm around my back this time.

I looked up at him in complete shock. What the hell was happening here? He'd never put his hands on me before, ever. Sure, a brush of a hand when I was dishing out food or a drink, but never this. Never this close.

I could smell the leather, tobacco, and some sort of spice coming off him. The smell was so damn intoxicating I leaned into him unwillingly.

He lifted my chin with his index finger, and my eyes went to his.

"You okay?" he questioned, breaking whatever spell had been over me.

I cleared my throat and tried to move back out of his grip, but he didn't allow it, holding me more securely.

"Yeah. Need to get Jennifer to the hospital, though." I nodded at her. "Xander says he thinks some ribs are cracked. I need to get her some x-rays and—"

He placed a finger on my lips, and my eyes flew back to his.

"This is how it's gonna play out. Hooch here is gonna take you ladies to the clubhouse. Then the doctor is gonna come and take a look. He'll be able to patch her up."

I glared, moving back an inch. Who the hell did he think he was, telling me how this would "play" out?

"But—"

He pressed harder on my lips, which got him another glare.

"No cops on this one. We're handling this in house."

I shook my head.

"I'll explain later. Hooch is gonna carry your girl to the car. Trixie, Spook's ol' lady, will meet you there. She'll get you fixed up." He removed his finger.

"You done?" I growled, because fuck him. One minute, he didn't talk to me at the table, and the next, he was … whatever the hell this was. *Um, I don't think so.*

"Yeah, babe. Know you wanna give me hell, but I've got shit to do. That shit is outside, so I need to get."

"Why the hell should I listen to anything you say?"

He pulled me against him, his lips coming to my ear, and every single nerve on my body went on high alert.

"Babe, let me help you." He grazed the shell of my ear with his nose, sending butterflies fluttering in stomach.

When he stepped away, I actually felt his loss, which was strange and a bit unnerving.

"Alright, ladies, let's get you the fuck out of here," Hooch said, giving me something to focus on.

FIVE

STIFF

"CUT THE ZIP TIES," SPOOK ORDERED.

We owned a massive amount of former military land and had brought the two guys to a small shed off the back corner of the clubhouse property, nestled back in the woods. We hadn't used it in quite some time, not having any need to, but these assholes had just given us a reason to dust off the dirt and give it a try again.

I stepped forward, flipping up my switchblade before moving behind the motherfucker who thought it was good practice to beat up small women. He was about two inches shorter than me but well-built; no way should he be beating on pixie girls.

"Yeah, untie me, you fucking bitch."

My first instinct was to slam the blade into the asshole's thigh. Instead, I cocked back my right fist and nailed him hard in the jaw. It happened so fast. One minute he was sitting on his ass, and the next, he was lying on the ground, spitting out blood.

"I'm 'bout ready to show you bitch, motherfucker," I ground out, slicing the ties around his wrists.

"You're a fuckin' pussy," he replied.

Wishing he'd stay quiet like his buddy, I retracted the blade and put the knife back in my pocket.

"*I'm* the pussy? You're the one bleedin'," I taunted as he rose to his feet unsteadily. He rolled his arms and cracked his neck from side to side. I wasn't sure if it was to intimidate me or what, but he fell far from the mark.

If the fucker wanted a fight, he could come at me. It had been a long damn time since I'd fought schoolyard style. That meant no tape, no ring, no nothing—just two men ready to beat the ever-loving shit out of each other. I had been in enough of them over the years to know exactly what I was doing.

"You done with the yoga?" I stood with my arms crossed, watching this idiot. Next, he was going to have me ordering him a fucking fancy coffee or some shit.

"Yoga?" Bosco questioned. "Really, brother?"

I shrugged. "I'm sure seeing a hot chick do it would be fun, but this is makin' me wanna vomit."

"Fuck you!" the asshole barked.

"Fuck you back," I told him to Bosco's amusement.

"Look at you, fucking Mr. Clean," the asshole chided. At this, Dawg full-out laughed.

"That's the best you got? Damn, you need more help than I can give ya."

The first three punches were in quick succession; one to the left of his face, one to the gut, the last to the right of his face.

He wiped the blood from his busted lip and charged me. That was one of several mistakes the man made today. The first was waking up.

Just as he got to me, I lifted my knee, hitting him hard in the jaw, then elbowed him in his spine, and he crashed down the cement floor.

I spit on the ground where the asshole lay. "Mr. Clean kicked your sorry ass, motherfucker." I kicked him in the ribs repeatedly, letting the images of Chelsea's sister race through my head: her on the floor, her cries of pain, her moans. I let it all take over as I kicked the asshole.

Bones snapped, and he screamed, but I couldn't stop. I was in a zone, one where part of me feared I couldn't pull myself out. Adrenaline pumped through my veins as memories of my mother getting the shit beaten out of her over and over again through her fucked up decisions crashed through me. Then came thoughts of Chelsea's father and the consequences his actions had put on his daughters. Everything rolled into me, hitting me hard.

As I continued to kick the limp man on the ground, words were spoken in the background. However, I couldn't register anything as I grabbed the asshole, pulling him up and giving him three savage punches to the jaw.

"Brother!" Spook yelled through the foggy haze.

"Stiff!" Xander screamed next.

Then I heard my other brothers all telling me I needed to stop.

Somehow, it registered and I halted. I dropped the dickhead. Then all I could do was look at the ground, my vision a bit hazy with red. Slowly, the room came back into focus, but my heart pounded so hard I thought it might beat out of my chest.

I stepped back from the heap of man as Spook came before me. Raising my head, I looked into my president's eyes.

"Brother?" he said softly, his concern evident.

I nodded. "I'm good."

"Care to tell me what that was?"

"Saw the little girl beaten. I …" I ran my hand over my head and down my face against my beard. Fuck, I really lost it with the asshole. "Sorry, man."

"I get you, brother, I get you. Take a break," Spook ordered, and I moved off to the side to stand next to Xander.

He checked me in the shoulder, not hard but enough to get my attention. "Damn, Mr. Clean, you can kick serious ass."

At his joke, I felt the entire fog I was under lift away. "I prefer Vin Diesel, but what the fuck ever."

"Vin? No fucking way, man. Chicks think he's the shit," Xander quipped as Boner and Dawg moved the half-conscious guy off to the side then zip tied his hands and feet together.

I fucked that one up. He probably wouldn't be able to talk for weeks from that shit.

"I am the shit," I retorted. This time, I checked him in the shoulder, getting a chuckle from him. "Fuckin' love havin' you home, brother." I flexed my hands, feeling the sting from the open cuts. They weren't oozing too badly, so I'd be fine.

"Here." Xander handed me a towel. "Rip it in half and put it over your hands." While in the service, he'd learned tons of shit. I was so damn proud of him, but really?

"Later," I told him. I'd get patched up once this shit was over.

He shrugged, tossing the towel onto the counter.

Looking back at the scene, I saw Dawg and Boner had the second man tied to a metal chair, his legs attached to the legs of the chair and his arms behind his back.

I pulled out a smoke, lit it, and inhaled.

"You already saw what happens when I let the brothers go. You wanna tell us where Gonzo is, or do you want the same fate?" Spook asked like he didn't have a care in the world. He had a way about him, always did, even as a kid in school.

"I don't know, man. He doesn't come around." Wetness—piss, I assumed—dripped from the chair in a stream, hitting the worn floor. This guy was the definite follower of the group. I couldn't believe Gonzo, or anyone for that matter, had even hired this pussy to do his shit.

"You've gotta be shittin' me," Bosco spat out, disgusted. "Fucking pissin' your pants? How the fuck old are you?"

"Talk!" Spook yelled, making the man jump. "Either fucking start, or we start tearing your fucking teeth out." This was going in a whole other spectrum of interesting as the minutes ticked by.

"He only communicates by phone or through Javier."

Boner kicked the chair, earning a flinch from the man and his attention. "And Javier is …?"

"Our connection to Gonzo. He's not due back for two days. Then he's supposed to meet us at Denny's place," he blurted out like we'd have a fucking clue who this Denny character was.

"Denny is …?" Boner probed, his patience wearing thin. I could tell from the fact that he'd pulled off his stocking cap and raked his fingers through his hair. He'd been wearing the covering lately to stop the habit. Obviously it wasn't working so well. Spook teased him about ending up completely bald like me, but Boner wasn't into that idea. Hey, not every guy could pull it off. It was a gift.

"Him." He pointed to the unconscious man on the ground.

"What time?" Boner asked.

"Seven-thirty at night," he instantly replied.

"Alright, you're meeting him along with us. Now, time for you to learn how the Vipers work. You do not come into our house, beating up innocents, especially innocent women. We don't play that shit. Now you feel the burn," Spook warned.

Then it began. We each took our shots. The asshole from before even woke up long enough for the guys to get their shots on him, too.

Chelsea's little sister might not be able to put all of her pieces back together, but at least on this end, after we let them go, these two would think twice before beating the hell out of a pixie girl again.

CHELSEA

NEEDLES—THAT WAS THE NAME of the man looking over my sister. He was an older man with a trimmed, gray beard and mustache. His eyes were chocolate brown, and he presented himself as very smart. I didn't know how one could do that, but he'd nailed it. But the name—Needles. I hated needles—hell, most of America did. Why the hell would anyone want that nickname?

When we'd arrived at the clubhouse, we had been greeted by a bombshell of a woman named Trixie, whom I vaguely knew from high school. After she'd escorted us to this room and Hooch had laid Jenn down, Needles had cut off her clothes before wrapping her in a blanket, only exposing the parts he needed to see. Then Trixie had left and hadn't returned since.

"What's that?" I asked Needles who held a syringe in his hand. Okay, so I got the needle thing, but come on.

"Just something to take the edge off. Your sister—"

"Jennifer. Her name's Jennifer," I quickly said. I'd noticed that everyone had called her "my sister." While that was true, she had a name, her own identity, and I would much rather they use it.

"Sorry. Yes, Jennifer is in serious pain. Her ribs are severely cracked. Fortunately—or unfortunately, whichever way you want to look at it—surgery isn't gonna help. This"—he tapped the syringe—"is gonna help her not feel so much pain."

"Okay," I mumbled. God, she looked so damn fragile lying there.

Needles gave my sister the injection, and within seconds, her taut body began to relax, her muscles losing the fight as she melted into the bed. I felt scared but relieved that her pain was alleviated.

"I'm not ruling out a concussion, but I have no way of knowing with all the other injuries. I'll be able to stitch some of the bigger cuts up, but for the others, I'll use liquid stiches. You'll need to put antibiotic ointment on them while they heal. She's gonna need a lot of rest and close monitoring. She can't be alone for a few weeks. It could take up to two months for her ribs to heal."

"She goes to school about thirty minutes away."

Needles shook his head. "I'd wait until she's coherent enough and have her contact the school or teachers to let them know there has been a family emergency and she had to come home. They don't need to know anything else. Most colleges will accept this and either have her make up the work or do it online." He chuckled. "In my day, we didn't have 'online.' Now you can buy anything and do anything on the internet. It's crazy."

Maybe if I weren't so upset about seeing my sister like this, I would have found it funny, too. Unfortunately, I didn't see the humor; I only saw her pain. I wished I could take it away and put it on me, instead.

Needles shook a bottle, and my eyes went to it.

"Pain pills." He gave me instructions on how and what to do for her then told me he would be back in the morning to check on her.

I liked him but wished I knew him better. He was nice and had taken good care of my sister, so that put him in the winning category for me.

Once he left, I gripped Jennifer's hand and let the tears flow. I let each one cascade down my cheek and splash to the floor. Then the tears turned into sobs. I couldn't stop them. I let myself feel the pain for my sister, every single moment of it. I allowed my strength to slowly dissipate, letting the grief take over.

Being so lost in thought, I didn't hear the door open and shut. As a result, I screamed when a large hand gripped my shoulder, only to look up into ocean blue eyes. Stiff.

I didn't know what I was doing and didn't care. I rose up and fell into his arms, soaking his shirt with my continued tears. He wrapped his arms tightly around my body, cocooning me. I had never felt safer in my life.

SIX

STIFF

DAMN. I INHALED CHELSEA'S SCENT, the smell of vanilla seeping into me and spreading throughout my senses like wildfire. I never knew I liked the smell of vanilla, but I damn sure did now.

I couldn't believe she'd stood and come right to me for comfort. When was the last time I'd given actual comfort to anyone?

I remembered. It had to have been Gabby when Xander came home from the service. Before that, though, I couldn't really remember anyone leaning on me like this. And I found that I liked it. Don't get me wrong; it was different, but different in a way I appreciated.

I gripped her tighter as her body shook. Looking over at the girl lying on the bed, my gut twisted. Even after taking care of the assholes who had beaten her to a pulp, my anger rose again. I wanted to do it all over again.

Chelsea began to settle from the sobs then stiffened as she pulled back and looked up at me. She came to my nose, but she was still little.

"I'm sorry." She tried stepping away, but I held her tight. I liked having her warm body against mine. Every place we touched, there was a heat that scorched me like nothing I'd ever felt.

"Don't be sorry. Like havin' you here." While I didn't understand it, I'd always done what felt good, and this was beyond amazing.

Her breath caught and eyes widened. "Stiff, I …" She didn't finish her sentence, looking away from my eyes, instead.

Not liking that shit, I said, "Chelsea, eyes."

Her eyes immediately came back to mine. Swarms of emotions I didn't really understand floated within them.

Her tongue darted out of her mouth, and she licked her bottom lip. Then she sucked that bottom lip between her teeth, and my cock hardened, pressing into the confines of my jeans. Chelsea's eyes hooded, telling me she felt this pull between us, too.

Fuck it.

I leaned down and took her mouth in a kiss that sucked the air out of her. Her taut body relaxed, melting into me, her hands now gripping the back of my cut. No doubt, if I didn't have my cut or shirt on, I'd have claw marks from how tight she held me.

She tasted like sweet fruit mixed with vanilla, and I couldn't get enough. The best fucking part, she kissed me back, giving as good as she got, meeting me at every turn. That turned me on more, making my cock painfully hard.

The kiss grew heavy and insistent as she rubbed her body up against mine. Each brush, each touch only sent me higher.

A cry came from the bed, and Chelsea instantly pulled away from me so fast I was still in the fog of her essence and let her.

She knelt down on the floor next to the bed, grabbing her sister's hand. "You're okay, Jenn. I promise, you're safe now."

A couple more moans then silence.

Chelsea's shoulders dropped as she turned and looked up at me from the floor. Her eyes were glistening, but I couldn't make out what from. Was it the kiss? Her sister? I didn't know, and I didn't like it one little bit.

"You need to go, Stiff," Chelsea said softly as tears pooled in her beautiful blue eyes.

I knelt down on one knee next to her, lifting her chin with my thumb and index finger. "Babe, she's gonna be okay." Sure, she would probably have a shit time dealing with it, but Needles told us that in time, she'd heal physically.

"I know." She closed her eyes, sucking in a deep breath.

A tear fell from the corner of her eye, and I swiped it with my thumb. The slight wetness on my skin did nothing to calm the burn I felt between us. I couldn't remember a time in my life when I'd felt this. I'd fucked a lot, but this gut feeling, this fire was something totally different. I felt a deep need to grasp it tight and never let go.

"Please, just let me be with my sister for a while," she pleaded.

I would give her this, give her some time, because I fucking needed some, too. I needed some space, needed to get the fuck out of here and get my head screwed on straight.

"See ya later." I released her and moved from the room, shutting the door.

With my hand on the handle, a war went on inside me. The feeling was so damn good, but like with all women, I knew it couldn't last.

My mother was the best example of that. She fucked men for money, drugs, or whatever else she wanted, never sparing my brother and me a thought. All women were the same. That was why I fucked and got out. No entanglements, no pressures of calling the next day—none of that shit. I needed to remember that.

I released the door, grabbing a smoke and putting it between my lips, then lighting it. Inhaling the nicotine, I let the burn hit my lungs as I stood, staring at the door. I closed my eyes then left, getting the fuck out of dodge.

CHELSEA

I LAY FAR ENOUGH AWAY FROM MY sister not to touch her yet close enough I could be here if she needed anything, which she hadn't so far.

The sheets smelled of smoke, reminding me of the kiss I'd shared with Stiff last night. Thoughts of that moment in time fluttered through my head. He exuded a scent of tobacco and leather that made my clit pulse.

When his lips touched mine, I'd willingly lost myself. In that moment, Stiff saw me as more than a waitress at a diner; he'd seen me as a woman. A living, breathing, and dare I say, sexy woman.

I'd let every fantasy I'd ever had of that man swirl in my head during that kiss, heating my body to the point of combustion. If it hadn't been for my sister's moans, who knew how far we would have gone?

Unfortunately, part of me was glad we'd stopped. Even though I'd wanted the man for years, I knew I'd never really have him, and I wasn't that type of woman. I wasn't one for one-night stands. I'd never had time for any of that. I'd always been working my ass off in order to make sure my family had what they needed.

I wasn't going to start being that woman now. So what if I throbbed. It didn't matter. Nothing mattered except my sister.

It was good, though. The way his lips took from me, the slight nips of his teeth, the taste of him exploding on my tongue—I tucked all of that away in my memories for later. I'd remember the tenderness of my lips and the slight sting he'd left me with, that he liked to be in charge. Even when I'd pushed, he'd pushed harder. I would remember each time he'd turned my head to dive in deeper and his panting breaths when I'd pulled away.

Yes, I would remember each and every moment of that kiss for the rest of my life.

"Chels?" my sister groaned, bringing me out of my thoughts.

I sat up immediately to see Jenn's eyes were swollen, black, blue, and an angry green to match. Stitches lined several places on her face, and I hoped she wouldn't have physical scars. I already knew she would have emotional ones.

She slowly lifted her arm, pain etching across her expression with each inch until she gave up and put her arm back down.

"Can you tell me what hurts?"

Her eyes came to mine, and even with the swollen eye, her brow rose, telling me that I just asked a very stupid question. Damn, I loved my sister. I'd missed her, too.

"Alright, got it … all over."

I rolled from the bed, the mattress squeaking. I didn't remember it doing that last night when I'd climbed into bed, but my head was still on Stiff, which wasn't good. I had a sister to protect and a father to murder. Shit, when my mother found out about this, she was going to raise holy hell.

The pill bottle sat on the nightstand along with a bottle of water. I moved to it and shuffled two pills out.

"Need you to sit up, Jenn. These are pain meds. They'll help you out."

"I don't …" she moaned, her words coming out a bit jumbled. "I don't know if I can."

Ever so slowly, I came around, lightly grabbing her shoulders. She cried out as she moved up, and I felt the tears well in my eyes. Those assholes needed to pay for what they'd done to Jenn. A lot of people needed to pay for this.

Once she sat up, I held up the pills, putting them in her mouth and making her groan. I'd thought she might have gotten her jaw broken, but Needles had said it was just hit pretty badly and would be sore for quite a while, making eating and drinking a little difficult.

As I lifted the bottle of water, she took from it, some dribbling down her chin to her shirt. Well, it wasn't her shirt. It had *Harley Davidson Motorcycles* written across it. Trixie tossed it to me when we'd brought my sister in.

Taking as much of her weight as I could, I laid her back on the bed.

"You wanna tell me what happened last night?"

Her breath caught, and then her breathing became a bit ragged as tears spilled from her eyes. My heart hurt so badly for her.

"Not really," she mumbled yet continued. "They got me at my apartment, hit me with something. The next thing I remember was a dingy hotel room where they hurt me."

I gripped my sister's hand in fear of what would come next. Still, I had to ask. "Did they …?" I trailed off, unable to even say the words.

She shook her head then closed her eyes in pain. "No, just the hits. Then they tossed me in the back of a car, and the next thing I remember was waking up as they threw me on the floor in your diner."

My body shook with rage. They'd gotten her at her apartment at school, which meant they knew where she lived, probably where I lived, too. They absolutely knew my place of employment. Shit, was anywhere going to be safe?

Then it hit me like a boulder. They had to know where Mom and Grams were.

I took the deep panic and pushed it into action, not letting it get me.

"I need to call Mom and Grams."

"No—"

I gave her hand a slight squeeze. "Jenn, those guys could go to their house and hurt them. I need to make sure they're okay." I didn't mean to talk slowly to her like she was a child, but it did come out that way.

"Yeah," she said on an exhale as she closed her eyes.

Trixie brought me clothes, too, so I could get out of my diner uniform. I rushed over to the discarded clothing on the floor and dug into my pocket. No cell. Crap. I must have left it in my purse … which was still locked up at the diner.

Looking around at the room for the first time, I noticed the place was clean and put together. I didn't know what to expect, but at the same time, didn't care. A dresser rested up against a wall with a window over it that had dark brown curtains. The carpet looked dated yet clean. Dark paneling covered the walls, and I was happy it wasn't a mess.

Unfortunately, there was no phone.

"Jenn, I'm gonna have to go out and see if I can find a phone or someone who has one."

"Are we staying here?" she asked.

"Right now, we're just playing it by ear, but my plan is to get you to Grams and Mom. I just haven't worked out all the details yet."

I gripped the door handle just as she asked, "Are we safe here?"

The feeling of warmth I'd felt from being wrapped in Stiff's arms came back, gathering in my belly and spreading throughout my body.

"Here, yes," I assured with absolute conviction.

Jenn didn't answer, and I left the room.

SEVEN

CHELSEA

AFTER WALKING DOWN A HALLWAY, I came out into a wide, open room. My attention went directly to the man sitting with his back to me at the bar and the beautiful brunette standing next to him. She leaned over, whispering something in Stiff's ear. Whatever it was made Stiff smile and my heart drop.

I knew he was a player. I knew he flirted with anything in a skirt. I knew that kiss was a one-time deal. I knew it; I just didn't want to know it.

She gave Stiff a kiss on the cheek, and Stiff swatted her ass playfully. Then the woman's cold eyes turned to me, and they assessed me from my toes to my head. I didn't know what I looked like, but I knew I felt like shit, like someone had ridden over my heart a few times. Why? Because after one kiss, it shouldn't hurt to see him with someone else. It was only a kiss. It meant nothing, and I needed to remember that.

"I'm done," the woman sneered cattily as Stiff turned around, his face not changing one bit. There was no regret, no guilt, no ... nothing. It was impassive, and that shit stung.

I sucked in a lungful of air as the woman slammed the door behind her as she left. There was no way in hell Stiff would get my goat. If it hurt from seeing him with someone else, then that was on me, not him. Like it or not, I had the ability to control my feelings. No one else.

With all the confidence as ever, I asked, "Do you have a phone I can use?"

He reached into his leather vest, pulling out a cell phone. "Yeah, use mine." His words came out a bit raspy, like he either hadn't gone to sleep last night or he had just woken up.

My heart jumped, not wanting to know the answer. After all, if he'd just gotten up, I was sure the brunette did, too.

Head held high, I brushed it off as I walked his way then took the phone out of his hand. "Thanks. I need to call my mom and Grams and—"

"Already took care of it. Had some brothers check it out last night. They stayed, keepin' an eye out. Talked to them a while ago and everythin' was quiet."

I expelled air in relief that they were okay. I'd felt the panic at the thought of something happening to them, but I hadn't let it fully penetrate. Knowing Stiff had taken care of that, knowing he'd taken the time to have his guys check on my mother and Grams hit me in the heart … hard.

It was an incredibly nice thing for him to do, and he'd done it without a word from me. That felt even better. I had to wonder, though, how he had found out about Grams and Mom. How did he know to go and take care of them? Regardless, the relief of them being safe outweighed those thoughts.

"Thanks," I whispered softly. "I need to tell them what happened to Jenn."

Regret filled my lungs. This was something no one should have to tell a loved one.

"'Kay," Stiff responded.

I stared down at the phone, my thumb pausing on the little bar to open up the screen to dial the number.

"I mean, it's not every day you tell your mother and Grams that the youngest in our family got the shit beaten out of them. And it's all because of our worthless piece of shit father." I clenched the phone, still staring down as my mouth seemed to lose the ability to shut the hell up. "I mean, hey, he always used me, anyway." I shrugged, looking up. "So I should be used to this, right? Once an asshole, always an asshole."

Stiff sat there, unmoving; no tick of the jaw, nothing in his eyes—just blank. I hated that; hated the stony expression of his face that I couldn't register.

"Never mind." I turned away and began dialing the number.

Just as I was about to press the green button, Stiff spoke.

"What'd your dad do to you?"

I stilled, all the feelings of what my father had done to me coming back and smacking me in the face: the betrayal, the heartache, distrust, lost love, and everything a child should have from a father, but I never had.

"He was a worthless piece of shit and still is," I replied.

"Didn't answer my question," Stiff retorted.

I turned back to him, seeing his attention was fully on me.

"Ran up a few thousand in credit card bills using my name and social."

He snapped his lips together then pulled out a cigarette, lit it, and inhaled. I watched as his Adam's apple moved when he swallowed. How that could be sexy on a man, I did not know, but on him, it was. Everything about him seemed to be.

"When'd you find out?"

Rolling my head from side to side, I felt a cramp in the side of my neck, most likely from sleeping wrong. I was surprised I had been able to at all.

"When I was nineteen and signed up for a credit card, I was declined. Then everything came out." Instead of allowing him to ask any more questions he had no right to the answers of, I hit the green button and called my mother.

"Hello?" my mother's chipper voice came through the other end of the line, and I turned my back to Stiff, knowing he was there yet not giving him any more than that.

"Hey, Mom. How are ya?"

"Chelsea, where are you? I don't know this number." Mom's happy tone deteriorated, and I hated that because I was about to make it worse. Some things in life sucked, but she needed to know so I could take Jenn over to her house later today and move in with them. Strength in numbers and all that. As a result, I needed to suck it up and tell her what was going on.

"I'm …" I thought then said, "with a friend. Mom, I …" A frog lodged in my throat, finding the perfect spot to make a home. No words came from my lips, only a small cry. I cursed my father once again.

The phone was snatched from my grasp, and Stiff stood in front of me as he spoke. "Hello, ma'am. Name's Stiff. I'm with Chelsea."

I could hear my mother's screams through the air, and I turned from panicked to angry. How dare he take the phone from me and speak to my mother!

"Give me the phone back," I growled, holding out my hand and tapping my foot in the ultimate bitch stance.

"Ma'am," Stiff stated with authority, and the sounds on the other end quieted. "Chelsea's fine, but she needs to talk to ya. I'm gonna have two of my boys come up to your door. One of them is Xander, my brother. Need you to follow them to the Vipers Creed clubhouse."

Stiff paused, and I fumed. If smoke could come out of my ears, I had no doubt it would be.

"Give me the phone," I demanded.

Stiff ignored me.

"No, ma'am. I promise you Chelsea's perfectly fine." His eyes roamed my body and sparked like they'd just woken up from a nap. It was intense, but it did nothing for my anger. "Just need you to come by."

"Yes, ma'am," Stiff answered.

Damn, I hated listening to one-sided conversations, especially when they involved my mother.

"Yes, ma'am." This time, he smirked with his answer then added, "I completely understand that you'll have my balls in a sling."

At that, my anger cracked. Damn, I loved my mother. Look up spitfire in the dictionary, and her name would be right there. Between her and my grams, I had great role models.

"Yes, ma'am. You'll be comin' to the clubhouse."

At this, I paused. Mom knew Stiff. Sure, being in a small town, mostly everyone knew everyone, but I hadn't thought Mom knew him well enough to know where he lived.

"Yes, ma'am." He removed the phone from his ear and held it out to me. "She wants to talk to ya."

I snatched it back from him, a sneer on my lips. "Mom."

"Chelsea Anne Miller! What is going on, young lady?" Crap. I hated when she pulled out the full name, and the young lady was a double whammy. It meant she was pissed. She would be pissed the whole way here. Then she would be pissed about my father. Then pissed about Jenn on top of that.

I needed to prepare myself for my very irritated mom.

"Calm down, Mom."

"I will not calm down," she snapped.

I blew out a breath. "Mom, will you please just come to the clubhouse? I promise I'm okay, and I know this is weird, but it's for the best." Was it for the best, or was I just going along with it because Stiff suggested it?

I shook my head and weighed everything. If I told her over the phone, she would be extremely upset, and I wouldn't be there to calm the beast. She'd also be hell-bent on seeing Jenn, which was totally reasonable, and getting here would make her already crazy driving worse. Telling her here, I could do it in person and cushion things more. Better yet, she could see Jenn immediately. I could also comfort her once she came down from the anger so she'd be able to tell Grams.

The scowl left my face. He was right, even if I didn't want to admit it.

"Young lady—"

"Mom, seriously. Please just come to me, and I'll explain everything. I promise."

"Fine. He says his brother is coming here. He a nice boy?"

I thought back to how well he had taken care of Jenn last night, his calm, and how he'd kept me feeling it.

I answered honestly, "Yeah, Mom. He's a good guy." I'd tell her why later.

Stiff crossed his arms over his chest, the stance utterly imposing. With his eyes narrowed, I wondered what the hell his problem was.

"When Xander gets there, just follow him. Okay, Mom?" My gaze never left Stiff's.

"I'll be there as soon as possible, and you'd better be ready to explain all of this."

"I will."

"Bye," she said curtly.

"Bye, Mom." I swiped the phone off and held it out to Stiff.

He released one of his arms then took it from me, sticking it back in his cut.

Hand on hip, foot jutted out—also known as bitch stance—I let him have it.

"How dare you interfere in my family business! If I wanted to tell her on the phone, that was my choice. You don't have a say so."

"Chelsea, knock that shit off."

Anger bubbled. "I'm not knocking anything off, Stiff. I appreciate the help with my sister, but that's where this ends."

"Oh, yeah? What're ya gonna do when those guys come back? You gonna get your bat and swing it around when bullets are flyin' at your head?"

"I can take care of my family," I argued. In actuality, I had no clue how I was going to do that. It was just the principle of the matter. Never once in my life had a man talked or acted like Stiff was to me. I'd never once dealt with a man who just was what he was: blunt, demanding, straight talker, and fixer of problems.

I'd always been the one to fix everything. Every time something went wrong, I'd figure out a way to make it work. I was damn good at it and had a shitload of experience. I took care of my family. *Me.*

"True, but now ya got us to help."

"What do you mean?" I removed my hand from my hip and crossed my arms over my chest, mimicking Stiff's stance.

"The moment those fuckers dropped your sister in the diner was the moment we got involved. Nobody does that shit, and until it gets sorted, you're gonna need to stay here."

"I can't stay here. That's crazy. I need to move Jenn into my mother's house, and then—"

"No. Not safe."

"If it's not safe for me and Jenn, how's it safe for my mother and Grams?" Arguing with Stiff was almost like a war I wasn't sure I could win. Although I was stubborn, he kept at me, meeting me at every turn.

"It'll be safe for them."

"What does that mean?"

"Woman." His tone turned very impatient, like he was done with this back and forth we had going on. Well, too damn bad; I wasn't backing out.

"Man," I retorted in the same tone.

"Dammit." He rubbed his hand over his sexy, bald head, and I forgot for a moment that he'd had a beautiful woman next to him mere seconds ago, kissing him. "Listen to me. Shit's goin' down. I need you here at the compound, and it's best your sister stays here so we can have Needles check on her."

"I have to go to work."

"No, not for a few days until we can figure stuff out."

"No? Did you really just tell me no I can't go to work? You're utterly insane if you think I'm gonna listen to your bullshit. I have to work. It's life. It's how the world goes around."

"Weren't you gonna take a few days off to take care of Jenn?" he questioned.

He had me there. I did think of that, and I couldn't lie to him. I'd evaluate why another time. It did piss me off to have to admit it to him, though.

"Yes, okay?"

"See? Problem solved."

"You can't just—"

He moved so quickly that scooting out of his path proved impossible. Then he wrapped his strong arm around my waist, crashing me into his hard body. Every hot inch of him that touched me burned through my clothes, and my breathing picked up along with his. The tension between us was combustible.

"Chelsea," he said gently, taking me off guard, "Need to protect you."

"Why?"

His nose was so close to mine as I looked up at him that I could feel the pull to rub the tip against his, but I somehow refrained.

"Don't know. Just gotta do it."

The air grew thick, vibrating through the space with each passing moment that we looked into each other's eyes. My lips suddenly felt incredibly dry, and I darted my tongue out to moisten them.

"Gotta stop doin' that," he murmured.

"What?" I asked, surprised I even had a voice at this point.

"Lickin' those sexy as fuck lips."

I felt the rigidness of his erection through his jeans, and it seemed to grow larger with each moment that ticked by.

I inwardly smiled to myself. Yes, he turned me on. Yes, I really wanted his lips on me again. Yes, I'd more than likely give him more, but the images of the snide look from the brunette lit my memory along with her lips touching Stiff's cheek and the way he'd smiled at her. If he thought for one damn moment that I would roll over and be like that, he had another thing coming.

I leaned in just as he loosened his grip on me, thinking I was giving in. Quickly, I moved out of his grasp and out of his range. Then I glared into his eyes, fire burning out of them. If it were possible, I would have lit him aflame.

"Keep your hands off me," I warned, hoping it came out as firmly as I'd intended.

"And why's that?"

Why did everything that came out of his mouth have to be so sexy? It wasn't normal. Why would a higher being give one man so much power? It wasn't fair to the rest of world, and having it directed solely on me …

I would not back down.

"Because I said so."

Damn, I sounded like my mother from when I was a kid and Jenn and I would fight over toys.

I shook the thought from my head. That route wasn't going to work with Stiff. I needed a different tactic.

Sucking it up, I replied, "Thank you for your help. I appreciate it, but we can't stay here. I need to be with my family."

"I'm not sayin' this shit to piss you off, Chels." God, the way my nickname came off his lips snaked under my skin, warming me. "I'm doing it to help you."

He wasn't going to let this go, and I needed to get out.

"I really need to go and check on my sister." I turned and bolted from the room, hearing a soft chuckle behind me.

"I cannot believe that man," I grumbled, closing the door to my sister's room, her busted eyes coming to me. Damn, Stiff had me so twisted I had forgotten to keep quiet.

Jenn groaned as she tried to turn to better face me.

Rushing over, I sat on the bed, touching her arm gently.

"What's going on?" she asked, but it came out in a broken mess. I didn't think the pain pills would have kicked in this fast, or maybe I'd been out with Stiff longer than I thought.

"Nothing," I reassured her. She needed to recover, not deal with anything else.

"See your eyes." Her words fell off a bit, but she remained awake. "You're pissed."

My sister always had a knack for reading me like a book. Unlike my mother who thought I held so much inside of me that sometimes she couldn't tell how I really felt about things, my sister had absolutely no problem at all. One look—good, bad, or ugly—and she got me. Always.

"Stiff," I began, lying down next to her on the bed. If I was going to tell her a bedtime story, I might as well get comfortable in the process. I stared up at the ceiling. "He thinks he can just tell me—us," I amended, "what to do and we're gonna follow. He says we have to stay here to keep safe, but dammit, Jenn, we're Millers; we take care of our own. I'll take care of all of us."

Jenn covered my hand with hers and gave a small squeeze.

I turned to her immediately, seeing pain etched across her face from the slight movement.

"You always …" She groaned. "You're always protecting us." Her eyes fluttered closed, and her breathing evened out. The meds completely knocked her out.

I turned back toward the ceiling, thinking, who in the hell did he think he was, telling me and my family what we were going to do? He had no right. No right to me. No right to even think I would listen to him. Millers always stood on their own two feet, never backing down from an obstacle.

The problem with this scenario was not knowing exactly who I was dealing with. Could he be right?

EIGHT

STIFF

"**S**HE'S BEING A PAIN IN THE ASS," I grunted to Spook as I walked into his office and shut the door. "Damn woman is hell-bent on fixing this shit by herself, but has no idea how the hell to do it." I plopped down in the chair in front of Spook's desk. Then I reached into my cut and pulled out a smoke, lighting it, and inhaling deep the burn filling my lungs.

His brow quirked. "And this is a surprise to you?"

I sucked in another lungful of nicotine, waiting for him to go on.

"Brother, she's been working her ass off forever at that diner. You know that. Her dad is obviously shit. You see how fucking protective she is with her sister. Fuck, you told me yourself she was gonna go after those two fucking men with a damn bat. She's got balls and determination. Can tell that already."

The damn man was right.

I blew out the smoke. "I get that, get her." It was unusual that both she and I had taken on the protector roles in our families, both working our asses off to provide. I understood her fierceness, also respected it. "She's stayin' here until the meeting with Gonzo's man."

Spook nodded.

"Her mom and grandma are comin'. They should be here in twenty."

"And you pulled that off by …?" He lit his own smoke, sucking in deep.

"Takin' the phone and dealin' with it."

Spook shook his head, but a smile played on his lips. "This is gonna be fun."

"What the fuck does that mean?"

"It's like a clash of the titans. Two strong ass people. Who's gonna come out on top?"

I looked him dead in the eye, exhaling my drag. "Me. I always fucking come out on top." Then I shrugged. "Unless she's ridin' me."

Both Spook and I laughed.

"Where's my daughter!" a feminine voice called loudly from the front door of the clubhouse.

I turned my head toward the sound, and the moment my eyes landed on her, I knew she was Chelsea's mother. Fucking spitting image of her, only years older: blonde hair, tits and ass, body, and the same piercing blue eyes that were fierce and glaring around the room, searching.

Bosco, Spook, Boner, and I rose from our seats as Xander and Hooch helped an older woman with gray, curly hair; a wrinkled face, and the same blue eyes as Chelsea and her mother into the room. Xander lifted his chin to me, and I did the same.

"Ms. Miller?" Spook asked, moving closer to the two women.

"Yes. Again, where is my daughter?" she repeated, not intimidated by the six-feet man in the least.

"Your daughter is here." I motioned for my brother to go and get her from her room. Damn, I loved having him prospecting for the club. "I'm Stiff, ma'am."

Her anger turned to me, one hand on hip, the other clutching a purse on her shoulder, reminding me so much of her daughter.

"Yes, young man, I know who you are. Know who all you boys are. What I don't know is why my daughter is with you."

"Oh, hush, Jannie," the older woman scolded. "You haven't givin' them a chance to talk." She looked at me. "Need a chair, son."

"Of course."

Hooch still had ahold of her as I moved to a table, pulling out a chair for her. She moved well but had a slight wobble at times. I grasped her other arm and helped her into the chair, and she set her bag on the table.

"Sit," she ordered, and I looked at Spook then sat.

"Yes, ma'am."

"Mother," Jannie called in warning, walking from the door.

"Now you stop that. I'd like to hear what this nice young man has to say."

Chuckles were heard from the guys because someone describing me as a nice young man had never been done in my life.

"Yeah, you nice young man," Bosco chided.

"None of that," the older woman commanded, and the laughter died. The woman was damn tough, especially if Bosco listened and toned it down. He was not an easy man to order. "You can call me Bee. None of that miss or missus stuff. Makes me feel old."

I chuckled at that. I could see where Chelsea got her determination, drive, and stubbornness, not to mention her humor.

"Bee, Chelsea'll be out here in a minute. It's best she—"

"Grams! Mom!" Chelsea yelled from behind me as she ran up and tackled her mother in a hug then gave her grandmother a soft kiss on the cheek. "I'm so glad you're here."

"Now explain to me why that is," Jannie responded, sounding about ready to lose her shit.

"Sit here." Chelsea grabbed the chair next to me as her mother took the one on the other side, Bee across from me. My brothers stood around us.

While Jannie looked expectantly at her daughter, Bee took in the men around her, and then her lips pursed.

"Something is very wrong here. These men are in guard dog mode, and I know we pose no threat, so who does?" Bee questioned, looking between Chelsea and me.

Chelsea began to speak, but all that came out was a garbled sound.

I moved my chair over next to hers, put my arm around the back of it, and placed my hand on her shoulder. Her body tensed then relaxed.

Bee's eyes narrowed, and I smiled.

"Last night, my brothers and I went to Charlie's."

Chelsea turned to glare at me, giving me the shut the hell up look. I stopped for a moment, giving her a chance to start. When she didn't, I did.

"We—"

"Last night, Jenn showed up at the diner." Then Chelsea let it all out in one giant rush, her back ramrod straight.

Jannie and Bee's faces turned stoic. I swore a fucking pin dropping could have been heard for the briefest of moments. That was, of course, until Jannie rose from her chair so forcefully it crashed to the ground.

The guys all came to attention quickly as Chelsea stood up, going to her mom. She wrapped Jannie in her arms, who was vibrating with such anger she had a high probability of exploding.

"Mom, calm, please."

"I will not calm. Do not ask that of me, Chelsea Anne Miller! First, I wanna see Jennifer. Then I will find your father and kill him my damn self!" Jannie raged as Chelsea tried rocking her back and forth to comfort her. It didn't work. Jannie was too far gone on the rage meter, and I couldn't blame her a bit.

"Mom, you can't go in and see Jenn like this. She's bad, really bad." At these words, the angry fire left Jannie's eyes, and motherly concern took its place.

"Why would they do this to her? I get it's your father, but why her? She's never done a damn thing wrong ever in her life. Hell, she doesn't even have a speeding ticket. Why her?" A lone tear fell from Jannie's face, which she batted away instantly, wrapping her arms around Chelsea and hugging her back.

"Because he's a dick, Mom. Always has been. There's no rhyme or reason why assholes are the way they are."

"We need a plan," Jannie determined.

"Ma'am," I offered, stepping in. "We're gonna keep you all protected. For now, we need Chelsea and Jenn to stay here at the clubhouse since they were the ones threatened. You and Bee can go back to your home, but we'll have two guys on you at all times, one for each of you."

Chelsea's face turned red as her mother pulled away from her. "I told you we weren't staying here," she ground out.

"And I told you it's the best way to keep you and your sister safe. Needles can help Jenn here, not—"

"Needles? Who is that?" Bee asked.

"He's the doctor who took care of Jenn when we brought her here. It'll be best for all of us this way, ma'am."

Bee nodded. "I'm fine with that. But whoever comes to my home better have manners and not gripe about my stories."

I chuckled. Damn, I liked this woman. "No problem, ma'am."

"Grams, I—"

Bee held her hand up. "You've taken care of everyone in this family for years. Yes, Millers don't give up. We stand on our own two feet and rise to the top. But, my dear, this is a situation where I don't think we have the resources to fight. Therefore, we accept their help with a huge thank you and move on. If they find your father, I'm sure they'll let you talk to him." Bee eyed me, and I got the meaning behind her words.

"Yes, ma'am."

"Done," Bee proclaimed. "Now, I'd like to see my granddaughter."

I went to help her, but Boner got there first, extending his arm. "Hello, Bee. I'm Boner."

Bee's face reddened. "You're kidding me."

"Not one bit."

She shook her head as she took Boner's hand. "Back in my day, we didn't have such sexual names." She turned toward me. "Don't think I don't know why they call you Stiff."

I burst out laughing.

CHELSEA

That arrogant, no-good—

"Chelsea, stop your stewing," Grams ordered, walking slowly down the hall with me behind her. How she knew what I was thinking, I didn't know. Grandmother radar maybe. "Look at the bigger picture here. Whoever is after your worthless father is bigger than we can handle. Getting help is not a sign of weakness. It's a sign of strength to accept it when you need it."

The damn woman and her wise words.

Sighing, I conceded my fate. I would be staying here with a group of badass bikers. What could possibly go wrong?

As we entered Jenn's room, the shit hit the ever-loving fan literally when a lamp smashed into a pedestal fan at the side of the room, clattering and clanging hard to the floor.

Jenn jumped, and I went after Mom. "What are you doing? Stop it!" I tried for quiet and stern, but I knew I fell short on the mark because of my anger over her not letting Jenn recover in peace.

"I can't believe those assholes did this to her!" Mom screeched as the door opened and boot steps flooded in. Great.

I ignored it, giving my full attention to my temperamental mother as I took in a cleansing breath.

"Mom, you have to knock it off and calm down. Yes, I'm pissed, too. Yes, I wanna cut off their balls and shove them up their asses. Yes, Jenn didn't deserve this. But, Mom, you can't be going off all halfcocked in attack mode."

Mom shook her head. "The hell I can't be in whatever mode I want. I'm her mother, and they hurt my baby!"

"Jannie, that's enough," Grams said, moving over to sit on the edge of the bed with Jenn. Tears spilled down my sister's face. "Hush there, young'un. You're gonna be just fine."

Jenn's tears fell harder, and again, I wanted to take that pain away from her.

I turned toward Mom. "Calm your shit," I demanded, low and stern. "She's been through enough and doesn't need you making this worse."

The starch began to seep out of my mother's spine as her face softened. I knew she was about to cry. We Millers were strong, but when one of us hurt, we all hurt. We all wanted to fix it, take it away. That was who we were, who my grandmother raised my mother to be, and who my mother raised us girls to be.

"Stiff and the guys got the two men who hurt Jenn," I whispered in her ear. "They took care of them. I don't know how, but I did notice cuts on Stiff's hands along with Boner's. Xander told me that Stiff would take care of it, and I have no reason not to trust that he didn't."

If I could, I would have knocked myself on the damn head. I was defending that man to my mother now. The sad part was that it was all true, and I couldn't knock that. As much as I hated it, score one for Stiff.

"I know. I'll calm." Mom let out a deep breath. "I just can't believe this is happening."

Heat hit my back, my body instantly coming alive. It could only be one man.

I inhaled deep recognizing Stiff's scent, and pulled slightly back from my mom.

"Ma'am, after you and Chelsea get done seeing Jenn, we'd like to ask you a couple of questions about her father."

Mom rolled her eyes. "Don't know much, but I'll answer what I can."

"Thank you, ma'am. We'll give you a bit then come get you," Stiff said.

Not once did I look back at him, but the loss of his heat … I hated that.

NINE

CHELSEA

WE SAT IN A VERY ORGANIZED OFFICE with wood-paneled walls and some type of deep brown carpet that looked to be twenty years old. Spook sat behind a monstrous desk while Mom and I took the chairs in front of him. Stiff leaned against the wall, his arms crossed.

The aura of the room presented dominance, but fear was kept at bay. If anything, I felt calm. Mom, on the other hand, had pulled herself together enough to be with my sister, but as soon as we'd set foot in this room, her body began vibrating with anger once again.

Gary Reese, my father, hadn't been good to my mother, and I felt bad for her because I knew she still loved him. I didn't know how or why, but she did. I'd caught her looking through old pictures longingly a couple of times. However, if I were a gambler, which I was not since I worked too damn hard for my money, I would bet it was the life they used to have that she missed the most.

When I was five or six, I remember game nights and even pizza nights where we would all be together as a family. Jenn had been little and would always screw up the game. Then I would get mad, and both Mom and Dad would have to soothe us. A few years after was when the change happened.

I looked back now and remembered my father passed out on the couch. I remembered shaking him and shaking him, but he would never wake up. Mom would tell me he was in a deep sleep. I knew now that he had been hopped-up on drugs.

The drugs tore us apart. Either that or his inability or care to ditch them.

My mother and father never married. They'd been together in all the ways possible, and I knew my mother loved him. They'd just never taken the leap, including my sister and me having my mom's last name instead of my father's. It was different, but it was something my mother had wanted, and it was what had been done.

"Have you spoken to Gary recently?" Spook asked, looking at my mother.

"No. Haven't heard from him since a couple of years after he stole from Chelsea."

"Stole?" Spook asked, and for some strange reason, I felt compelled to look over at Stiff, who nodded at me. I turned back to Spook.

"Credit card theft when I was a kid. He took out cards in my name and racked up the balances."

"Asshole bought expensive stuff, pawned it, and took the cash to buy drugs," Mom growled.

"True. Cops found items from the card statements at pawn shops across the state." My gut twisted at reliving my father's betrayal, but I powered on. "He went to jail for a short time, got out, and we haven't heard from him since."

"How long ago was that?" Stiff asked.

"When I was about twenty, so about ten years ago." Wow, that number hit me in the chest like a sharp knife. I hadn't heard from him for almost ten years. That shouldn't hurt, and I should be grateful, but he was still my dad. Even if he was messed up, part of me always wanted him to be there for me. It was a pipe dream, though.

"It's been about eight for me. He came around after he got out, apologizing."

My mother's words surprised me. She patted my hand, obviously feeling my growing tension.

"His family wanted nothin' to do with him, and I didn't need him around, messing up my kids' lives any more than he already had. I kicked him out and haven't heard from him again."

"Either of you know where he may be?" Spook asked.

I shook my head, but Mom spoke.

"The only place I can think of is his friend Patrick Samuelsson's. Last I knew, Pat lived out in Lake of the Woods in Petersburg, Kentucky, but with all of this so close, something tells me he's much closer to us."

"Agreed." Spook's eyes penetrated, looking between my mother and me. "Gary has gotten in bed with a powerful man in the drug business. We know he owes him money, but my guess is he's selling for him, too, because that's usually what happens in this situation. Either way, he's hiding in the shadows from this man, and he'll sniff him out sooner or later and take his hide, even if that means coming after the four of you. That's why we made these arrangements."

"Shouldn't Mom and Grams stay here, too?" I asked.

"Thought of that, but the guys on them will keep them safe. And something tells me Bee wouldn't be too kind about leaving her place."

Mom chuckled. "True. She'd do it for the girls, but she loves her house. Been there for fifty plus years."

"We're on the lookout for Gary and also the guy behind all of this. Needles will take care of Jenn, and Stiff here"—Spook nodded to the big man— "will take care of Chelsea."

My eyes narrowed, and Spook chuckled, not saying a word.

"I—"

My mother squeezed my hand so hard it caught my attention, and I turned to her.

"Let it go," she said, and I closed my eyes, finding the calm within.

"Fine."

"Fine," Spook returned. "Once your visit is done, Jannie, my guys will follow you back to the house."

"Thanks."

"Is this where we're gonna stay? Because I need to run by my place and get a few things." As I gestured around the wood-paneled room, the question was aimed at Stiff who'd followed me back after saying good-bye to my mom and Grams.

Jenn still lay there, sound asleep, no doubt the visit from them wearing her out. Hell, I felt a bit wrung out, but I powered through.

"No. You'll be stayin' in my house."

The room momentarily spun, and when I looked at Stiff, I swore he'd grown horns and was laughing at me like some cartoon devil.

"I agreed to staying here, not staying with you."

Stiff shook his head. "Damn, woman, you're stubborn."

He stepped toward me, and I stepped back. Each movement he made, I countered it, but inside, my pulse began to pick up. I felt like I was a lamb, and Stiff was the big panther, stalking his prey. While I knew I shouldn't want to be the prey since I had no time for it, my body had other thoughts, tingling in places that should stay dormant.

When I sidestepped him, he was too fast and caught me around the waist, pulling my back flush to his front. I inhaled, which was a mistake. It did nothing to calm my libido that decided to go into hyperdrive. The air seemed to have compressed, exerting every bit of its force on Stiff and me.

I struggled, but he held me fast, his other arm coming around my chest and holding me to his rock hard one.

"What are you doing?" I tried for annoyed, but it came out breathy and wanton—hell, even needy. How long had it been since I'd had an orgasm that wasn't self-induced? So damn long I couldn't remember it.

His lips touched my ear, and I jerked. Not from pain, but from the pleasure his hot breath elicited. My thighs tingled in a way that sent sparks to my core.

"Showin' you why you're stayin' with me." He darted his tongue out and licked the shell of my ear, and my body almost liquefied from the touch. My knees felt a bit wobbly, but I held strong.

"How are you gonna do that?" I whispered, waiting for my brain to kick in at any given moment.

He nibbled on the lobe of my ear then moved to the spot right behind it. Pleasure shot up my spine as sparks cascaded over my skin. As he suckled that spot, my knees really did give, but he held me securely to him, not letting me fall.

He used his tongue to trace my neck to my collarbone, sucking and nipping the entire time.

"Because, with you close, I can watch you. Protect you."

My brain had a small spark. "Why? It's not your responsibility."

His grip tightened, and his lips came back to my ear. "I'm makin' it my responsibility. I'm makin' it my problem to solve."

My head lulled back against his shoulder. "Why?"

"Woman, you're fuckin' lucky I find this sassy, stubborn mouth of yours sexy." He moved to my cheek, giving me a slight kiss there, and my brain engaged.

"I'm not some whore," I said, stiffening my back. "You can't just play with me."

His grip tightened so much I could barely breathe, but I managed.

"Who said I'm playin'?"

"I saw the woman earlier. I'm not her."

He chuckled, which I didn't find funny in the least. "Rita? She tried to get on my dick all night but couldn't, not when your face was the only one I saw when I closed my eyes."

Oh, God. My struggles left me as my head spun. Trust was such a hard thing for me, always had been after my dad left us. I had always trusted that he'd keep my mom, sister, and me safe. He broke that, damaging a part of me.

I tried afterward to trust men, but each one of them turned out to be a frog in a sea of toads, one worse than the other. My choices in men weren't the best. I fully admitted to that one. But it wasn't like I was going to marry the guy, or even date him for that matter. Besides, I fully believed the men here would protect us, so the small building block of trust was there. I just couldn't get too sucked into him. As my father said, "You'll never be anything. No man will ever want you." So I knew it would never last.

Still, what would be wrong with having some fun, easing some tension while I was here? It didn't have to turn into anything. I'd never really done casual before, but Stiff was hot, like seriously hot, and the way his hands touched me … I just knew he would be able to help ease this fire inside of me.

"You think I'm gonna believe that?" I retorted, not relaying any of my thoughts.

Stiff turned me in his arms, my nose coming to his chin. As I looked up, I saw his eyes were blazing holes into me. His grip tightened, and the shallow rise and fall of his chest, along with his erection poking into me, told me he was burning. For me. How did that happen?

"Let me show ya." His hot lips came to mine in a fierce kiss that sucked me under the instant our flesh touched. He consumed my mouth, his tongue taking ownership. I swore he touched every inch inside of it, demanding more from me, and I gave in willingly.

He snaked his hand up my back to my neck then threaded his fingers through my hair. He massaged as he went, his rough hand strong and determined.

One thing I'd always loved was my head rubbed. As a kid, I would bargain with Jenn for her to rub it. It'd been a long time since I'd had this. I let every thought sweep away then focused on breathing and standing upright.

Stiff pulled away, his forehead pressing against mine. I gasped for breath as he began inhaling deep. With my eyes closed, I could feel his breath on my lips, cool against the wetness he'd left, sending more shivers through me.

"Sooner I get shit cleaned up at my place, the sooner you're in my bed." Stiff's rough voice penetrated the air.

I should have been appalled—hell, my stubborn 'I am woman, hear me roar' side wanted to be, but I melted, wanting to be in his bed. I wanted to forget the shit in my life, even if for a small moment. Maybe that would help me focus on a plan of action.

I reached up and gripped his leather and shirt. With utter boldness I didn't know where I'd obtained, I stood on my tiptoes, kissed the tip of his nose, then whispered in his ear, "Then you better get cleaned up."

He growled. Yes, growled like the panther I thought he was. His lips crashed into mine in another scorching kiss so hot I gripped his clothing in fear I would fall. Then he tore away and pushed me away from him.

"Got shit to do," he said, moving toward the door. "That was hot, Chels. Don't fuckin' lose it. I'm comin' back for ya."

He stalked out the door as my heart thumped hard in my chest.

Moving to the bed, I sat down, my hand over my heart, feeling the pumps.

"That was hot," my sister confessed, jolting me from my spot to look down at her on the bed. Her cut lip tipped slightly.

"I didn't know you were awake."

A sound came from her throat, and I was hoping it was a chuckle, but it sounded like a pained one. "Saw you two and didn't wanna interrupt."

"Jenn!" I pretended to scold.

She knew everything about me: the good, the bad, and the ugly. While that was fine with me, I was happy the kissing stopped before we'd gone any further. One thing I didn't ever want to do was to get intimate with a man in front of my sister. No thanks.

"Oh, shut it," she stated, closing her eyes. "You deserve to be happy, sis."

I reached for her hand and held it loosely. "I wouldn't call this happy. I would call it getting lost in the moment."

Her eye lids lifted. "Whatever way you spin it, that right there, sister, was happy. Hell, bliss."

"Jenn, he's part of a motorcycle club, and I saw a woman all over him and kissing him on the cheek this morning," I started.

"Shut it," Jenn said again. "I heard everything he said, so don't feed me a line of bull. Gotta take life as it comes. Never know when something fucked up will happen to you and you'll end up like me."

I knew she was trying to joke, but I did not find it funny at all.

"What happened to you will not happen ever again, Jennifer. I swear to that."

Hell, if I had to drop my life just to go up and play bodyguard so she could finish school, I wouldn't think twice about it. She would finish, and she would get her degree. She wanted it too much, and I refused to let my father fuck that up for her. By any means necessary, she would get that piece of paper.

"I love you, but you need to start living in the moment."

I stared down at her in shock. "I've been living."

She gave a slight shake of her head. "No. You've been surviving. I'm not saying this guy is the one, but you need to live and experience things. All you do is work, sleep, take care of us, work, sleep, take care of us … Repeat, like, a million, gazillion times. I'm not saying give the man your heart and declare your undying love for him or anything like that." I chuckled as she rolled her eyes. "I'm just saying we're here for a while, a few days, a couple of weeks. Might as well have fun."

"I thought you were doped on pain meds. How are you pulling all of this out of your ass?"

"I am on meds, and they're nice. I can almost think about moving, but when I do, the pain returns. So if I just lie here, I feel great."

I gave her hand a small squeeze. "Sleep. I'll get us sorted on where we're staying then somehow get to my place to get us a few things. Is there anything you can't live without?"

"Diet Coke," she responded with a slight smile. "Haven't had one since I was grabbed. Maybe that's why my head aches so badly."

"I'll make sure to stock you up. Sleep."

If she were resting, then I could figure everything else out.

TEN

STIFF

I FUCKING HATED CLEANING. Never had a reason to when I lived by myself, but as soon as I decided Chelsea and her sister would stay here, I went on a mission and enlisted Xander to help. He was a prospect after all, so that helped with telling him what to do. It also helped that while in the Corps, he'd learned to take orders well.

In three hours, the place looked livable.

"Smells better in here," Xander said, spraying some blue shit around the place.

"Easy with that."

"Fuck, man. You gotta get the funk out and rid of the damn sock smell. You always had nasty feet," Xander chided.

"Fuck you. I did not. That was your scrawny ass," I fired back.

"Scrawny? I'll fucking show you scrawny." Bottle dropped and forgotten, he came at me, but it wasn't hard, just a shoulder to the gut. This was fucking around, not actual fighting. We'd had our go-arounds. Sure, I busted my ass for him, but he had a thick skull like me, and we collided at times. Those usually ended up with us being black and blue.

We wrestled, me catching a couple of soft hits to the side, and I threw a couple at Xander. We each pulled away, laughing. I'd missed this when he'd been gone, missed him.

Xander fell onto the couch and tossed his boots up on the coffee table that was not clear of all the garbage.

"So, got a thing for this one?" he asked, twisting the cap off a beer and tossing it on the table.

I glared. "You'd better pick that shit up."

He grinned. "Nice deflect."

"Zip it." I plopped into the recliner.

The room wasn't grand or anything like that. All of the brothers lived here on the compound in block buildings. They were nice, at least nicer than some of the rooms in the clubhouse, but it wasn't the Ritz. I had a huge seventy-two-inch TV hanging on the wall with a cabinet below for a Blu-ray player and my movies. I had a new couch that was charcoal gray. Everything in here was new. My room inside the clubhouse, not so much. But in my home, everything was, from the fridge to the toilet seat. All installed by me.

I didn't have shit growing up, living from place to place. This was the first home I really knew. It meant the world to me, gave me a sense of stability in a world filled with chaos.

I joined Vipers Creed officially when I turned eighteen, but I'd been around the club with Spook for as long as I could remember. We'd become friends in high school, even with him being a year older. Then, that year felt like forever; now, it was an afterthought. I'd had Xander to support, a mother who didn't give a shit, and this club gave me purpose, stability, a family. It also had given Xander a home when I moved into the compound. It had been more than I could have asked for. Still was.

"Stiff's got a hard-on for the waitress," Xander taunted.

I shot him a glare that he laughed at. Most men wouldn't dare. My brother, on the other hand, knew I might punch the hell out of him, but I'd never really kill him. At least, I didn't think so. If he kept this shit up, there were no guarantees.

"Shut. It."

"What's the big fuckin' deal? You've got women comin' and goin' all the time."

Exactly. Easy fucking pussy that meant absolutely nothing except to get my dick wet and to get off. Chelsea, she was different. Yeah, I wanted my dick wet and to get off, but there was this keen sense of knowledge that came from her. She knew the hard knocks of life. She'd lived them, told them to fuck off, and grown a pair of her own balls so big she didn't let shit get in her way. Then she knocked down any bitch who did.

That, I fucking admired. That made me harder than granite. Add in the tits, ass, and face with her fiery personality, and I was a fucking goner.

"Fucking hell. Is Old Stiffie ready to turn in his house mouse card?"

Damn, was I ready to turn in the mouses? A house mouse was a woman around the club who serviced the brothers in any way they needed: sex, blowjob, hand job, cooking food, cleaning the clubhouse—pretty much whatever. In return, they got protection from the club.

I'd had my share of mouses, women, whores, and strippers in my time, but not one set me up like Chelsea had with only a damn kiss. I fucking craved to have her in my home, under me. Her sister would be in the guest room, and Chelsea would be in mine.

When I kept my lips sealed, Xander laughed harder.

Normally, I'd have some witty fucking comeback, but he had me stumped for a moment.

"Alright, brother, I'll let you off. Let's talk about tomorrow night."

I leaned farther back in the chair then rolled my head from side to side. "What about it?"

"Dawg and I are gonna case the joint again tomorrow. Today, there wasn't any movement. Then what?" Xander replied.

Prospecting, Xander was only privy to some shit going down, not everything.

"You're not going in tomorrow. You're here with Chelsea and her sister."

Xander rose, yelling, "What the fuck!"

I'd spoken with Spook earlier and asked him about leaving Xander back. The man just got out of the military, and I knew his fellow teammates had issues that he'd joined the MC. Not that I gave a shit, but my brother had honor that I wasn't ready to tarnish just yet. Keeping him clean had been ingrained in me for so long it was natural.

Protect Xander. Period.

"Look, I need someone to stay here. Count yourself lucky you're not on Bee and Jannie duty." I had no doubt those two women would be a handful.

Xander groaned. "Is it because I'm a prospect or your brother?"

I turned toward him, my eyes telling him the answer.

"Dammit, Stiff." He raked his hands through his hair.

"Why don't you head home to Gabby? I got this."

His boots sounded on the carpet until he was next to my chair, and I looked up at him.

"Gotta stop treatin' me like I'm a kid, Stiff. I'm good with this shit."

"I know that, but I need you here, and that's what it'll be."

"Fine." He held out his hand, and I clasped it, squeezed, and released. "Later."

"Later."

I lifted the footrest and kicked my feet up. Chelsea was due here in about thirty minutes. I had time to kill.

CHELSEA

"You'll walk down to the fourth house. That'll be Stiff's," Trixie instructed, coming into Jenn's room.

"I can't believe—"

"Believe it," she said. "These guys, they're something else. Best advice I can give ya is to roll with it."

"Roll with what, exactly?" I questioned as she held out a bag, and I looked inside. Score. Women's shampoo, conditioner, and deodorant. At least when I shower, I wouldn't smell like a man. That was all I could find in the small, attached bathroom.

"With Stiff …" She paused for a moment then continued, "There's a lot more to him than what you see."

"Oh, I saw, alright," I mumbled, setting the bag on the dresser.

"Saw what?" she asked.

"He said it was nothing, and it doesn't matter, anyway," I retorted.

"Be patient. Have fun. And I have to say, I've never seen Stiff like this. Earlier, he didn't even have a line for me, and he only does it to get under Spook's skin. Okay, I've gotta run. You have your stuff and know where to go."

"Thanks," I told her, meaning it yet confused at the same time.

"Anytime. I live here with Spook, so we'll see a lot of each other." She smiled so warm I felt comfortable with her. It wasn't fake like Mitzi. No, this one was completely honest.

"Bye."

"Bye."

Once she left, I washed myself and gave my sister a sponge bath, or tried to at least.

Needles came by and looked my sister over. He changed her dressings, which I'd already done. Yes, I cut my eyes up at him a couple of times, but he was doing his job, and I tried to give a little. It was so damn hard to let others help. I needed to start letting that part of me open up more, even if difficult.

I also called Charlie and told him I was taking a few days off for the first time in my life. That hurt, but it also felt liberating. Hurt that I'd never done it before. Liberating because my feet could always use time to recoup.

Charlie was pissed, though not at me, of course, and chewed my ear off for a bit, wanting every small detail. When I told him Jenn and I were staying with the Vipers, he calmed a bit. I didn't know if I should feel good about that or run.

Now I stood in front of the structure Trixie had told me to go to, and well, I really had no other word for it. It was a huge, concrete, brick building that matched several down the line. The outside of this one was clean, but nothing stood out for it to be unique. I knew the Vipers Creed owned this old Army compound for years. However, I'd never been in it, never had a need to.

The clubhouse was a huge gray building, I believed around three levels. There were also thick walls around the entire perimeter with guards in tall, parapet things by the gate. A lot of drab, military gray was everywhere except for a couple of houses that had some flowers in pots, but not Stiff's.

I felt cold yet warm if that were possible. Cold due to the starkness of color, but warm from feeling safe. I didn't have to worry about the ugliness just outside the large gates that barricaded this world away from the rest.

The front had a slab of concrete for a porch with a steel door. Very inviting—not.

I knocked politely, then thought better of it, balled my hand into a fist, and banged on the door. No one on the other end would hear a small knock through the thick steel door.

The hard metal opened in a whoosh, blowing my hair back with the gust of air-conditioned air.

I pulled the tendrils away from my face and stared into the ocean colored eyes of Stiff. The man looked as if I could be his next three meals and he wouldn't be happier.

"Come in." He stepped back from the door, but not out of the way.

I sucked in a deep breath and had to brush by his body to get through the door. The man took up at least half of it, so getting through the space was a challenge, but I made it.

The space had the normal living room furniture—couch, chair, an over the top TV—but it was clean, like someone had been in there just moments ago, cleaning the hell out of the place. It even smelled like fabric softener of some sort. The bitch in me wanted to ask if the brunette had come in and cleaned, but I wasn't going there. He'd said some nice things to me, and I needed to put that woman out of my head.

The door snapped shut, and then I felt it—the force of the room hitting me from every angle, bouncing around like live wires. The crackle was so palpable it could almost be heard.

I dropped my bag and wrapped my arms around my body, feeling the need to shield myself. I wasn't afraid. No, this was more powerful, something on a cosmic level that I'd never known existed.

Strong hands came to my shoulders, and I let out a small gasp. He kneaded them, easing the tension until there was none. Then he cascaded his roughened fingertips along my neck, making small up and down strokes. The room became incredibly warm, and my heart beat like a jackhammer.

Each caress awakened tiny bits of my skin that added tingles, building in intensity like snowflakes landing on the ground, forming into a huge ball.

I shut my eyes, no longer able to keep them open, his touches both calming and arousing.

Lost in his touch, I yelped when he picked me up bridal-style like I weighed nothing and strode over to the couch. He sat down then placed me on the seat next to him, my legs on his lap.

"What are you doing?"

He reached for my feet without answering and tore one of my tennis shoes off. I squirmed away.

My feet were the one thing on my body that I hated to show off to anyone. Many women here in Tennessee loved the comfort of flip-flops. Me, not so much. With as many years as I'd put in on them, they were rough, callused, and gross.

I periodically gave myself a pedicure because there was no way in hell I was spending money on something like that when I could do it just as easily. However, it had been a couple of weeks since I'd done my last one, and I knew those puppies wouldn't be pretty.

"Stop," he commanded, bringing one of his arms across my hips to hold me down. He was strong; I had to give him that much. "Talk. Why can't I take your shoes off?"

"Why do you want to?" I responded.

"I know you're on 'em all the damn time. I wanna rub them."

Oh, hell no.

"No, Stiff. I'm fine. Please just leave my shoes on." Thank God I still had a sock on.

"Do your feet hurt?" he asked, and I almost lied. Then his face gave me that 'don't you dare' look, and I didn't know him well enough to know what he'd do.

"They always hurt."

"Then I'm rubbin' them."

I picked up my knees and tried to get away again. "Please, Stiff, really I'm fine." I looked around the room, the television catching my eye. "Why do you need such a big TV?"

"Because I want it, Chels. And nice deflection. I'm rubbin' them. End of story. Either I do it with you lyin' there, relaxed, or I tie your ass up so you can't move, but either way, I'm takin' care of you."

While my belly warmed at the thought of someone even wanting to take care of me, I couldn't let him see my callused feet. He would throw me out and never look back. Plus, I was here to check out the place for Jenn and myself. I'd left her at the clubhouse, and Xander was supposed to bring her here in a while.

Then it hit me. Wasn't it just a short time ago that I wanted him to go away? Yeah, I did, because this couldn't happen. Okay, fine. Let him rub my nasty feet. Then maybe he'd let Jenn and I go to my grams' house, instead.

"Fine." I smirked and stopped fighting to his astonishment.

He shook his head then pulled off a sock without batting an eye. He then pulled the other shoe and sock off, tossing them to the floor, and again, nothing. He pulled one foot into his hands and began rubbing. I knew he felt the hardness in spots; he had to. Nevertheless, he said nothing, just stared at the television like this was a normal thing.

"Do you bring lots of women to your place to rub their feet?"

Smack my damn head. Why the hell would I ask a question like that? I didn't want or need the answer to it, so why? Why, why, why! I was seriously a glutton for punishment.

"Babe, the only chick who's been in here is Gabby, my brother's girl. Oh, and Trixie. That's it until you. Jenn will be the next."

I stilled. "You've never had women in here?"

"Nope."

Anger welled up. I'd had enough men in my life screw me over. I was not in the market for another.

"Don't lie to me," I practically growled out, and his head snapped toward me.

His hands kept moving, yet one gripped a little more tightly in warning. I might have been hot, but I caught it.

"Ain't got no reason to lie to you, woman."

"Man," I barked back, "don't feed me a line of shit. At least be honest with me."

"You want honesty? Fine." He grabbed both my ankles and pulled me onto his lap, wrapping his arms around my body and immobilizing me. "Never had a reason to have a woman here. Clubhouse, all the fuckin' time. Here, no. This is my home. You don't shit where you live."

"Well, technically, I'm sure you shit in the toilet." My damn mouth got the best of me, and as soon as the words left my lips, I clamped them shut. Damn, damn, damn.

He chuckled. "Alright, smartass, so I shit in the toilet. What I don't do is bring women back here."

"Then why am I here?"

He snaked his hand up my back. "Still tryin' to figure that out." His eyes dropped to my lips as they parted. "Now I'm takin' those fuckin' lips."

And he did. God, did he. The foot rub was a distant memory as his mouth took mine, and I didn't fight it. I couldn't. The pull between us was too great, and every time his lips touched me, my brain went to Jamaica, or maybe Florida. Hell, it went somewhere other than the present place, and I rather liked it there.

ELEVEN

STIFF

DAMN WOMAN TASTED LIKE HONEY; bona fide, right out of the beehive, honey. So damn sweet each taste had me craving more, needing more, wanting more. Her mouth was a fucking drug I could get high on for days alone.

She nipped at my bottom lip, earning a growl from deep within my throat. That one sound sparked something in her, something hungry.

Hot and sexy as hell, she gripped the sides of my head and moved to straddle my hips, her heat blazing against my hard cock. And I just held her tight to my body, but she didn't need any help. Her tits smashed against my chest, her hard nipples poking me.

With Chelsea, I had to fight for control. She didn't placate me and follow my lead. No, she demanded that I earn that submission from her. And fuck, I loved that.

If she thought she was going to win, though, she was sadly mistaken.

Gripping her wrists, I pulled them behind her back, clutching them with one hand. She pulled away on a sharp intake of breath. I took a few, too. Then a small smirk appeared on the left side of her lips mischievously, and I knew I was in over my head.

The way her fucking hips worked in a steady rhythm over my erection was unnerving, and unnerved was something I didn't do.

I released her arms, lifted her, and flipped her back to my couch, crowding in on top of her.

"Think you're running the show here, Chels?"

She gripped my cut and T-shirt hard. "I'd let you run it if you'd get your ass in gear."

Chelsea lifted up and suctioned her lips to mine. I fell on top of her, trying not to crush her yet knowing I was, anyway. She was still moving, so she was getting air.

I rose, straddling her body now. She panted and brought her hands up to reach for me, but something was off. Before, she couldn't wait to get away from me, thought of every way to leave the clubhouse. Now, all the sudden, she was on fire.

I gripped her hands and held them to her stomach. "Gotta say, lovin' this fire." I paused for a moment. "Fire … That's what I'm callin' you from now on."

"Why?"

"Because that's what you are, baby. Hot as hell—fire."

She planted a kiss on my cheek. "Whatever."

Something was definitely off.

"But what's goin' on?"

Chelsea blinked rapidly, and an adorable stain of red came to her cheeks, but her words were fierce. "I'm feeling the need to let loose a little."

"Why's that?" Not that I wouldn't fuck her, but there were so many depths to this woman, and this was another one that I felt the urge to get to the bottom of.

She let out a gust of air. "If you don't wanna do this, I'll go."

"The fuck you're goin' anywhere."

Her eyes shot to mine.

"Wanna know how it changed."

"You feel this, don't you?" she asked quietly. The "this" being the sparks between us, the pressure that was due to intensity forming diamonds in the rough. The volcano that was going to erupt once I slipped my dick into her wet heat.

My cock jumped at the idea.

I leaned down close, our noses only an inch apart. "Yeah, Fire. I feel it. Don't know what the fuck it is. Never felt it before. But I do now. I get you. Just gotta see where this leads us."

"Yeah," she whispered then went for my lips again.

As I snaked my hand up her shirt, I felt the softness of her flesh jump with each brush of my fingertips. I met her bra-covered mound and squeezed. It was a handful with none of that artificial shit that felt like balloons.

I pulled the cusp of her bra down, finding her nipple and brushing my fingertips against it.

She broke away and moaned, arching her back into my touch. Her hands met my bald head, rubbing, and I couldn't hold it back anymore.

I pulled her arm, making her torso come with it. Wasting no time, I yanked the shirt off and removed her bra then let her fall back to the couch, her tits doing a sexy as hell jiggle.

I squeezed her breasts hard and rough, so much so the small mound that overflowed my hand began to turn a beautiful pink.

"Oh, God," she moaned, grabbing my wrists as her body arched into my touch.

The rosy tip called to me, and my mouth found its purchase. I sucked, nibbled, and swiped my tongue all over while kneading her breasts.

Her grip on my wrist tightened, and I went to the other peak then sucked it in deep.

Her hips bucked, but mine held them down, not giving them any wiggle room. Her eyes were burning with the fire she would be referred to from now on. She was fire when she was pissed, happy, and fucking horny. Lucky for the both of us, I liked each one of them.

She tried to push my hands off her breasts and down her body, but I held fast, giving her a warning squeeze that was even rougher than I'd already given her.

"Stiff, please," she moaned.

That fucking moan, along with my name being in it, broke me. I rose from the couch, unbuttoned and pulled off her jeans and underwear, fell to my knees, and then devoured that pretty, bare pink pussy of hers.

"Oh!" she yelped as I turned and twisted her until her pussy was right against my mouth, being devoured by me. The fucking woman tasted like a woman should: hot, ripe, and wet. I sucked down every drop she gave me.

She reached for my head. No doubt, if I had hair, it would have been pulled pretty fucking hard.

"I'm gonna come!" she screamed as I took the little hard bud and sucked with everything I had until she burst into the flames of fire she was.

Chelsea's body shook, her eyes shut, head thrown back, fingernails in my scalp. Her body completely lifted from the couch as she screamed, moaned, then screamed again as the shocks hit her. I couldn't take my eyes off her, but I began to slowly bring her down by licking her inner lips, still keeping her aroused yet gradually letting her fall.

I watched as she slowly came back to herself, her eyes finally fluttering open, only to stare down at me. I couldn't help smiling.

I started to insert two fingers. Then, surprised by how damn tight she was, I only added one.

"Been a while," she panted out breathlessly, obviously reading my mind.

"How long, Fire?"

"Years." She let her head roll back to the couch and closed her eyes as her pussy sucked my finger in greedily. She was going to be fucking magic around my cock, but I didn't want to hurt her.

"Best fuckin' news I've heard in a while." Knowing I was the only man who'd been inside this pussy for years turned me on to a point I'd never experienced before. It made me want inside her right fucking now.

Willpower of the gods allowed me to attach my lips to her clit again, thrust, and finally get two fingers inside. Fuck me, she was tight. I had fucking girth, so I'd need to go slow or at least fucking try to.

Chelsea's pants echoed with the laps of my tongue and fingers. She arched, and I felt another climax coming, so I backed off, earning a very disgruntled groan of protest.

Sliding my fingers out, I saw they were drenched. Her eyes came to mine, and I licked every single one of those fuckers.

And there it was … that fire blazing in her eyes. Her desire and want were calling to me to come and take my fill.

I rose, and with record speed, tossed my leather and shirt on the chair. Then I unbuckled my belt and pants, letting them fall to the floor. I didn't bother with underwear today, so my rock hard cock stood at attention.

Chelsea's eyes widened, and I smiled.

CHELSEA

HOLY SHIT.

Feet to the floor, I leaned in. I was pretty sure if I tried to put my hand around his cock, I wouldn't be able to touch my fingers.

"Fire, if you're gonna get that close, ya may as well make good use of your mouth."

My body thrummed from his words. It might have been a while since I'd had any sexual relationships, but I knew what to do in the bedroom. Never once had any complaints.

One thing I was a sucker for was sucking on cock. It wasn't like I was at bars, trolling for someone to suck off. I just kept the men I was with happy.

Looking up at him through my lashes, I gripped his cock and took it all the way down my throat, not gagging a bit.

When his lips touched mine, I'd decided I was all in. I'd show him exactly what I was made of, which had already scared one man off.

"Fucking shit," he groaned as his body went stiff. Maybe that was how he'd gotten his name.

I chuckled at the idea.

"Think that's funny, do ya?" He threaded his fingers through my hair as I pulled back.

I would let him think he had this, but with my tongue and lips, I could change his mind.

He maneuvered me, bucking his hips, thinking he had me where he wanted. That was when I started in with my tongue.

Down the underside of his dick as I sucked around the bulbous head. With my hand, I reached down and cupped his balls, rolling them, then reached out my finger to rub the sensitive area between his sac and asshole.

"Fucking shit!" he called out, giving up a little pressure he had on my hair.

I continued giving him everything I had. I pulled him out and ran my lips roughly up and down his length. Then I sucked in just the tip until his knees wobbled.

The next time I took him in my mouth, his pubic hairs tickled my nose as I kept my gag reflex at bay. I could usually go about twenty seconds, which was pretty damn good in dick-sucking time.

He pulled out of me so abruptly I fell to the floor, catching myself with my hands.

"Fire," he said in almost a warning, reaching for his jeans, pulling out a condom, then placing it over his shaft.

I was in awe watching it, because I'd never known those things stretched so much. Surely, he had to get extra wide or something. No regular condom would do the trick.

I snapped myself back to reality when I was lifted in the air, my arms going around Stiff's neck and legs going around his hips.

"Fuckin' gonna kill me after that shit you just pulled, but I gotta go slow so I don't hurt you."

He carried me through the living room, kitchen, down a hall, and into another room. When my back hit a bed, I realized we were in his bedroom.

Stiff slid between my thighs as I lifted my knees, inviting him in. He slid his arms under my shoulders, his hands cupping the back of my neck. Then I felt his heat at my entrance.

Painstakingly slow, he eased into me, and my body accommodated his girth rather quickly. With each small back and forth thrust, he went deeper inside. Also, with each movement, he awakened nerves inside me that lit up like a burning blaze.

None of the men I'd had before compared to Stiff's size, and the stretch and burn only added to my pleasure.

Holding his solid arms, I tried not to dig my fingers into his skin, but it was damn hard. I felt it then—his hips and mine aligning. He was in to the hilt, and he just sat there for a moment, a look of pain etched across his face.

"Gotta move," was all the warning I got before he began.

I'd had sex. I'd made love. I'd fucked. But never in my life had any of that compared to this right here. Put all three of those into a blender, set that sucker on high, and put it in a shot glass—that was what this was.

I felt him everywhere. Not just inside my body, but along my skin, burning me, searing me, ruining me for any other man.

Rocking my hips, I got in sync with him, and the more I did, the harder he pumped in and out. Sweat dripped off his face down to my body, and I wanted to lick every damn drop off of him.

His eyes came to mine, and I was lost. As the swirling depths sucked me in, I erupted, screaming so damn loudly I was sure to be embarrassed his brothers had heard me at some point, just not at this one.

He got up on his knees, and his thrusts grew more out of sync as he gripped my hips.

He tossed his head back. "Fire," he breathed out.

I'd never seen a man come like that and never thought my name sounded as sexy before.

Stiff spilled inside of me as I tried to calm my breathing, a slight sheen of sweat covering me now, as well.

For long moments, he stayed planted, like leaving the comfort of our connection would be too difficult.

Finally, he pulled out, and we both groaned. Stiff fell to the side of me and pulled me into his arms, holding me tight. I snuggled in, enjoying someone taking care of me and my needs for once.

One time of him inside of me—one—and I could feel the patter of my heart change, but I needed to remember to protect it. I knew it would be an uphill battle, because lying there with Stiff's arms around me, I felt that muscle inside me tighten.

TWELVE

CHELSEA

*T*HUMP, THUMP, THUMP.

I popped my head up from Stiff's chest, my breathing back to normal and my body feeling sated in a way that should be illegal.

"Fuck," Stiff growled, rolling from the bed and grabbing his jeans. "Better get dressed. Your sister's here."

He tugged them on as I scrambled from the bed to the living room, only to hear the thump on the door again.

"Shit!" I muttered, grabbing my clothes then putting them on in record time. I ran my hands through my hair to get some of the tangles out when one caught between my fingers, and I had to pull hard to get it out.

Stiff had an ease on his face that I had never seen on him before. It was as if he were calm, maybe even happy, but of course, everyone was happy after they'd been laid. Hell, my body felt great, so I probably looked the same.

Regardless, I was another conquest for him, a simple release. He'd said he felt something, but I had to remember who I had just been in bed with—the man who was rumored to hit anything in a skirt. I might be in jeans, but same concept.

I shook my head then finished with my hair and made sure all of my clothes were on right.

"I don't even know where she's sleeping," I said.

"You'll see it in a minute, Fire," he replied, grabbing me around the neck and pulling me to him before he kissed me breathless.

When he released me, I wobbled a bit on my feet, trying to find my balance. My mind was just as unsteady. Never in my life had a man kiss me breathless like every time he did.

The walls I'd set around myself were beginning to fall and crumble around me, but I couldn't allow that. I couldn't accept that whatever this was between us was real. After all, nothing in my life was ever real when it came to men. That had been proven over and over again.

"Fucking love that look on you." He softly touched his lips to mine then went to the door right as more pounding came.

Stiff swung the door open to reveal an amused Xander holding my sister in his arms, her head resting against his wide chest.

"Took you long enough." He smirked, walking in then eyeing me. He shook his head knowingly, and I felt the heat creep up, but I didn't back away from his eyes. He shook his head again as he walked through the house.

That was when shame and embarrassment hit me like a load of bricks on my head. Xander knew better than anyone how Stiff acted. Me, I probably looked pathetic and weak to him from giving in to desires that I'd had for so long.

I pushed that down and followed close behind.

"Be careful," I told him unnecessarily.

"Woman, if you tell me one more time to be careful with your sister, I'm gonna have Stiff tie you up and stick a fucking gag on you."

I stopped dead in my tracks. "You wouldn't," I gasped, my hand coming to my chest, even though my clit, fully sated from Stiff, began to throb at the thought. My eyes flitted to Stiff, and I was unable to stop them.

With his index finger and thumb, he brushed the sides of his lips in a move that was so damn sexy it should be videotaped and sent to porn shops around the world.

He clucked his tongue. "Don't know, brother. She's pretty fuckin' good with that mouth."

Xander chuckled while I glared; the warm feeling that resided in my belly seeming to flutter way.

"I can't believe you just said that in front of your brother," I snapped to his amusement.

"Babe, he knew it the moment he entered the place."

While I doubted very much Xander knew that I'd sucked Stiff off—well, almost off—the house did sort of smell like sex.

Damn.

"Leave her alone," my sister said with a groan, "and lay me down please."

Her words snapped me out of my rollercoaster of emotions, putting all the focus on her.

"Like she said, let's go."

I followed as Xander went down the hall to the first door on the left. The door was partially open, but he pushed it with his boot the rest of the way. The room was simple yet very clean and new. The furniture was a dark wood, the posters of the bed and the lone dresser matching. The bedding was a soft bluish-gray and looked seriously comfortable. A television was mounted on the wall, but other than that, nothing. No pictures on the walls or decorations of any kind. Guess this was a man's room.

I scooted around Xander then pulled the blankets and sheet down. The crisp, white linens didn't have a wrinkle in them, and they smelled like dryer sheets.

Xander laid my sister down.

I'd changed her into a pair of sweatpants and a loose T-shirt after her bath earlier, and her small frame seemed to be engulfed by the bed.

I sat gently on the side of the bed. "How are you feeling?" I asked her, brushing the hair away from her face, seeing the bruising was even worse than the day before.

"Like I got run over by a truck." The corner of her lip tipped up, telling me she was joking, but I still hated it.

"You're gonna be fine," I whispered softly. "I promise."

"I'm really sleepy," Jenn replied drowsily.

I'd given her a pain pill before coming over to Stiff's place in hopes that when she was moved it would help lessen her pain. It seemed to be kicking in.

"Sleep," I told her, but her eyes were already closed and there was a slight rise and fall to her chest.

"She'll be fine."

I jumped at the sound and whirled around toward Stiff.

"You scared me."

He smiled as Xander walked back in, carrying a small bag, reminding me that my sister and I had nothing with us. He set the bag on the bed, slapped his brother on the shoulder as he passed, then left the room. The loud thud of the door echoed, telling me he'd left the house.

"I need to go to my place and get some things. Is there any way someone could watch Jenn and you give me a ride over?"

"Yeah, babe. I'll get it together."

"Thanks," I said, reaching in the bag and pulling out my sister's pills, taking them over to the dresser and setting them out.

I felt a bit awkward. Here, I'd just had sex with this man, felt so damn good, and now I almost didn't know how to act, which was seriously unusual for me. I'd never had this problem before. Then again, I'd also never had a one-night stand or a … whatever the hell this was. A couple days thing? I needed to pull my shit together.

"She's fine. Come with me." Stiff held out his hand, and I bit my bottom lip.

Slowly, I walked toward him, and he tugged me into his body.

I tentatively looked up at him, seeing heat blazing in his eyes, and his growing erection pressed into my thigh.

"Already?" I asked.

While I didn't have a long list of lovers, I'd had zero who could go a second time only fifteen minutes after he'd just climaxed.

His lips came to my ear as I pressed against him. "Fire, I'm nowhere near done with you." He kissed me long, hard, and deep. Then he pulled me into his room and showed me exactly how much he wasn't done with me.

STIFF

You've gotta be shittin' me.

I pulled up my dually truck to the address Chelsea had given me, and what I saw was not happening. A single-wide trailer sat in the vast area of several other trailers. While I'd lived in several growing up, this one had to be one of the worst, at least from the outside.

The paint was peeling, the metal underneath showed rust holes, window screens had holes, and while clean, scratches were all over the place. The wooden stairs leading up to the front door needed to be scrapped and new ones put in to replace them.

I stopped and threw the truck into park. "This is your place?"

Her spine stiffened and shoulders drew back, not liking my tone, which hadn't been intentional.

"Yes. I'll just go in and get a few things." She reached for the door handle, opening the door, and I shut off the truck and climbed out, following closely behind her.

"You don't need to come in," she called back.

I grabbed her arm, and her eyes flared at me, burning me to my soul.

"Chels, didn't mean anything by it. I'm guessin' you pay rent, and I was pissed that the person you rent it from isn't keepin' it up. Got nothin' to do with you, babe."

She let out a huff of air. "I know it's not a lot, but it's mine."

I gave her a soft squeeze, pulled her in close, and kissed the top of her head. "Get that, babe. Let's get your stuff."

I really didn't mean to be a dick about it, but in my mind, I plotted all the things that needed to be fixed, putting each of them on my to-do list. Not to mention, I needed find out who the fucker was who owned this place and beat the shit out of him. My boys and I would see to that.

Chelsea jingled the key in the lock for long moments, and I looked around her.

She looked up. "It gets stuck sometimes."

Fucking, fuck me. You've got to be shitting me.

Even her damn lock that was supposed to keep her safe was broken. Add that shit to the list, too.

"I've got it," I said in a very clipped tone, reaching for the keys.

I pushed my way through, hoping like hell the rickety stairs would hold both mine and Chelsea's weight.

"No, wait!" she called out, keeping the keys. "There's a trick."

I watched and waited as she stuck the key between the door where the lock met the jamb, wiggling the key. Sure as shit, that fucker popped right open.

Chelsea turned around and smiled wide at me. While she was being a smartass about getting it open, I couldn't help feeling as if that smile had hit me in the chest like a boulder.

The second thing that hit me was her lock was shit and needed to be replaced yesterday, along with her door.

She walked in first, and I followed behind, shutting the door.

A scent of the beach or the ocean instantly hit me, and as I turned toward the room, I stopped dead. I was at the beach minus the sand at my feet and the water crashing against them.

Hanging on the light blue walls were large prints of the ocean, the waves crashing against the shore. One was of a beautiful sunset spread across the horizon of the water.

Chelsea had oars and anchors on the walls in a way that looked really good. The two couches were covered in light blue fabrics with large bright blue, red, and yellow pillows thrown sporadically along them. Under the small coffee table was a dark tanned rug that covered almost the entire floor of the living space, the color reminding me of sand. A glass bowl sat on the table with sand, stones, and shells inside.

Looking at the kitchen, I saw it was decorated in much the same theme.

"Have a thing for the beach?" I asked in amusement.

She smiled and bit her lip. "Yeah, somethin' like that."

"I can tell there's a story here. Hit me." I really wanted to know more about her, so if this was her thing, I needed to know.

She moved into the kitchen, tossing the mail that we'd picked up on our way here onto the counter. Then her eyes lifted and met mine.

"Always wanted to go to the beach." She shrugged. "So I brought the beach to me."

My chest tightened from her words. She was finally letting me in, and it only made me crave more.

"Ever been?" I asked.

She shook her head. "I'll get there someday." Her tone was absolute, and I had no doubt she would have her toes in the water and ass in the sand one day. If I had anything to do about it, it would be sooner rather than later.

I only smirked.

"Why don't you have a seat, and I'll pull together my stuff?"

I wasn't going to sit; instead, I followed her down a small hallway to her bedroom, the beach theme continuing. Lots of light blues, yellows, and reds graced the pictures of the beach on the walls.

She turned around and jumped, surprised to find me right behind her, her hands coming to my chest. "Crap!"

I grabbed her wrists. "Calm down, Fire. It's all good." I brushed my lips against hers, fully admitting to myself that doing that one gesture was better than kissing her and fucking her. It felt more intimate, and I felt closer to her. From the way her breath caught, I figured she liked it, as well.

Being in her space and seeing her holding her breath because she didn't know if I would kiss her senseless or let her go was a hell of a turn on.

"Yeah," she breathed out, and I released her. She then went to a small closet, grabbed a duffle bag, and began throwing things in. "How long do you think we'll be there?"

When she asked, my first thought was forever, which knocked me on my ass. I'd never had a forever or a thought of it, and fuck me, I liked it … a lot.

"Plan for a couple of weeks."

She snapped her head up. "Really? That long?"

"Yeah, Fire."

Her eyes held mine, and unspoken desires flashed between us. I was positive that if I had anything to do with it, her beach would be coming to my house.

THIRTEEN

STIFF

WE ROLLED UP TO DENNY'S PLACE TWO hours before this Javier guy was supposed to show. Xander and Hooch had kept eyes on the place all day and seen nothing out of the ordinary. They'd also had a chat with the two morons who seemed to be on task for this.

I'd gone to my mother's earlier, knowing Xander would be busy. She wasn't there and hadn't been for a while; undeniably missing in action.

After I got back from that dead end, Spook sat us down, and we planned, making sure every exit was covered. Javier would definitely have backup, and all the wire taps we'd placed on the house and the idiots' cells hadn't shown anything about them being on to us. Yes, it was a sneak attack, and the five guns on my body proved I was ready.

When the black Town and Country with fully tinted windows pulled up to the house, we all braced ourselves. The front doors opened, and two beefy guys stepped out of the car. Then the man on the passenger side shut his door and went to the rear, opening it.

A strongly built Italian man—I supposed he was Javier—wearing pressed pants and a suit jacket got out of the car, buttoning his jacket as he did. The two brutes searched the area, and since we were hidden in the house next door, we weren't detected. Its occupants had won a free meal at a local steakhouse that could only be used tonight. Lucky them.

One brute went into the house, Javier following, while the other brute stood at the door, hands in his pockets.

I looked at Spook who nodded. Then I slipped out the back door with Hooch and Dawg on my tail.

Pulling the Taser from my cut, I aimed it and fired. The man at the door fell into a heap on the ground with a hard thud. We stopped, waiting to see if either Javier or anyone else in that house would come out because of the noise. When no one did, it took all three of us to fucking move the guy. Hooch tied his hands behind his back with zip ties, and then tied his feet together, leaving him on the side of the house.

I lifted my arm, giving the all clear sign. Hooch and Dawg then went to the back door while Spook, Boner, Bosco, and I tagged the front. With Spook's nod, I turned the door handle, thinking it would be locked, but the fuckers were stupid. It opened with ease.

Spook went in first, gun in hand, while the rest of us followed behind him, our guns at the ready. The two assholes we'd beaten the shit out of were sitting on the dingy sofa. Javier stood in front of them as his guard made his way in front of Javier. It was like a well-orchestrated play. Good for them.

"Javier?" Spook asked in a quiet tone.

"What the fuck is this!" he exclaimed, moving to the side of his guard. "Who are you?"

"We're the Vipers Creed MC, and we have some business to discuss with Gonzo."

A crooked smile appeared across his lips. "Oh, yes, the assholes who keep callin'. What didn't you understand about Gonzo not returning your calls?" His tone was causal, like getting bombarded happened all the time. Fucker.

"Too bad we're persistent. Need to talk to him," Spook replied.

"And you think coming in here with your guns pointed at me is going to accomplish that?" Javier arched a brow.

"Well, this could go two ways. One," Spook started, "you call Gonzo and make a meet. Or two, we take you and piss everyone off, which isn't our intention." Spook clicked his tongue. "What should we do?"

"He's not going to like this," Javier snapped, reaching into his jacket.

I aimed my gun right at his head. If he pulled out anything except a phone, he was on ice.

"Easy there," he said with a small smile playing on his lips.

Javier pushed buttons on the phone then held it up to his ear. "It's me," he reported. "It appears that the assholes who've been trying to get to you, beat the shit out of Denny and Dwaine. Now they're here looking for you ... Yeah." He grinned. "Yeah."

I had no clue what he was smiling about, but I didn't like it.

"All they want is a meeting." Javier looked at Spook. "What is this in regards to?"

"Becky Collins and Gary Reece."

Javier's smile disappeared, and his brows furrowed. Then he repeated the information to who I assumed was Gonzo on the other line.

He listened then said, "We know Becky is his"—he nodded his head at me—"mom, but what the fuck does Gary have to do with anything?"

"Those idiots"—Spook threw his arm out, indicating the two men on the couch—"decided to find Gary's daughter at school, who did absolutely nothing and hasn't heard from her father in ten years, and beat the shit out of her. Then they threw her at the feet of her sister, warning her, as well. The sister is under our protection; therefore, so is the woman these assholes beat up. It was all done because they are Gary's kids."

The "under our protection" thing hadn't really been in the works at the time, but it was now, so it was all true.

"Since these two beat the hell out of her, we beat the hell out of them, and all of this leads back to Gonzo. So we need a meet to clear all of this up. Fuck, I'll even talk to him over the phone at his point."

"You hear all that, boss?" Javier asked then nodded, but it was more to himself than to anyone else. "Yeah." Javier pulled the phone from his ear then held it out to Spook.

I stepped up and took it, handing it to my president. We took no chances with his safety.

Javier just chuckled.

"Spook," he relayed into the phone. "Could have avoided all of this if you'd returned my call … Right." There was another pause before Spook said, "These two women have no idea where their father is, haven't talked to the fucker in years, and know full-well he's a dick. They'd have no problem giving their father to you if they knew his location. I even talked to the mother and grandmother, and they know shit, either. Your beef is with Gary, not them." Spook paused, and then his eyes narrowed on the two assholes on the couch. "You're fuckin' shittin' me."

The two men paled as Spook's anger pulsed off of him in waves, penetrating the room. Even Javier felt it and took a step back, his guard more on alert.

"Fucking hell," he growled. "I'll deal with them."

The assholes on the couch made a move, but Hooch and Dawg were on them from behind, pulling their guns away so fast the fucking shocked looks on their faces were laughable. Gonzo needed to hire better help if he wanted to have good business.

Spook looked at me then nodded at the men. I waved over Bosco, and the four of us instantly subdued the two idiots. I made good use of the zip ties that were handed to me, tying them the same as before.

I expected more of a fight from them, but with Hooch and Dawg's guns at their heads, they complied. I thought it was a stupid move considering the look on Spook's face and the anger pouring off of him. We might just be using the old shed again.

Spook looked at Javier. "I understand … Good. They have nothing to do with this … Right." Spook turned to me and nodded.

Gonzo was off my girl's ass, or so he said. I didn't believe it, didn't trust it, because I had absolutely zero reason to. Not only did I not trust Gonzo, but now that Chelsea was officially under our protection, which would be spread wide, she was on the radar for anyone who wanted to get to us or me. Add to that whether my mother was really fucking over Gonzo, and no way would I trust that he wouldn't use Chelsea in some way. That wouldn't be happening, though. No fucking way.

"Becky does not have Stiff's protection or the club's. She's into this shit on her own, and we do not back her one single bit. We'd fucking tell her that if we could find her, but the slippery little bitch got away from us."

I felt nothing as he talked about my mother. She was a stranger to me, just another woman in a long line of users. And as much as it sucked, she'd end up dead. I hated that for my brother. He'd always deserved a woman who cared about him, but he had Gabby now, and it was time to break all the old ties holding us back.

"Good. Then we're done," Spook announced. He held out the phone for Javier, who stepped up and took it then placed it to his ear.

Spook waited as Javier spoke to Gonzo.

After he hung up, Spook announced, "Those two assholes weren't supposed to go after Jenn or Chelsea. They were told to find Gary and thought his kids were the best way. They need to pay retribution."

Bosco cracked his knuckles beside me.

"Gonzo doesn't feel the need to go after the two women. Becky, on the other hand …" Spook's eyes came to mine. "You'd better brace yourself, brother."

I nodded. What else could I do? I had no other option, and it was time this was done. I was done with all of it and wanted to move on.

Spook turned back to Javier then held out his hand. Javier took it, and they shook.

"We're taking care of these two." He nodded to the men. "You can go."

Javier looked at the men then at Spook, lifted his chin, and walked out. Business with him was done. While I was fucking ecstatic to have another go at these two dickheads, I really wanted to head back home where I knew Chelsea would be.

Gonzo may have told us he wouldn't go after Chelsea or her family, but I wasn't taking any chances. Her ass was in my place, and I needed to explain it to the brothers I knew would take my back. Spook was probably already thinking it, but at least now it would be spread throughout that Chelsea's family had our protection.

The biggest part, however, was I just got her, and I wasn't ready to let her go.

CHELSEA

AFTER LEAVING MY PLACE and coming back here, I took care of Jenn. When I went to lie next to her to sleep, Stiff came in, picked me up, and took me to his bed with him. Confliction punched me in the gut.

Yes, I'd had sex with him, but that didn't mean I needed to sleep with him. It was so intimate. Too intimate. My mind screamed at me that it was a bad idea, but my body was pulled to him like a magnet, unable to resist. Ultimately, I decided it was only one night. I could let myself get lost just that once. As a result, for the first time in a very, very long time, I fell asleep, curled up to a man. Better yet, to Stiff.

He woke me up by fucking me hard and fast, saying he had shit to do. I couldn't complain, because it was wonderful. Every time he touched me, it was wonderful. He even kissed me before he left, which shocked me at first then warmed me. It was sweet in a Stiff way.

On the flip side, I had to wonder if I was just a convenience for him. I was staying in his house, and he didn't have to do anything except lay his lips on me for me to get hot for him. I hated that thought, hated that I even had to think it, but it was probably true, and that settled in my gut like a hard, pointy-edged rock, cutting me from within.

After he left, I changed Jenn's bandages, and then she called her advisor at school, who told her she'd talk to her professors. With that out of the way, I lay with Jenn, putting on *The Hunger Games*. No sense in not using the massive television Stiff had in the room, and I'd heard great things about the movie and had really wanted to see it, just never had time. I had it now, and with Jenn taken care of, I took it. It was surreal yet wonderful, relaxing even. I couldn't remember a relaxing day ever.

Better yet, it was simple, and that was the best part. Grams always told Jenn and me that we would find our happiness in the simple things in life; the moments we shared together, the memories we created. While I hated the reason I was here,

I enjoyed this time and tucked it into my memory bank. It was a moment I could find good and treasure it.

When the door to Jenn's room opened after nine o'clock, I popped my head up from the pillow while movie number three—*Mockingjay - Part One*—played in the background. Stiff stood there, leaning his large body against the doorframe.

Damn, he was sexy. Every single inch of him from the top of his bald head to his boot-covered feet. The way his arms flexed under his sleeves and his jeans hugged his thighs. Now that I knew what those jeans covered, my desire for him only heightened.

I looked over at Jenn who was sound asleep.

Stiff nodded to the TV, and I turned it off. It was purely for selfish reasons, though. My grams was big on telling us to follow our guts, and mine was telling me that whatever Stiff had needed to do, it had to do with my father, and I wanted information. I wanted to know if, by chance, he'd found my father.

"Didn't have to do that," he said as I climbed from the bed.

I moved past him and went through the door. He followed behind, shutting the door with a soft click.

I thought better of going to his bedroom, and instead, went into the living room where I parked my ass on the couch. He sat next to me and grabbed my legs, hoisting them up and pulling off my socks. I flinched, and it took everything in my power to keep myself from pulling my feet out of his grasp. He gave a slight chuckle like he knew my confliction, and in return, I glared at him and leaned back, putting my head on the armrest of the couch.

With the first touch of his strong, warm hands, I lost it, and a moan escaped.

"Told ya you'd like it." He smirked in the sexiest of ways.

Needing to stay on task, I asked, "Did you find anything out about my dad?"

"Nope." His answer was short and terse. I didn't quite like it.

"Where have you been all day?" The damn question came out of my mouth before I could stop myself. Once again, my body and mind were at war when it came to Stiff.

His eyes found mine. "Babe, that's club business."

My temperature rose. "What the hell does that mean, 'club business'?"

"Fire, I'm gonna lay this out for ya because I want it to be clear."

A slow shiver fell over my skin, and not one that I liked. Still, I kept quiet and let him speak.

"I get you don't know much about the club. I like that, but gotta clue you in. When I tell you it's club business, that means I'm not tellin' ya where I've been or what I've done."

My stomach fell to my feet as images of the brunette floated into my brain. I didn't want to care, and I should have never put myself in a situation to care. It was a stupid mistake on my part, one I knew would end up costing me. How much, I wasn't sure yet, but it would.

"Bottom line, babe," he continued, "not knowin' keeps you safe. If it's somethin' you need to know, I'll tell ya. It's not me being a dick; it's how it is here. Trixie only knows what Spook needs her to know. When I find your father, I'll deal with it, just like I did with the men who hurt your sister. None of that will come back on you or your family, though. Therefore, I won't be telling you about it."

My mind reeled. Being an independent woman, I'd been in control of everything I possibly could in my life. I fully admitted that I thrived on knowing what was going on and when. Consequently, I wasn't sure how I felt about Stiff knowing and doing things and not telling me.

I couldn't deny that his words also cut into my heart. With no choice, I learned the hard way to stand up for myself and fight for me and my family. My mother ingrained that in me at a very young age. Not in a bad way, but she'd given me the skills and knowledge to deal with real life issues. She'd taught me to save money, be smart about my surroundings, keep trust close to the vest, and numerous other everyday things that every human being should know but unfortunately didn't.

When my father left us, I grew up faster because my mother had to work all the time, and it had been my responsibility to take care of my sister. That was before we'd moved in with Grams, which was the best move my mom could have made.

It didn't mean the lessons weren't ingrained in me; they were. I wasn't soft. I loved fierce and deep. Nevertheless, I was undone by the thought of a man taking care of me, protecting me, and keeping me safe when I'd done it all by myself my entire life. Still, I let the warmth of it spread through my body and into my soul, cracking part of the hard shell around my heart as it pulsed and throbbed.

Stiff said nothing, only went back to rubbing my feet, giving me time to absorb his words. Unfortunately, the more I did, the more the warm, fuzzy feeling dissipated.

The realization hit me like a throat punch: he wasn't my man. Even though I was living in the moment and keeping my memories locked up tight, this right here would be all I had of Stiff. I'd have a couple of weeks to feel that, and then it would disappear like everything else.

I felt the tears sting the back of my eyes and bit them back. I refused to let them fall.

I would take each rub, each touch, and store it for when this was over.

FOURTEEN

CHELSEA

STIFF'S HEAD LAY BACK ON THE COUCH, his posture relaxed and hands still cupping my feet but not moving. The slight rise and fall of his chest told me he was asleep.

Carefully, I pulled my legs out from his lap and rose from the couch.

He looked years younger, the lines around his eyes and mouth almost disappearing. His tanned, bald head was perfectly shaped, making him look hotter than should be legal. For years, he'd come into the diner, and for years, my heart would speed up. Now, here I was, in his house with him.

I let out a huff of breath, pulled a blanket from a nearby chair, and put it over Stiff's body then set off to check on my sister.

I MOANED AS I WAS LIFTED from the bed of its own accord. Or, at least I thought it was. I felt like a floating cloud in a sea of bluish green, the same color as Stiff's eyes. Almost like I was on a flying carpet from the kids' movie *Aladdin* that jostled me around a bit.

My cheek hit something hard and warm, and I nuzzled into it, inhaling the smell of spice. I loved that smell. Loved it better than the beach. If I could smell it forever, I'd happily give up going to the beach.

The carpet around me hugged me tight, but it didn't scratch me. Instead, it was soft, almost like skin. My body settled gently on the cloud as warmth hit my back and wrapped around me. I liked it. Loved it. And I fell back asleep.

MY LEG WAS LIFTED AS calloused hands moved up and down my flesh, causing goose bumps to form, but I wasn't cold. No, I was burning, on fire.

The hand on me bent my knee and pulled it behind me slightly. Not uncomfortable, but an unusual position to sleep. Then I felt it, warm and hard, touching my core.

"Fire, baby," was whispered in my ear, and thoughts of Stiff came to me: his touch, smile, and how he took care of me and my family. My arousal grew, and I wiggled my hips into the hardness.

Kisses trailed across my neck, up my jaw, and to my ear.

"Wake up, Chelsea." Stiff's voice rang in my ear, but I didn't want to.

The dream was too good, too perfect. If I opened my eyes, I would ruin it; it would be gone. I couldn't lose it.

A nip came to my ear, and I yelped as Stiff chuckled.

"Wanna fuck you, but not gonna do it while you're sleepin'," he said softly in my ear, and I groaned or maybe moaned—I couldn't tell which.

"Don't wanna," I whined. Yes, whined. I was not a whiner, but in this instant, it floated out.

Stiff's body shook with laughter as he continued his assault on my neck. His lips, tongue, teeth, and hot breath cascaded up and down my flesh as if he were making out with my body, not needing any of my help to do so.

I pulsed between my legs with each swipe.

He brought his hand around and cupped my breast, giving it a hard squeeze. Damn, that felt good, and my hips swirled, telling him so. Then I reached up and placed my hand on top of his, letting him know I was awake.

"See? My Fire wants my cock."

I dug my nails into his hand, his words turning me on. I loved a rough talker in the bedroom. It was one of my biggest turn-ons. However, my other lovers hadn't cottoned to the idea even after I'd told them time and time again.

"I feel you wet, hot, and ripe for me, baby."

I let out a whimper, trying to put his cock inside of me by moving my hips. But each time I got the tip right where I needed it, he moved away, teasing me, taunting me.

"Words. Tell me what you want," he growled, squeezing my breast and running the head of his dick between my folds.

My breathing picked up as the arousal spiked.

Seeing no point, I didn't hesitate. "I want you to fuck me."

His dick hit my clit in the faintest of ways, and as he moved back, I tried chasing him, wanting more of the hot flesh. Once again, it didn't work to my utmost frustration.

"Yeah, you do. Wanna see that fire burnin'." He wrapped a strong arm under my body and around my waist while the other still hung on to my breast like letting go would be painful.

Stiff gave me no preamble, no warning. He thrust hard inside of me, letting me feel him deep in my core.

With my leg up, I was wide open for him, allowing him ultimate access, which he took. Each shift of his hips became harder and more intense, as if he were on a mission and the only way to accomplish it would be to break me in two. I would let him, too, as long as he didn't dare stop.

"Fuck, your pussy's so fuckin' tight. So fuckin' perfect for my cock."

He moved the arm wrapped around my waist down to my core. With the pad of his fingers, he rubbed hard on my clit just as his penis hit the one spot inside me that sent me flying.

He kept moving as my pussy clamped his cock, and my head flew back to hit his shoulder, eyes closed as I screamed out my release.

"Now it's my turn."

Before I could breathe or think, he rolled me onto my stomach, his cock still inside of me. He then pushed my legs together, placing his knees on either side of mine.

With the tight grip I had on him, I felt full, so damn full.

"Like my cock hittin' those fuckin' walls, filling you until you blow beneath me?" He placed his hands on the small of my back, holding me on each side. Then it started.

Stiff pounded his flesh inside of me almost as if he were marking me, branding me, owning me. The build happened rapidly, and I felt the quiver in my pussy again.

Stiff grabbed my hair harshly and pulled my neck back. A normal woman would probably hate this, but thank Christ I wasn't normal. The tugs of sharp pain from my scalp moved all the way through me like bolts of electricity to my toes. The act only amped up my arousal, and with one look into his eyes as well as his hard thrusts, I lost it.

He held my hair tight so there was no moving my head. He also had my hips plastered down, so no movement there, either. All I could do was take it.

A sharp sting came to my ass, and I erupted, my entire body setting off like I'd been attacked by lightning bolts from the sky in the worst storm imaginable. Except, I liked this storm—no, I loved.

As I began to come down, sucking in breath, Stiff continued thrusting, taking what he needed from me. He pushed in to the hilt and stilled. The sexiest part was when he groaned my name.

FIFTEEN

CHELSEA

"**C**OME ON; XANDER'S WATCHIN' JENN. She'll be fine." Stiff pulled me toward the door by my hand, but I gave him a bit of resistance.

I had no issues with leaving Xander with my sister. I did, however, feel very unnerved about going to hang out with the guys.

I didn't hang out. Never had time. And that made me a little socially awkward. At work, it was different. There, it felt like home, so I was in my element. Here? I felt so out of place I could be in Switzerland.

"Why don't I just stay here and you go?" I offered.

I'd been here a couple of days, and each time he took me was better than the last. He made it very hard to keep the sexual aspect of our relationship separate from feelings. And hanging out with his boys wasn't going to help my situation.

This pull between us grew with every passing minute. I tried keeping that lock on the chains around my heart, even throwing away the imaginary key, but it didn't help. Therefore, I feared that seeing Stiff in his element at the clubhouse, actually being with him there, would make things worse.

"Chels, freaking go with the man," Jenn demanded. "You need to get out for a while. And besides, after the visit from Mom and Grams today, I need to sleep."

Both of them had come by for a visit. They'd only stayed about an hour, but with the laughter between us, I could see the light coming back into Jenn's eyes. She was making progress, slow and steady, even getting up to use the bathroom with little to no help from me. She groaned yet kept pushing herself, and seeing the spark that was Jenn coming back filled me with so much happiness … even if right now she was intent on throwing me to the wolves.

I glared at her. She smiled.

"I'm tired."

Jenn rolled her eyes then winced before bringing her attention back to me. "Seriously, Chelsea. Go. Get out. And if you don't go, I'll make farting noises the entire time so you can't watch the TV."

Stiff chuckled, and I let out a huff of exasperated air.

I threw my hands up. "Fine. Let's go." I bent down and kissed the top of my sister's head. "I'm gonna get you back, brat."

"We'll see. Now go," she ordered.

"I don't remember you being so damn bossy," I retorted.

"Well, you've always been a pain in the ass. I don't remember a time when you weren't."

I felt the urge to smack her in the arm then thought better of it.

"Shut up, brat."

"Back at ya, PIA."

I chuckled, moving past Stiff who stood in the doorway. Then I heard the slight click of the door being shut.

We walked down the hallway to the living room where Xander sat on the couch, his booted feet up on the coffee table, hands clasped behind his head, elbows sticking out.

He looked over at us. "See, Stiff? You two are perfect for each other. She's a pain in her sister's ass, and you're a pain in mine."

"I'll give you a pain up your ass," Stiff retorted, pulling his boots on and latching them up as I grabbed my tennis shoes and tied them.

"Sorry, buddy. Don't swing that way," Xander said, garnering a grunt from Stiff. "Gabby's gonna come over in a bit."

I hadn't met Xander's woman Gabby yet, and I was a bit excited to meet her. Sounded strange, but Xander had been awesome with my sister, and curiosity had me wondering about the woman he'd snagged.

"No fuckin' in my house," Stiff warned. "I mean it, too. You fuckin' think of gettin' in my bed, I'll hang you by your balls. Then I'll let the brothers at ya."

I looked up from my shoe at Stiff who stood with arms crossed over his chest, legs apart, glaring down at his brother who began to chuckle.

"You think I want in that bed after you two have been at it like rabbits? No fuckin' thank you."

Heat blazed in my cheeks. It wasn't a secret or anything, but just throwing it out there made me a bit uncomfortable. Therefore, I did what Grams taught me. I faked it.

"Sugar, you surely don't want in those sheets, then."

Both Stiff and Xander burst out laughing. It was the best sound ever.

"Bam!" A feminine voice I recognized as Trixie's screamed as pounding came from something hard.

Looking over at it, I noticed she was banging her hands on the table in front of her, her head flapping from side to side with delight.

We'd just stepped into the clubhouse, and even though I'd been there, I'd never really taken the space in fully. My gaze tracked across the wide open space to see a low hum of lights cascading down on the room. Tables were scattered throughout with chairs at each of them. A long bar sat on the other side of the room with loads of liquor and a pool table off to the side. The scents of stale booze and cigarettes permeated the air like a thick haze.

My focus went to the circular table where Trixie's back was to Stiff and me as she whooped and hollered her excitement, sitting on Spook's lap. Around the table were Bosco, Boner, Hooch, Dawg, and a couple of other men I hadn't met yet. They didn't come into the diner, or if they did, I didn't recognize them.

"Hey, Stiffie! You gonna get in on this action?" Bosco called out, and heads turned toward us, still smiling.

On the inside, I wanted to shrivel at their assessment of me, but being a Miller, I didn't. I squared my shoulders and put a smile on my face.

"Hey." I waved with my right hand stupidly, instantly wanting to take it back yet knowing I couldn't.

"Fuck no. Trixie cheats!" Stiff roared, but it was in laughter, not anger.

I looked at Trixie. Her beautiful smile lit up her face, including her green eyes that glinted of mischief. Her long brown hair fell below her shoulders and had such a shine to it I wanted ask how in the world she got it that way. Of course, I didn't, but maybe at some point.

"Don't listen to him," she called out. "He has no idea what he's talking about."

Her laugh was infectious, and I felt my lips tipping up as we walked closer to the table.

"Bullshit!" Stiff hollered, making me jump. "Don't fuckin' believe her. Fuckin' card shark, this one. Took us all for a ride the first time she was here."

When the entire table broke out in laughter and Trixie bit her bottom lip, I knew he was right.

"You're a card shark?" I didn't know much about her. People talked in the town, but I'd never heard anything about this until now.

"So they say." She shrugged. "I know how to read people's tells when they play." She turned and mock-glared at the table. "These guys just give it away."

That was pretty cool. I'd never learned to play cards, so I had absolutely no clue about them, but tells had been what kept me going at the diner: a foot tapping when a customer thought I took too long getting them their drinks or the tapping of fingernails on the Formica. I may love the sound of the plates scraping across it, but I did not appreciate the finger tap. When I heard that one, I made them wait just a bit longer because I knew the tip would be shit, anyway.

Trixie turned back to me. "We don't play for money anymore since I wipe the table with these guys. Felt bad takin' it all the time."

"Bullshit," Boner said. "You didn't feel bad. You just got tired of hearing us bitch."

Trixie smiled. "That, too." Then she lowered her voice and put her hand on the side of her mouth like she was whispering something to me, but she wasn't whispering. "They're a bunch of big babies."

Spook grabbed her ass hard, and Trixie yelped while the guys around the table laughed. I felt a twinge of heat in my cheeks.

Trixie started batting Spook's hand as he held her closer. The love in his eyes could have busted out. I was happy they'd found that.

Looking around the room, I didn't see a baby in the mix. No, I saw huge men who looked as if they could crush a car with their hands. However, from the way Trixie talked to, interacted, and joked with them, they did almost seem like teddy bears, even if Stiff and Boner had scrapes on their hands the other day like they'd beaten the hell out of something or someone.

"Shut it, woman," Spook ordered, gripping Trixie's hair, pulling her back, and stealing a searing kiss from her.

"Fuckin' hell. Get a room," Boner groaned, tossing a poker chip at the two, but they didn't stop, or more like, Spook wouldn't let her stop. No, he deepened the kiss, and the hotness factor in the room went up a thousand degrees.

By the time Spook pulled away, Trixie looked dazed and confused.

"Throw somethin' else at us, and I'll beat your ass," Spook warned Boner who laughed.

"Don't get your panties in a bunch," Boner retorted.

Damn, these guys seemed so down to earth and nothing like the badass persona they put off. Not to say they weren't badasses, but I liked this side of them. They were in their element exactly like I was at the diner. This was where the real them shined through, and the ease was remarkable.

Stiff pulled up a chair. "Sit," he ordered me, and I raised my brow in question. I knew I didn't look like a dog.

"Oooo ..." came from the table. I forgot we had an audience.

I gulped, but I wouldn't let him or anyone else railroad me. I'd worked too hard to allow that to happen.

"Don't be a pain. Sit. Take a load off," Stiff said in a nicer way, so I sat.

I was at the table with the poker players, but there would be no way I would play.

"Two beers," Stiff called out, but I didn't know to who.

When I turned to see, that fucking brunette from the first night came strutting out with two beers in her hand. I clenched my hands on the table then immediately moved them under it.

Her eyes met mine knowingly.

Even turning my head back to the group around us, I still saw out of the corner of my eye as that woman brushed her tits that were practically falling out of her low-cut, hot pink shirt against Stiff. I hated it to a point where my leg started bouncing up and down uncontrollably like I'd eaten a shit-ton of sugar and the high had taken over.

"What the fuck?" Bosco asked, his hands flat on the table. "Who's shakin' everything?"

I snapped my head up and controlled my leg. His eyes met mine then looked to the side of me, and then they narrowed. I found this act strange and didn't know how to read it. When the terse, "Stiff," came out of his mouth, everyone turned to him then to Stiff. I kept looking at the table, pretending the cards were the most exciting thing in the world.

Bosco knew I didn't like the woman. He knew I had a hard time with her being around Stiff. He'd read me like a book, which made me a bit unnerved.

Out of the corner of my eye, I saw Stiff lift his chin to Bosco, waited a beat, shrugged, and then took the bottles from the woman.

"Thanks," he muttered as she grabbed his arm.

"Wanna go back and play?" she asked, and my leg started bouncing again uncontrollably.

My nails dug so deep into my palms I wouldn't be surprised if I had blood coming from the wounds.

Are you fucking kidding me right now? She wanted him to go "play"? Was this place like this all the time?

Heat traveled through my veins like hot lava ready to erupt.

Fuck it. I might only have him for a short time, but I had him now, and she was not going to take what was mine.

I rose from the chair, the scrape of the wood to wood contact had eyes coming to me. I didn't give a shit.

I turned, facing the woman and Stiff. Then Stiff's eyes flashed to me as I tilted my head.

"Oh, fuck," Stiff muttered as I walked closer to him. He had that right. He must have seen the fire breathing, seething out of me. "Fire, it's all good," he said, but my eyes were focused on the bitch in front of me.

"If you rub your fucking tits on him one more time, I'll get out a knife and pop them," I warned then heard Trixie's laugh behind me.

The woman's lip turned up in disgust. "And you are?" She cocked her hip snottily.

"Chelsea. I'd say nice to meet ya, but my grams always told me that lyin' isn't right."

Stiff placed his hand on my arm as he pulled me against his hard body.

The woman smirked. "Oh, I get it. You're the woman tonight." She flipped her hand in the air. "Whatever. There's always another one."

My stomach dropped as my temper flared.

"Bitch, you've got one thing right. He's mine for right now, which means keeping your damn hands and tits off of him. When it's done, have at it; use my sloppy seconds." The words flew out of my mouth before my brain even registered what I was saying.

When the grip on my arm tightened and I looked up at Stiff, something told me I'd fucked up.

His eyes blazed with anger, and a tick came to the right side of his jaw. I reran what I'd said in my head. Maybe I had gone a little too far with the sloppy seconds thing—he wouldn't be sloppy for anyone. However, for this level of anger, I didn't know what I'd done.

"Rita, out," Stiff barked without looking away from me. He pulled my arm, not hard, but determined, and I followed as he led me through the hallway and into the room my sister and I stayed in that first night.

He slammed the door behind us, and I knew I was in trouble. Shit.

SIXTEEN

STIFF

WHEN IT'S DONE, HAVE AT IT; *use my sloppy seconds.* Her words rang through my head like alarm bells on a fire truck. I couldn't put my finger on why they pissed me off so much, but they did, and I rolled with it and let it feed me.

Chelsea turned to me, her eyes a mask of confusion.

The burn inside ached, and it slammed me in the gut like a two-by-four.

"You ready to get rid of me?"

Her eyes widened as I took a step closer to her, and she took a step back. Smartest thing she could've done at that moment, but I didn't let her get far.

"Ready to throw me out?" I asked.

Her face held the same confusion as her eyes squinted, but she kept her mouth closed. For me, though, this was an old wound that, until this moment, hadn't arose since I was younger. Something about Chelsea had made it come to the surface and seared me just like it did all those years ago.

"If I could just get rid of you and your worthless brother, life would be so much better!" my mother spat at me while Xander backed up against the wall, me in front of

him.

I kept silent, knowing a single word would set off her fury more, and that wouldn't be good.

"All you two do is cost me money!" she continued.

She was totally wrong because I worked my ass off to keep us boys fed. However, instead of disagreeing with her, I remained quiet, still protecting my brother.

The slap across the face came hard and fast. My head whipped to the side, and I could feel the tear to my chapped lip. Again, I stayed quiet, hoping that she would run out of steam.

Two more slaps came before a pounding on the door.

"Go to your room and shut the door. Don't you dare come out," she ordered as Xander slinked across the wall, trying to get out of the living room.

Then I saw it. My mother changed from angry to calculating, and I knew a man was on the other side of that door and what my mother was about to do. I didn't give a shit as long as she left me and my brother alone.

"Stiff, I didn't ..." Chelsea started, snapping me out of the thoughts of the past. "I didn't mean anything bad."

"You didn't? Wanna get rid of me? Throw me to whoever wants me? Is that it?" I asked, unable to stop myself, the control I normally had flying from me. "Give me to Rita because I'm your nasty, sloppy seconds!" I roared, and she took another step back.

"I didn't mean—"

"Didn't mean, what? What you said?" I barked.

She crossed her arms over her chest, pushing her tits up, the V-neck exposing them. "Stiff, I know this is a short fling. I get it. Pretty soon, when this mess is cleaned up, I'll go to my mother's or my place, and it'll be done."

That felt like a blade to the heart, which I couldn't understand.

"So, what? You're already writing me off when we're just getting to know each other, Chelsea?"

Her face turned alarmed as she shook her head. "Okay, wait." She put her hands palms up out in front of her. "Let's talk about this, because we aren't on the same page, and we need to get there."

"No shit," I barked out. We were on different fucking planets, it seemed. "Somehow, you got it in that pretty, little head of yours that once this situation is over, you're going back to your life the way it was before … without me. So, let me educate you." I had no idea where the hell all this shit was coming from, but I felt it and it needed to be said. "When this gets done, I'm not goin' anywhere except in your bed in that trailer. You're at work, expect to see me. Expect that you'll be with me on your days off. Expect that our nights will be together either at your place or mine … every night."

She gasped in a breath and clutched her neck with her hand, her jaw dropping open. Guessed it was good she'd seen me with Rita, because this shit needed to come out.

"Don't know where this is goin', Fire, but get this … I like it, you like it, and neither one of us is gonna fuck that up."

She blinked, but it was so slow her eyelids actually fluttered open. When she kept quiet, I kept right at it.

"Yeah, Rita brushed her tits against my arm. I get that you don't like that shit, so it stops."

She came unstuck. "Ya think?"

"Think what?"

"You think I liked her tits touching you? Brushing against your arm and the smile you gave her? She wants you, and it pisses me off!" Her voice rose with each word she spoke until the last one almost came out on a roar. "You're inside of *me* at night, not her. She shouldn't be touching you!"

It made me the biggest dick on the planet, but I liked this—the jealousy. It proved to me that she was really in this. She felt what I'd been feeling. She was willing to fight. That was what I needed—a fighter. In this life, in this world, only the strong survived, and Chelsea was that—a survivor.

"Exactly, so fuckin' words like someone havin' me when you're done better never cross those fuckin' lips again, woman. You're the only fuckin' pussy I want," I said, my control seriously slipping.

Not sure how we got to that point, but my cock throbbed, and when Chelsea charged me, her arms going around my neck and our lips crashing together in the fiercest fucking kiss I'd ever experienced, I lost the last shred of control I had.

I turned her then pressed her hard against the door. She tore at me, and my body left hers long enough to take my shirt and cut off then hers. Our lips were then in a tangle, both fighting for superiority, but I wasn't backing down. No, my control had been severed, and Chelsea was going to find out who I really was.

We each tore at the others pants, unbuttoning and pulling them down. We did this all without breaking the kiss. I then gripped her around the waist, lifting her with ease, and her legs wrapped around my hips. My dick knew exactly where it wanted to be and slid home in one hard, angry thrust. I knew I hadn't put a condom on, and I didn't give a shit.

Using the door as leverage, I gave her no mercy. Her body was mine. Her lips were mine. Her pussy was mine. I took, and she gave.

"Stiff!" she cried out, the sound music to my fucking ears.

"My name on those lips," I ground out, moving my hands to her ass then lifting and using gravity to slam her back down on me hard.

Each time she cried out, her nails made indentations in my skin.

"Fuckin' hot for me. Always fuckin' hot for me." The tingle hit my spine, but I wasn't ready to let it go yet. "Fire, come for me."

She screamed, her pussy clamping down on my cock so hard I could barely move, but I did, pushing far into her body before I released.

Sweat coated both our bodies as I panted with my face in her neck, inhaling her scent. Thank Christ for the door to keep us steady.

I'd fucked a lot in my day, but this angry fucking … I made a note to make sure we did this often.

I lifted my head and pressed my lips to hers. Not like before, though. No anger, only her and me. Nothing else in the world mattered.

She kissed back, bringing one of her hands to the top of my head.

I pushed away from the door and took her to the bed. I laid her on her side before lying next to her, still kissing the hell out of her. Who knew how long we lay there, simply kissing. No matter how long it was, it didn't get better than that.

I brushed Chelsea's hair away from her face. Her eyes were closed and her breathing even, adorable and relaxed. She'd fallen asleep on me, and all I could do was lie here and watch her.

Her face was so angelic, and I fucking loved the freckles that went over her nose. I thought back to the times I'd seen her working so damn hard with a smile on her face. But those smiles weren't the ones I received from her now, making most of those at the diner fake. She showed me the real ones after I made her come, when she talked to her sister, even the smirks she gave me in the clubhouse. All of those were real, the ones I wanted on her face, not the made up bullshit hiding the woman underneath.

Lying next to her, I'd seen her relaxed for the first time, and I had to wonder if it was the first time she'd been able to do it in all her years. I wanted her like this—the pressure off her and getting to live her life.

Inside, I felt good. Lying here, holding her in my arms felt right. For the first time in a long ass time, I felt a calm within myself. Chelsea had given that to me. Now I needed to make sure she saw it and felt it, too.

The feeling was strange, though, because I'd never experienced it before. I'd had some form of it for my brother, but this was different, deeper, more real.

Chelsea stirred then opened her beautiful blue eyes, looking up at me. "Hey," she whispered.

"Hey," I responded, my hand on her cheek, our bodies facing each other.

"Did we make up?" she asked with a genuine grin.

"Yeah, babe. But straight out, this is somethin', and I'm not fuckin' anyone but you. I'm too old for games, so I'm tellin' ya flat out. This feelin' I have inside me when you're around, I'm not lettin' it go, which means I'm not lettin' you go."

Her eyes glistened. "I still don't know what that means. You wanna be my boyfriend?"

I chuckled at that. Damn, she was funny.

"I don't do that shit. I'm your man. You're my woman. End of story."

"You've known me for years, came into the diner; why now?"

I stared into her eyes, feeling a pang in my chest. "I saw you." I soothed my hand down her cheek. "I don't have an answer. Maybe my brain finally caught up with my eyes."

I'd just claimed her as mine, and I wasn't sure if she fully got the extent of it yet. Hell, I wasn't sure I got the full extent yet, either, but it was done.

She grinned then bit her bottom lip.

"We've gotta talk about somethin'. I came in you without a condom. You on the pill?"

When she shook her head, confliction hit me. I didn't know if I was happy about that or not.

"But I've been told by doctors that I won't be able to have kids," she uttered so softly her fear came out with every word.

"Why?" My gut tightened. It sounded like something she would want.

"I have something called endometriosis. It causes infertility, and I'm high on the spectrum scale, so the doctor told me that my chances of conceiving are very slim unless I have surgery."

I rubbed my thumb against her jaw. "How'd you find this out?"

"I thought I was pregnant."

My thumb stilled. "What?"

The thought of another man fucking my woman, let alone planting their child inside of her, flipped something inside of me, and pissed off didn't seem like the right word for it.

"A couple of years ago, there was a guy I saw sometimes. Anyway, the condom broke, and I was late, so I went to the doctor. Even though the test came back negative for both pregnancy and STDs, he found the endometriosis."

"Do you want kids?"

Her eyes welled up. "I'd thought about having them one day, but ..."

Wanting her to finish, I prompted, "But, what?"

She looked into my eyes, and whatever she saw, she must have liked, because she continued.

"Kids have never been in my plan. A man has never been in my plan."

This shocked me, but with her independence, I could see it. Too bad her plans had just changed.

"What's your plan?" I moved my hand down her face to rest in front of us.

She swallowed. "Grams always said we needed to have goals, something to strive for. My goal is simple: save money for a down payment and get a loan to buy my own house."

While that was a great goal, I thought for sure her goal would be something else.

"Not the beach?"

She chuckled. "You'd think that'd be top on my list, but it's not. One day, I'd like to go, but I've worked too hard in my life, and I want something to show for it. A home."

I smiled at her. "I think that's a great goal, Fire. How close are you to gettin' it?"

"Pretty close. In another couple of months, I should have enough of a down payment for the bank to take a chance on me."

I knew better than anyone that having a home meant security, safety. I had never felt that until I'd moved here to the compound.

"That's good, babe."

"Speaking of that, I really need to get back to work. I know my sister still needs help, so I'm thinking—"

I pressed my fingers to her lips, not wanting any talk of her leaving, knowing that was where she was going with this. "Give it a couple more days."

Surprisingly, she nodded, shocking the shit right out of me.

"A couple, but I have to get back. I have bills to pay."

"I get you. Let me work some things out first. Need to make sure the diner is covered, that you're covered."

"Thank you." She leaned over and brushed her lips against mine. I fucking loved that shit.

"Stiff?" she questioned.

"Yeah?"

"Are you clean?"

"I always glove up, but I'll get checked to make sure."

"Thanks," she whispered. After a few beats, she found her voice again. "You really wanna give this a go?"

I smiled. "Yeah, Fire, I do."

She smiled, and damn, it was beautiful.

SEVENTEEN

CHELSEA

"You're shittin' me," Stiff growled with a menace that would make the Devil quiver.

"Wish I were. Didn't think she'd be stupid enough to come here," Boner answered, lighting a smoke and inhaling as he stood at the door of Stiff's home.

"Fuck. Me, neither." Stiff rubbed his bald head as Xander came up to the door, anger etched in the lines of his face.

I didn't know who "she" was, but I had a feeling I would find out really soon, and I knew I wasn't going to like it.

I rose from the couch and moved toward the door, my hand instinctively going to Stiff's back. He jolted like my touch shocked him then settled, some of the starch going out of his spine. That small moment was a beautiful thing, but I had to quickly store it and focus back on the task at hand.

"Why the fuck is she so stupid?" Xander grumbled, his eyes flashing to me then back to his brother. "Can't believe this shit."

"Where is she?" Stiff asked.

"Hooch has her in the courtyard. Didn't want her inside, because fuck knows what this is," Xander answered.

Stiff turned to me. "Got shit to deal with. I'll be back." He brushed his lips over mine, stepped away, and moved out the door.

I stood there, watching as Boner and Xander followed suit. I then watched as Stiff moved to a set of picnic tables far enough for me to only see a figure of a woman, but there was no way I would be able to hear what was said.

My curiosity got the best of me, and I ran quickly to check on my sister, who smiled at me as she watched some show on television. I loved that she was feeling better. She still ached and had a hard time moving, but it would come in time.

"I'll be right back," I told her.

"Okay," she replied.

I slipped my feet into my tennis shoes sans socks and pushed the laces into the top of the shoe. Then I opened the door, the bright sun feeling really good on my skin.

Yelling could be heard, and I saw Stiff's arms were motioning in the air, pointing somewhere, but I had no clue where, because it looked like a wall. Maybe he was trying to convey outside the wall. I didn't know.

I walked closer, and Spook's eyes then Boner's came to mine.

"Stiff," Boner called out as he lifted his chin to indicate behind him.

He turned, his eyes flaring. "Chels, go back in the house."

My feet stopped moving, and I was angered and hurt by his dismissal. How dare he order me to go somewhere, and how dare my feet listen! This wasn't the Stone Age. Him telling me to do things in the bedroom was different. I didn't like being shut out of things. I needed to be in the know for self-preservation.

"Who's this?" the woman asked.

I leaned over, looking around Stiff, and my breath stilled.

Sores. All over her face were red sores; some looked new, and some must have been there for years. She looked about sixty-five with her sunken in face, bones standing out prominently. Her lips were chapped and cracked, and the corner of her mouth tipped up in what looked like a disgusted look, and my first reaction was to ask, *What the fuck are you looking at?* but I refrained.

As the woman stepped out from behind Stiff's large body, it took every bit of self-control I had not to gasp. Her body was frail, all bones and loose skin, no fat anywhere on her. Her hands shook, and her body twitched at different intervals.

Stiff caught my attention as he made his way toward me, but something about the woman made me unable to take my eyes off her. She gave off an untrustworthy vibe, and that thought felt like spiders against my skin, setting me on edge.

"Chels." As Stiff grabbed my arms, my attention went to him and his beautiful eyes. "Babe, need you to go back into the house while I deal with this."

"Oh, come on, Wes. Introduce me." The woman's voice came out deep and throaty, like she'd smoked cigarettes every moment of every day since she was twelve.

What shocked me, though, was her use of his real name. I hadn't heard anyone call him that since high school.

"Shut it." This came from Xander, who Stiff was blocking my view from.

"Who is that?" I whispered to Stiff.

The woman had all the signs of a meth head, and my gut clenched. I thought I knew who she was, but I didn't want to be right.

"My mother," he answered.

I closed my eyes, letting the bomb hit me.

"You don't need to see this."

I opened my eyes and asked, "Is she okay?" already knowing the answer yet hoping I was wrong.

"No, Fire. She's not. Hopped up on ice, and I need to find out why the fuck she's here."

I lifted my palm to his chest, placing it there, feeling the need for that connection with him. He placed his hand over mine, and I felt a warmth I never wanted to let go of.

"Sorry," I whispered.

Stiff bent down and brushed his lips over mine. "Been that way for as long as I can remember."

My heart broke for him. My father did drugs, but he split before I'd seen too much of it. It made me wonder if he looked the same way as Stiff's mother now.

"Oh, how cute," she taunted. "Wes got himself a whore."

Stiff's eyes changed in a flash. One moment, they were soft and warm, and the next, ice formed over them in a way I didn't like. He kept ahold of my hand but turned around to face the woman.

She stood with her arms crossed, oblivious to the number of big men around her and either not caring her son was pissed or too high to notice.

He released my hand and stalked toward the woman in the long strides of a panther. "What did you say?" he snapped. "You have the nerve to call my woman a whore when all you've ever done was whore yourself off to any man you could? You wanna see a whore? Look in the fuckin' mirror."

I wrapped my arms around myself, lifting one hand to my mouth to bite on my nail. There were so many things wrong in this situation, but the only thing that stuck out in that moment were the words "my woman." Those two words came with so many questions, though.

Hope fluttered, which was totally stupid, but I didn't stop it. I was too invested in the scene.

"I kept a roof over your head," she snapped back, and Xander laughed. Yes, full-out laughed.

"You did shit, woman. Stiff took care of everything. You were just too fuckin' high or had some dick inside of you to notice or care. He's right, though. Don't call Chelsea a whore," Xander threw out.

So much information was coming at once, and I needed to process it all.

"I can't believe the disrespect!" the woman yelled dramatically.

Bosco rolled his eyes; Boner ripped his stocking cap off and ran his fingers through his hair; and Spook stood there, unmoving and unflinching.

When that didn't work in getting attention, she turned to Xander.

"Xander, baby, you know I did the best I could."

I watched Xander's disgusted reaction and realized quickly there was no love lost there. I felt bad for them—Stiff and Xander—even if they'd turned out to be decent men.

"That stopped working on me when I was twelve, Mom," Xander told her.

"I can't believe this." She turned to Stiff, anger flaring in her eyes, the erratic behavior turning up about a hundred notches. "I came here because you told Gonzo

I didn't have your protection." She waved her arm out to the boys. "None of your protection, and now he's after me! Stiff, you know what he'll do to me if he catches me. I need you to protect me!"

There was downright fear in her eyes, and I couldn't blame her after seeing what my sister had endured. Then the cards fell in place for why Stiff and Vipers Creed had been so keen on helping me. They'd already had a serious interest in it due to Stiff's mom. This whole scenario hadn't really been about saving me or my sister, rather to kill two birds with one stone.

As much as my heart desired to be more than another skirt, I was a right place, right time thing for Stiff; nothing special. And he'd never told me anything.

Emotions welled up inside of me. Doubts about anything ever being real filled me. I had to fight back all the feelings of worthlessness and remind myself not to get attached. This was supposed to be my chance to let loose, not my forever.

"You did this to yourself," Stiff argued, his shoulder brushing mine, and the woman's fierce eyes turned on me.

She pointed her finger at me. "I know you. You're that waitress at the diner."

Would it be rude to say duh? Yeah, it probably would be.

"You mean to tell me you're shackin' up with her instead of keepin' your own mother safe!"

Stiff's arm came around my shoulders, giving me a squeeze. "You don't take her shit on. This is why I wanted you away from this," he said to me.

Did he really want me away from this? I knew my place. I was nothing more than a hard working woman trying to make my way in the world. The school of hard knocks gave me lessons at every turn. When this—whatever it was—came crashing down, I would still be the waitress at the diner. And she would always be his mom.

The thought hit me harder than I wanted it to.

I swallowed hard, whispering, "Are you gonna let someone hurt her?" Stiff had been so protective of me and Jenn—hell, even Mom and Grams.

"I can't help her, Chels. We'll talk about this in a bit. I need to get her the fuck outta here before it gets worse."

"How much worse could it get?" I asked.

"You have no idea, Fire. I need you to go back to the house. Can you do that for me?"

I nodded, not wanting to be a part of this pony show anymore. I wanted my sister and to be away from Stiff's mom.

I turned and began to walk away when I heard, "Such an obedient little dog."

I whirled. "Did you just call me a dog?"

She laughed. "Nice puppy," she replied.

I went to retort, but before I could, Bosco came up behind the woman and smacked her on the back of the head. She fell to the ground in a heap, and I gasped, jumping back.

Bosco's eyes came to mine, and something glimmered in them that I didn't recognize.

"I just knocked her out. She needed to shut the fuck up."

I was relieved for the small miracle but couldn't help feeling strange.

EIGHTEEN

STIFF

"**W**HAT DO YOU WANNA DO WITH HER?" Spook asked, looking between Xander and me.

My mother had woken up and spoken to us, not providing us with any good information. She knew the first name of the supplier and Gonzo, saying she had a prepaid phone, but she had nothing on her.

I turned to Xander. "Know she's a bitch and a piece of shit, but we can lock her up here."

Xander looked at me like I'd grown three heads, and I felt that way. "What, let her wither away under lock and key?"

I shrugged. "It'd be better than what they'll do to her."

This decision was all about Xander, but I wouldn't tell him that. I'd put it on me and carry that load. I'd carried it for years and had no intention of stopping where he was concerned.

My brother was a tough man, strong man, but he'd always loved her, always wanted her to be a mom. I fucking hated the woman and knew that ship had sailed, but if I could lessen the pain that he would feel, I'd do it. I'd suck up my anger and lock her up, feed her, and keep her safe, even though I'd said I wouldn't.

"She's not gonna get clean," Xander concluded, looking over at our mother, who sat on the picnic table, fuming.

"Didn't say she would, even though we won't supply her with drugs. But if we lock her up, she can't come back on us and bite us in the ass. No tellin' what she'd do to save her own ass. Could be a number of things, and having her here eliminates that threat. And we"—I used the term "we" here yet specifically put it on me—"won't find out her fate."

Xander shook his head, pinched the bridge of his nose, and held it. I waited, letting him process it.

"Yeah," he finally said softly.

I turned to Spook. "Can we lock her in the safe room? Get Needles to come in and help get her off the ice?" I had no fucking clue if that was even possible. Drugs weren't my thing, so I didn't know the first step about getting rid of the shit. She'd been on drugs for as long as I could remember, but I would do this for my brother—try one last goddamned time.

"Done," Spook said, nodding to Hooch.

We had a small room in the basement that was padded and only had a mattress and toilet. Back when Spook's father had been in charge, he had put in a room to hold those who had done us wrong. It normally didn't get used now, but it would be good for my mom.

"Wait … What's goin' on?" my mother questioned as Hooch grabbed her small frame. She kicked and screamed to be let down.

I turned to my brother, whose brow was tight as he watched our mother get carried away.

"Xander," I called, grabbing his attention. "Never made a promise to you I couldn't keep, so you gotta know I can't here. But this is the only option other than handin' her over to Gonzo. Don't know if it'll do a damn thing, but it'll be better than what he'd do."

He lifted his chin, and that was done. Spook would set it up to have someone bring our mother food and such, and Needles would have his people do what they had to do.

I didn't want to think about the fact that I had just let the one woman I despised the most into the only place I had felt safe. The woman who never allowed me that feeling while growing up, yet I was allowing her to stay here, invading my sanctuary.

I closed my eyes, sucked in a breath, then grabbed my smokes and lit one up.

Spook came up next to me.

When he said nothing, only stared at the same green grass as me, I said, "Chelsea wants to take Jenn to her mom's and go back to work. You think we can trust Gonzo?"

"We trust no one but our own."

While this had rung true to me for many years, I now wanted to include Chelsea in that circle.

"How can we do that for her and keep her safe?" I asked.

"Where's she gonna sleep?" he countered.

I smiled. "My bed, of course."

Spook chuckled. "We can set up cameras in the diner and get a tail on her. Workin' this important to her?"

I nodded. "Yeah, it is."

"Alright, brother, we'll make it work." He slapped my shoulder, gave it a squeeze, then left.

Xander's boots came into my line of vision, and I raised my head.

"Don't know what's gotten into you, brother. Don't really know how I feel about all this. But, man, who the fuck needs Superman? You've always been a fierce protector. Some things never change."

"You think that?"

"Wouldn't say it if I didn't."

I inhaled my smoke, letting it penetrate in deep.

"Brother, it's in your blood, in your soul. You protect. Just like you'd protect that woman of yours from a damn hangnail if she had one."

His words were like a knee to the balls, knocking the wind out of me. Then I thought about it—her being hurt and me having a way to fix it. I would do it in a heartbeat and not bat an eye.

I only nodded.

He placed his hand on my shoulder, giving it a squeeze, and then he walked off.

I looked up at the sky, having no fucking clue if I'd done the right thing or if I had fucked us all.

CHELSEA

"Yeah, Mom, it'd be great for you to come by." I held my cell to my ear, thankful one of Stiff's boys had gone to Charlie's and gotten it for me.

"Grams and I will be there in a bit," Mom replied, and I was happy they'd decided to come.

Stiff had texted me, saying he had to work at the shop, and that was four hours ago. With what I had seen of his mother, though, I wanted him to come back now. I needed to make sure he was okay, and keeping myself from texting or calling him was hard.

I'd even plugged in a movie for Jenn and me to watch, but all I'd done was curl up on the couch while my sister sat in the recliner. I didn't ever remember actually watching a single minute of it, too worried about Stiff.

"Sounds good, Mom. See you then."

"Bye." After she clicked off the phone, I tossed mine to the couch beside me.

"Sounds like they're coming to visit," Jenn said, her head tilted toward me without pain etched in her features. I liked that.

"Yeah."

"What's wrong? You've been quiet. Hell, since you came back from wherever you went, you've been off. Talk to me," Jenn ordered.

I let it all out, not holding a single thing back, even telling her how twisted in knots I felt from not knowing if he was okay.

Jenn kept quiet, listening to every single word. She always did. I could count on her for anything, and this was no exception.

"Damn, Chels." Damn was right. "So, let's see here. You got yourself a man, which I have to say is wonderful. Don't know him well, but he's been awesome with me, so he gets lots of points in my book. And his brother is hot."

"He has a girl."

She lifted a brow. "I know that. I can still look at him. I may have bruises and some rib issues, but I'm not dead, Chelsea. Hell, half the men here are hot."

I chuckled, something I didn't think I'd be able to do with my mood being the way it was. "Very true."

"Anyway." She paused. "You really like this guy?" Her tone came off hesitant.

I sat up from the couch and rested my back against the soft cushion, looking at my sister. "Yeah."

"Okay, yeah isn't gonna cut it here, and I know he's good in bed. I can hear you with the television on and the door shut."

A blush crept into my cheeks, but I powered on. "Yes, he is, but there's more to him than that."

My sister got a glint in her eye, a spark that I'd missed. "Keep goin'!" she all but yelled at me.

I rolled my eyes. "He's … We're a lot alike in a lot of ways." My sister stared at me, waiting. Shit. "He's very protective of the ones he cares about. He's a hard worker and didn't give me shit for having a house decorated as the beach." Jenn laughed, and I smiled. "He also didn't knock down my goals, and he doesn't think less of me because I work at Charlie's."

"Wait a minute." My sister's hand went up, index finger extended. "Less of you? Why the hell would anyone think less of you?"

I shrugged. "I don't have a fancy degree like you will, and I've been doing the same thing for years. Not really any room to move up with employment opportunities. Don't get me wrong; I love it there, love Charlie."

"Then you shouldn't give a shit what anyone thinks."

I shook my head. "You don't get it. I don't give a shit what others think. I give a shit about what Stiff thinks."

The light bulb dawned on my sister. "I get it."

I knew she would. She always got me.

"What are your thoughts on school?" I asked hesitantly. She'd only used Stiff's laptop once to log into her portal at school to make sure her classes were there.

She sucked in deep then winced. I hated that for her, and my stomach cringed.

"My professors are good this semester; told me I can do all my work online. They all record their lectures, so those will be available to me, too."

"That's good. There's only a couple of months left of the semester."

"Yep. Once I get going, I'll get busy. I'll finish."

One thing still scared me. "You have summer classes and another semester to go, Jenn," I reminded her. "What do you plan on doing?"

"I don't know," she murmured softly. "When I called my boss, I had to take time off. He was a dick and let me go, saying he needed to fill the spot. So, as of right now, I have nothing. I'm not going back to the apartment, though."

Barbed wire wrapped around my heart and squeezed. Those assholes had taken more away from my sister than just her health. I hated that, hated them. Hated my damn father.

"It's only a half-hour to forty-five minutes' drive depending on traffic. You could live here and commute. And for work, I'm sure Charlie would hire you."

She sighed heavily, like everything was weighing her down. "Let's just take it one step at a time."

"The apartment is month to month, Jenn. If you want, I'll go up, get your stuff, and work out everything with your landlord."

Jenn stayed quiet for a while before speaking. "I love you. You know that?"

"Yeah, little girl. I know that."

"We're Millers, and we make things work, but Chels, it's already the middle of the month, so I'll have to pay for next month, and I won't even be there."

Damn, this would take a bite out of my money and probably set me back a few months from getting my own place, but my trailer had been my home for so long I didn't give a shit. I'd do anything for Jenn.

"I'll get it taken care of." I rose, walked over to my sister, then leaned down to kiss the top of her head. "Everything will work out."

NINETEEN

CHELSEA

WHILE MOM AND GRAMS WERE visiting with Jenn, Xander stopped by, saying he had to check up on me. Once he saw my family there, he joined in, and I ended up laughing so hard my stomach hurt, tears running down my face. I hadn't laughed that hard in my life.

I'd needed this. I'd needed my family around me to make everything disappear just for a little while, to put life back to normal, or at least our normal, for a time. However, then the door burst open and Stiff prowled through, his face an empty mask. The laughter died, and all eyes went to him.

"Hey," he grunted, and I wanted to take the emptiness away.

Even with the doubts, I felt the pull between us, and I couldn't fight it, so I followed my instincts. I rose, walking right over to him, wrapping him in my arms, and holding on tight. It took a few beats before he did the same then rested his cheek on the top of my head. I felt his body relax from its tautness, and that made me relax a little for him.

The room was silent, but I knew they were there, watching, waiting. Still, I didn't want to let him go quite yet. Therefore, I stayed planted on the spot, holding him and inhaling the smell of tobacco and leather. I'd never been into anyone who smoked, but with Stiff, it was him, so I liked it.

His cheek moved away from my head as he spoke. "You two gonna be around for a while?"

"If you need us to. I have the day off," my mother replied as I pulled back to look up at Stiff, wondering why he'd asked that.

"Need to go out for a while. Want Chelsea to come with me. You good with stayin'?"

I drew my brows together in confusion as to where he would want to take me, but I kept quiet, not wanting him to get wound tight again.

"Sure," my mother replied.

It was Grams who asked the question I wanted the answer to. "Where are you taking her, young man?"

To that, he gave a sexy grin, his arms still securely around me, flexing. "Need to go for a ride. Want her on the back of my bike."

"Really?" I asked breathy. "I've never been on a motorcycle."

"Then it's about time we get you there," he replied, looking down at my shorts and tank. "Need you to change into jeans, boots, shirt, and jacket. If you don't have one, there's one in my closet."

I thought about what little I'd brought with me and realized something. "I don't have boots. I only have my tennis shoes."

"Those'll do. We'll get ya some boots later."

I nodded, and he gave me a squeeze then released me, giving me a sign to get a move on. So I got a move on.

After glancing at my family then moving quickly to the bedroom, I changed, pulled my hair into a low ponytail, and headed back out to the living room. Stiff looked as if he hadn't moved an inch, but he now had on a leather jacket. Me, I had to wear one of his, and all of them were huge on me. I found the smallest and went with it. I hoped it wasn't too hot outside for all of this, or I'd sweat my ass off.

Even though I thought of this, excitement bubbled in me. My first bike ride, and I was lucky enough to be on the back of Stiff's. No fear came through, only happiness.

"Let's go," he ordered after looking me up and down, seeing my shoes, and shaking his head.

I rolled my eyes. It wasn't like it was a shock. I'd already told him what I had. Whatever.

I kissed Jenn and Grams on the cheek then Mom, telling her exactly where everything was located, and left with Stiff.

Stiff grabbed my hand, walking out to the large row of bikes parked in the lot. This gesture was simple, yet to me, it meant so much more. The warmth flowed as my heart squeezed.

He sidled up to a black and silver bike. It had a huge windshield and a small skull emblem by the engine. The bike had a seat on the back and bags that hung off the sides. It was hot.

"Swing your leg over and get behind me," he said casually.

With as much grace as I could muster, I threw my leg over, wiggled my ass in the seat, and got comfortable.

Looking down on either side, I noticed he had these little pegs for my feet to go on, so I placed them there.

"Wrap your arms around me," he ordered.

This I did without any hesitation. Stiff was rock solid, and I loved having him pressed against me.

Stiff took off like a shot, the large metal doors of the compound opening as we neared. He lifted his hand to the guys, and we were off.

The moment the wind drifted through my hair, I fell in love with being on the back of Stiff's bike. I'd thought I'd love it just from being close to him. I was wrong, so very wrong.

As the wind came from every different direction, tangling my hair and hitting my cheeks, freedom hit me like a physical force, almost knocking me off the bike. I felt as if I were flying high above hell, soaring.

With each mile that passed and the sun shining down on us, I fell deeply in love … with the bike, of course.

I squeezed Stiff, and he squeezed my hand. It was sweet—him acknowledging me and giving me this part of him.

I noticed a few things while riding. One, Stiff held his arm out to those on motorcycles, but only to the ones on Harleys. For the ones who flew by us on those motorized crotch rocket things, he never lifted his hand. I made a mental note to ask him why later.

Also, when we were on the highway, he was so focused on who or what was around us, but then, when he turned on the back roads, his body visibly relaxed. I assumed it was because of all the cars, but I didn't know for sure. Another thing to ask him.

We rode for a really long time, and I enjoyed every second of it, living life. It was amazing. I didn't clock how long we were out. I was so thrilled to be exactly where I was that it didn't matter. Therefore, when we pulled up to an older cabin that had a lake behind it, I was floored by our location. Living in Dyersburg my whole life, I'd never been here—hell, hadn't known it existed until this very moment.

The old cabin was exactly that—old. The wooden planks covering the outside were discolored from years of weather. The roof had peeled up shingles, and the window screens had so many holes in them I wondered why the owner didn't just take them out. The porch knocked me on my ass, though. It wrapped around the entire structure made of very wide, rounded logs. It was gorgeous.

Stiff stopped the bike then cut the engine. "Hop off, Fire," he said, and I listened, swinging my leg up and off.

My body felt stiff from the ride. When my feet hit the ground, I felt the need to brace on to something, as they felt like Jell-O. I bent my knees and straightened them, even lifted my arms to stretch them out. I never knew being on a bike could make your muscles ache.

Stiff put the kickstand down and got off, his dark shades covering his eyes. Then he reached out and took my hand.

"Come on. Wanna show you somethin'," he said, pulling my hand.

We stopped as I took in the view. Trees lined the area except straight in front of us where the blue lake shined from the sun. Every once in a while, I could hear the water moving just a touch. The other side of the lake had vibrant green trees, and the side we were on had been mowed down so the grass wasn't that tall. Out from the land and into the water was an old dock that looked rickety. I hoped Stiff didn't think we were going out there on that.

I followed along as Stiff began walking with his hand still latched in mine. Sure enough, he walked us right to the dock and began to walk on it.

I pulled back, and his head snapped toward me.

"That doesn't look safe," I said, and his brow lifted.

He leveled his intense gaze on me. "You think I'm gonna let anything happen to you?"

I exhaled. "No." That word was the honest to God truth. I didn't think for a second he would let anything happen to me. I felt it in my gut and down to my bones.

"Right, come on."

The wood creaked under our steps. It was only about five feet across, and as Stiff plopped down on the edge, bringing me down with him, I braced for water impact. When it didn't come, relief hit me. I could swim, but I just wasn't in the mood to test out the water.

Stiff swung his beefy legs over the side, and I was surprised he didn't touch the water. I followed suit.

Without a word, we sat.

And sat.

And sat.

Stiff remained quiet, and I took that as he didn't want to talk. Maybe he needed this break from all the shit going down, some solitude. If I could help him with that, I had no problem doing it.

I took off my jacket and rolled my jeans up. It was warm, but not so hot that I wanted to jump into the water. I listened to the birds calling each other in a musical dance just like in *Mockingjay*, along with others who squawked once and disappeared. Frogs or toads croaked as a breeze fell over me.

"Guess you figured out my mom's a bitch." He broke the silence after a very long time.

"I got that."

"Yeah, she's tied up with Gonzo, too, and I don't trust her."

My gut twisted as I recalled her words about someone hurting her. She might be a bitch, but she was still his mom, and I hated thinking that Stiff had thrown his mom out, only for her to get hurt.

"Gonna tell you some shit. It stays between us. I'm trustin' that you'll keep it that way." He turned his head to look at me.

"Of course," I answered without missing a beat. I could give him that.

"Didn't put her out. Locked her up in the clubhouse. It won't be pretty, but gonna have Needles do whatever the fuck he does, and maybe he can get her clean. If not, then not."

I reached over to Stiff's hand resting on the edge of the dock and laid mine on his. He took it a step further and entwined our fingers then lifted our connected hands to his mouth, kissing the back of my hand before putting it down again.

My heart fluttered. It was such a simple gesture, but so much was packed behind it. It would be one of those moments I would never lose.

"Why did you do it?" He sighed, and I went on. "You seemed as if you wanted her to leave."

"Xander. He didn't need that on him. You saw what they did to your sister, an innocent. Our mom's anything but." He shook his head, letting out a deep breath. "Couldn't do that to him. She's a bitch, and I fuckin' hate her, but I couldn't deal with seeing the look on Xander's face when she came to us in a body bag."

"Why did you change your mind?"

He looked at me. "Seein' you with your mom." My heart squeezed. "You had it good with her. Xander and I never had that. Xander always had hope, and I didn't wanna be the one to kill it."

I squeezed his hand, but what I really wanted to do was wrap my arms around this man and hold him. However, he wasn't done talking, and I wanted him to continue. If he needed to get this out, then I wanted to give him that chance.

"Always had his back except when he was overseas. That I couldn't control, but other than that, always."

"Do you think it's a bad thing?"

His eyes came to mine again as he shrugged. "Don't know."

"We can only do what we can, Stiff."

"Yeah, babe, I know." He turned back to stare at the water, going quiet on me again.

I decided to fill the silence. "My mom's great, but my dad, not so much." I let the memories of my childhood fill me. "Not all the time, though. There was a time when he was around, and he played board games with us. I remember *Chutes and Ladders* because I always landed on the damn chutes." I gave a little chuckle. "Mom always worked. My dad couldn't keep a steady job to save his life. He was fired from McDonalds and Burger King. He had a job in a factory once, but that didn't last long, either. Then, one day, he changed, stopped trying. Started lyin' on the couch, clicking through the television.

"I'd run up to him and try to get him to play, but he always told me 'later.' It was always later. Then later became days, weeks, months … until I didn't ask anymore and got my sister to stop, too."

Stiff let go of my hand and wrapped his arm around my shoulders, pulling me against him. I loved feeling the hardness of him, so strong, protective.

I continued, "He became really moody, and nothing my sister, mother, or I could do was right. He yelled a couple of times; he threw things. When he picked up the television like he was the damn Hulk or something and heaved it across the room, shattering it into a million pieces, was the day my mom put him out. Well, she waited for him to go out then changed the locks on the trailer."

I shook my head, remembering the sounds of him yelling through the door invaded me. "He pounded on the door and yelled. Mom called the cops. Then it got so bad we moved to a different trailer. It didn't take Dad long to find us there, so we moved again. Six times, we moved everything we owned. The last place was Grams' house."

"Why'd you wait to go there?"

I chuckled. "Mom's stubborn."

He shook me a bit. "Go figure."

I looked up at him, smiling. I knew I was like my mom, and I was proud of it.

"Grams hated Dad. She got out her shotgun and told him, if he came around again, she'd put a bullet in his chest."

Stiff grinned. "Remind me not to fuck with her."

"Yeah, she's of the mindset to shoot first, ask questions later."

"Yep, me and your grams will get along perfectly."

It made me warm inside that he was thinking about further on, not the here and now.

"Jenn and I didn't see him, but I guess Mom did. She protected us from that. Grams protected us from that, or so they thought. With the credit cards and now with Jenn, I just wish he'd go away," I confided.

"I've got boys lookin' for him."

I turned toward him quickly. "You do?"

He leaned over and kissed my forehead, another one of those moments that I locked down in my memory bank. "Yeah, Fire, I do. He's underground, so Spook's callin' in some other guys he knows who can hunt him out. We'll get him."

"What are you gonna do with him?"

I hated him for what he'd done to my sister, my mom, and me. I knew I'd said I wanted him dead, but could I really live with that on my conscience? Not that Stiff would do it, but it was the first thing that flitted into my head.

"Don't know yet. Figure that out once we find him."

Conflicting feelings hit me, but I would have to stash away those thoughts until it became my reality. Right now, it was just a possibility.

"You good with that?" he asked.

"Don't know. Kinda up in the air about it," I answered.

He pulled me to him more tightly, and I reached around his body. This was the hug I'd wanted to give him, and he was giving it to me, instead.

I felt the warmth, the fluttering of my heart, and wetness want to spring from my eyes. Damn, I loved his strong arms holding me.

When he pulled away, part of me wanted to grip him and tell him not to go, but we were right next to each other, and I was too rational.

"I've gotta ask you something," I told him.

"Shoot."

"Your mother is in with Gonzo and so is my father. Did you get with me just because of that?" I hated that my voice went had gone soft, but if he answered this question a certain way, I knew I'd be crushed.

"That was luck, Fire. One good thing out of this fucked up mess. I'm with you because I want to be, not because of anything else; know that. Having you entangled in this shit wasn't the way I'd like it to happen, but it is what it is, and we move on."

I liked that answer. I felt good with it.

"Okay," I said quietly.

"What do ya think of this place?" he asked, holding my hand again.

I looked back out at the water, the sun dancing off its surface. "Beautiful."

"Yeah. I used to bring my brother here."

This revelation caught me off guard. "Really? Do you know who owns it?"

"Then, nope. Now, me."

My breath caught, and unable to prop my knee up because we were too close, I turned as much as possible toward him. "You're kidding me."

He turned to me and gave me the sexiest smile I'd seen on him yet. "Nope." He accentuated the 'P' with a pop of his lips, and even that was sexy. Then he turned back toward the water.

"Are you gonna live here?" I asked.

The house needed so much work, but I could envision what it could be, given the right TLC.

His eyes bore into mine like drills trying to find oil. "Didn't. Plans have a funny way of changin', though."

I felt the blush, but this time, not only did it hit my cheeks, it hit every part of my body. My heart thumped so damn hard I swore it would come out of my chest.

Needing his lips on mine, I quickly moved to where I was straddling Stiff and pressed his back down to the wood. Then I crashed my lips to his, and he brought his arms around me firmly. He could, of course, have stopped me, but he didn't, thank God.

Long and deep, I kissed him, letting every emotion I felt pour through my lips. He met me at every move, and I felt like a teenager getting kissed for the first time.

Amazing how I'd kissed him several times, but this one felt different—closer, intimate.

I drew it out until my breath failed, and I gasped for air. Then I opened my eyes, looking at this gorgeous man below me, and my heart expanded.

TWENTY

STIFF

Fuck me. Being with Chelsea was like a drug, and I was so damn high on it I never wanted to climb down. I almost understood what addicts felt like.

Me, Stiff, biker, man, supervising mechanic, kissing a woman stupid for a fucking hour on a dock. The same dock I used to bring my brother to when we needed to escape. This place held so many different memories for me; some good and some not.

Chelsea had single-handedly wiped all the bad away, only giving me good.

Then, riding with her hot pussy against my back, her arms around me and hands stretched across my abs—fucking heaven. I never really believed in all that before.

The life I grew up in had made it hard to think there was a higher power at work, but something had to be there for Chelsea to have been put in my life.

Damn, I sounded like a fucking Hallmark card. It was the truth, though. She'd helped me turn a shitty day into a great one just by being her.

Once we got back, I showered while she went to see her family out and check on Jenn. My dick throbbed with the need to be inside of her, to take her and make her mine.

Chelsea strutted through the door, confidence beaming in her eyes, and then she shut the door behind her. She reached for the hem of her shirt and pulled it off in a whoosh then reached behind her and tugged off her bra. Fuck, her tits bounced, and her nipples were ripe.

She moved her mouth as if she were sucking on something. Surely, she wasn't eating. She had my dick's attention, and he was ready to play.

I lay in bed, the sheet tenting from my massive erection, just watching her. I got off on her taking the wheel. What I liked better was we weren't fucking high on emotion. For this, we could take our time.

"Whatcha got?" I asked, and she smiled coyly, not answering. Instead, she unbuttoned her pants then shimmied them down her legs along with her underwear, displaying her ripe pussy for me.

Wanting to move, I kept still, wanting to see what she had up her sleeve.

At the end of the bed, she crawled up until she reached my tented sheet. Fucking hot didn't even cut it. The way her tits jiggled was amazing. The best part was the fire burning in her eyes. She had a mission, and I was going to let her achieve it.

She pulled the sheet down my legs, my cock mere inches from her lips. She sucked again on whatever was in her mouth.

"May wanna spit that out," I told her.

She shook her head. "You don't want me to."

That was when she opened her mouth and took me fully inside her. But this wasn't like the last time. Oh, no. This time, my cock was burning hot, not in pain but aroused to the point I wasn't going to last a minute with my cock inside her mouth.

"What's in your mouth?" I groaned as she sucked me in farther, the spike of my orgasm right there on the brink.

She popped up. "Your cock."

"You little smartass."

She moved her mouth back around my cock, not letting me get out another syllable. The burn was like nothing I'd ever experienced.

Sucking hard and fierce, she then rolled my balls gently with her hand.

I felt it, couldn't stop it—the roll in my spine down to my groin.

"Oh, fuck, baby," I called out, giving no warning as I burst inside of her mouth.

She milked me, sucking me down until my dick began to soften. Then she licked me clean before pulling her eyes up to mine. She stuck out a small piece of something red.

"Cinnamon Fire Jolly Rancher."

"You little minx!" I said, grabbing her then flipping her so her pussy was at my mouth. Then I ate until she screamed my name.

"Got it all set up. She's good to go back to work. Talked to Charlie, and he's gonna make sure he's there on her shifts. He's a former Marine, so I know he'll kick ass and protect hers," Spook assured.

This would be good news for her, but I was a selfish bastard and didn't want her leaving. The past three days since our visit to the lake had been kickass, but Chelsea had been practically vibrating to get back to work. The shit was so ingrained in her it was almost like a physical restraint to keep her from going in.

"Charlie said she can start tomorrow with the lunch shift. Said she'd know what time."

I didn't like it, but I'd do it for her.

"Got it."

"You takin' her, or do I need to rearrange shit?" Spook asked.

"I'm takin' her. I'll work it out at the shop. What about Jenn?"

"Needles said she can go to the mother's. Everything else now is just healing time. There isn't much for him to monitor anymore. And since we already have eyes on Jannie and Bee, we'll have them on Jenn, too."

"Thanks, brother." The words didn't feel like enough, but they were all I had at the moment.

That was the reason I'd wanted to be a Viper all those years ago. Brotherhood—a family I could depend on no matter what I needed. Fuck, he'd taken on my mother, and now he'd busted his ass to get all of this ready for Chelsea—for me. Spook was a good man. None better than him.

"Anytime." He looked down at his desk then back up at me. "Your momma's havin' a hard time. Needles had to give her some shit—"

I held my hand up, halting him. "I get it, man. I do, but I can't go there. She's safe, and Needles or whoever he needs to can take care of her. Straight out to you, brother, I did that shit for Xander and Xander only. Don't need to hear about it."

Spook nodded in understanding. His mother was a handful, too, and he'd had to deal with her.

"Gotta split and tell Chelsea."

"You need anything, let me know." Spook rose from the chair as I did. He stepped around and held out his hand to me. I shook it then went on the search for Chelsea.

"There you are, young man," Bee commented from my couch with a cup of tea in her right hand. "Been waitin' for you to come around."

Why she was waiting for me was anyone's guess, but I liked the woman. Loved her quirkiness.

"Yes, ma'am." I smiled, turning to Jannie and greeting her then Jenn and Chelsea.

"Talked to Spook," I announced.

Chelsea looked around the room at her family, and I smiled. I loved how she was thinking, giving me the 'in front of my family' sign. She'd caught on quickly to the biker way of life. I fucking loved that.

"You can go to work tomorrow."

She hopped up from her spot on the couch and ran into my arms. If I'd had any doubts of how important this was to her and not a way to get away from me, I knew it was shit now.

She wrapped herself around me securely, and I did the same before kissing the top of her head.

She looked up at me. "Really? It's safe?"

"We're workin' it out." I then nodded over to Jenn. "She can go to Bee and Jannie's."

"Thank God," Jenn said, giving out a deep sigh.

I turned toward her. "Not enjoyin' it here?"

"Don't get me wrong, big man; the views are great, but I want some familiarity." She smiled big. "Not to mention, you two need privacy because, Chels, you're loud."

Bee coughed on her tea, and Chelsea broke from my hold and ran over to her.

"Grams, you okay?"

"Fine, fine. At least someone is gettin' something."

It was my turn to burst out laughing.

Chelsea's eyes turned to me, something working behind them. Tentatively, she asked, "This mean I can go back home?"

"As long as my ass is next to ya in your bed."

"Stiff, I highly doubt you and I are gonna fit comfortably in my double bed." Her cheeks stained pink in that sexy-ass way she did when she was embarrassed. Fucking adorable.

"Then we stay here." It was better for me, anyway. "I take you to work, pick you up, and we sleep here."

Out of the corner of my eye, I watched as Jannie ping-ponged back and forth between us, her eyes alert. I didn't have a clue if Chelsea had talked to them about us. Hell, we were having a hard enough time with it. But I didn't give a shit, either. I was who I was and would be who I was with Chelsea, family there or not.

Chelsea came up to my side, putting her arm around my waist and her head in the crook of my arm. "I'm a bit of a pain in the ass, I've been told."

"That's true," Jenn piped up, obviously feeling better.

"My brother says the same thing about me. All good, Fire."

Chelsea smiled up at me.

"Fire?" Jannie asked, not skipping a beat.

"Yeah." I didn't owe anyone any explanations for how I felt or what I thought. Her family or not, I wasn't ready for that shit yet.

"So, you two are together?" Jannie asked.

"Oh, don't be stupid," Bee quipped, all eyes going to her. "He's had a thing for our girl since the first time we met him. Seems now that she's cottoned to the idea, and they're together." Bee was a wise woman, and I liked that Chelsea had that in her life.

"Are you moving out of your trailer?" Jannie asked, and Chelsea stilled in my arms.

"No." The single word came out pained, like she didn't know how I'd feel.

I handed out an answer that would solve both our problems.

"Seems smart to pack up your shit and move it here. That way, you can save up for what you want." It seemed like the logical thing to do, even if she hadn't given me a true yes on everything. I didn't give a fuck. I'd get her to come around sooner rather than later.

Chelsea's other arm wrapped around me, and she burrowed into my body. I fucking loved that shit.

"Thanks," she whispered.

TWENTY-ONE

CHELSEA

"**A**BOUT TIME YOU GOT YOUR ASS back here," Charlie said when I walked into the diner with Stiff right behind me.

It had only been a few days, but a hell of a lot had happened during that time. Now I felt like I was coming home. The diner was a constant, and now I was back.

Charlie strode up, wiping his hands on a towel. His gray hair was slicked back and a smile made wrinkles around his eyes. When he opened his arms wide, I fell inside of them. He smelled of grease, meat, and Charlie.

"Missed you," I whispered.

"Same here, girl. Talked to your man. I'm here when you are. I've got your back." He gave me a hard squeeze then stepped back.

My heart filled so full it almost burst. Charlie was the first man I'd trusted after my father had crushed that trust. He had never let me down in thirteen years, and I knew he wouldn't ever, no matter what life threw at me.

"Thanks."

Charlie's attention went to Stiff. "You stayin' or leavin'?"

"Leavin'. Got some shit to do."

I felt a small pang of disappointment, but it moved away quickly and changed to something else when Mitzi came out of the back with a huge smile on her face, making her way to Stiff.

"Hey, Stiff," she said sexily, totally ignoring me.

"Hey," was his response. No sexy come on. No other acknowledgement. I liked that a hell of a lot.

Mitzi stepped closer, obviously not liking his response, and trailed a finger over his arm.

Grams had me watch a rodeo once where the bull attacked one of the riders. Then a clown guy came over, wearing all red, and led the bull away. I felt like the bull as a red haze covered my eyes.

"Don't," I ground out just as Stiff pulled away from the touch.

Mitzi's focus came to me. "What?"

I stepped in her space. "My man. No running your hands on him. No trying to get in his pants. No getting near him," I snapped.

Mitzi's eyes widened. "I … He's your man?" she asked.

"Yep. Remember it."

She gave me a small scowl then marched off to her tables.

Stiff put his arm around me and pulled me to him. "Easy there, Fire," he said gently.

My body hummed, and it took me a few beats to get myself together. When I did, I looked up at Stiff.

"Don't like that."

"I get you. Now get to work."

And work I did.

Sometime later, when the bell rang over the door and I looked up, old man Darren walked in. His eyes caught mine, and a wide smile came across his face.

"Chelsea, you're back!" he practically cheered, moving toward me, and I smiled at him.

"Yes, I am," I told him then ushered him to a table in my section. "Have a seat."

"Thank you, young lady," he replied, sitting down and scooting in over the plastic.

"What can I get ya?" I asked as I pulled out my pad and pen.

When he didn't say anything, I looked at him. He had a gleam in his eye.

"That smile of yours sure makes an old man's day," he remarked, and I felt like I was home.

My world fell into a pattern, and Stiff proved to me at every turn that he wasn't going to let me down. He would take me to work and pick me up most days. Other days, one of the brothers would bring me. Xander or Hooch came around at times, scoping things out in their man way. Even Stiff came in and ate pretty regularly. I enjoyed having him in my space.

After two weeks, Jenn's recovery had improved greatly. She was doing school work online, and I'd talked to my landlord and was moving my stuff out of my trailer next week. While I'd miss the space I had created, I was happy to stay with Stiff. In doing so, my bank account would increase by four hundred and fifty bucks a month, starting next week. That was huge in my world.

That wasn't to say I didn't have a plan B, because that was who I was. If things went south for some reason, I always had my mom and Grams; although I hoped down to my bone that I wouldn't. Trusting Stiff this much wasn't the easiest thing I'd ever done, and I needed that safety net.

In all the time we'd spent together over these last two weeks, I'd never asked once about his mom. Not once had Stiff let me down or wronged me during this time, and I figured, if there was something I needed to know or he wanted to share, he would tell me. I trusted him to do that for me.

I did ask about my dad, though, to which Stiff told me, "He's slippery." That meant they hadn't found him yet.

Stiff and the guys went up to Jenn's place at her school, packed her up, and brought everything to Grams'. She was still up in the air about other classes, but I would be damned if she didn't get back to it. That degree was hers; I would make certain of it. Come hell or high water, this setback would not cost her the degree she wanted. Then again, she was slowly getting her fighting Miller spirit back, so I didn't think it would be much of a fight.

The bell over the door chimed, and in strode Boner with the stocking cap and big shades. He whipped them off, coming right toward me.

"I'm your ride. Stiff's got shit going on at the shop," he told me, plopping up on the bar seat.

"No problem." I turned to the back. "Charlie!" I called into the kitchen, and he turned toward me. "I'm going."

"Later, girl."

I smiled, grabbed my things, and headed out to Boner.

My feet were barking at me. The small break from being on them still had them on rebellion. I hoped it wouldn't take them long to figure out we needed to work now. I was lucky, though. Stiff rubbed them a lot. He didn't find them gross, but I made sure to scrub them really good in the shower. That was more for me than him.

"Ready," I said, seeing Mitzi giving me the stink eye out of the corner of my eye. Whatever. She was just pissed because none of the guys now sat in her section. And now that they knew me, tips were even better. I protested, but it got me nowhere. They were all very insistent and Bosco even more so.

"Let's go."

Boner led me out of the building, his eyes watchful. It had been weeks since my sister had been hurt, and with no sign of my father, I really didn't think that anything would happen. It made Boner feel better, though, so he did.

He moved me to a black four-door Jeep and opened up the passenger side for me. Gotta love southern hospitality. Stiff did the same when we weren't on his bike, but those were becoming seldom since I loved riding.

Boner closed the door, rounded the hood, and jumped in with me. Then he fired up the engine, and we were off.

"Boner?" I asked.

"Yep."

"Can we stop by my place so I can pick up a few things?" Despite wearing mostly my uniforms, I wanted some of my yoga pants and tees, even if Stiff was dead-set on me wearing his.

He shrugged. "Sure." He turned the Jeep in the direction of my house.

"Can I ask you something?"

"Shoot."

"How come none of the brothers come and pick me up on their bikes? Whenever you or anyone besides Stiff come, you always have a vehicle. Is there a reason for that?" I'd learned many things during my stay with the Vipers, but there were still things I had questions about.

"Yep. Don't ride on the back of a man's bike unless you're his woman. You're not mine, so we don't ride."

This made sense. I had only seen Spook with Trixie on the back of his. The others, I hadn't seen anyone.

"Is that a rule or something?"

He chuckled. "Yeah, Chels."

"Why don't you have a woman?"

His chuckle died, and I instantly regretted the question.

"Never mind," I said quickly.

"It's all good, Chelsea. Long story. Don't really wanna talk about it. Maybe some other time."

"Okay," I replied.

We rode the rest of the way to my place in silence. When we pulled up, it looked exactly the same: beat to hell, rusty, and way used. However, it was mine, and I knew the inside was better than the out.

"I'll just be a minute," I told him, grabbing the door handle.

"Hang on there. I'm comin', too." He rolled out and came behind me as I inserted the key into the new lock Stiff had put in. He'd wanted to change the door, but since I was moving, he'd decided not to.

I opened the door wide and stopped dead. That was because someone wrapped an arm around my neck, tucking my back to a front, and placed a gun at my temple.

Boner pulled a gun from somewhere. The gun at my temple left, and two shots were put into Boner.

I screamed as Boner's gun went off, pinging somewhere in the room as he crumbled to the ground. My heart pounded as I tried to get out of the hold to help him, but I couldn't.

A black boot kicked the door shut. Then I was turned, and the lock on the door was bolted. The arm around my neck released me, and I turned around to see my father, or at least a version of him.

The man before me looked similar, but the years had not been kind. His face was sunken in to the point he didn't have cheeks, the skin concave. His eyes were wired, looking everywhere, unable to settle on one thing. He had the same sores as Stiff's mom on his face. He also had no meat on his bones, his T-shirt hanging loosely. He needed one about three sizes smaller.

Not only that, but he had a gun pointed at me.

"Dad?" I asked.

"Money." He sniffled and moved his head around frantically. "I need money. He's comin' for me, and I need money."

He kept repeating himself, and I wasn't sure if he was high or if he was coming down from one. I didn't know much about drugs or their effects, so I was winging this.

"I don't have any money."

He waved the gun frantically at me, and I stepped back with my hands up.

"Bullshit. Don't you lie to me." He aimed the gun up and down my clothes. "You were workin'. You've got somethin.'"

I did. I had about two hundred dollars from tips for a twelve-hour shift, but he didn't need to know that. I just needed to calm him down and get the hell out of here to check on Boner.

"I did, but I don't have any on me."

That was when my father shot at my feet. I jumped a mile high and moved into the kitchen, farther away from him.

"I can't believe you just shot at me." I gasped, surprised as hell. How could a man do that to his own daughter?

"I can't believe you're still fuckin' talkin'. You don't wanna end up like your fuck-buddy out there; you'd better give me your fuckin' cash!" He punctuated each word, growing louder and louder.

Fear hit me, but I hid it because that would not help me in this situation. Obviously, talking wasn't going to help, either.

As much as it killed me, I reached into my purse and pulled out the bills, holding them up to him.

He stalked closer and tore them out of my hand. He stared at the money then shook it at me. "This is all you have!" he roared like it was my fault I'd only gotten two hundred bucks today. I thought it was a pretty good take.

"That's all I have."

"Lying bitch!" His arm holding the gun came up.

I tried to get away from it but couldn't before he landed a hard blow across my cheek. I fell hard to the tile floor and held my face as warm liquid ran through my fingers.

Anger mixed with the fear, but this was a battle I wasn't going to win. He was too far gone to care about anything except the money. I had no doubt he would shoot me just like he had Boner. As a result, I kept my temper in check and slowly rose from the floor.

My father picked my purse up off the floor and shuffled through it. He found my checkbook and put it in his back pocket then opened my wallet. He found my ID, my lone credit card, and a few more dollars inside of it. He took it all and put it in his back pocket. He even opened up the small zipper and grabbed the change, too.

"Stupid, lying bitch!" he roared at me.

No, this wasn't the man who'd played board games with me when I was younger. This wasn't the man I remembered at all. This man, I didn't know.

"I need more!" He grabbed me by my shirt and shook me, and I brought my hands up to his wrists.

"I don't have any more." It was true. I didn't. All of my money was locked up at the bank. I went often, and thank the gods I'd gone yesterday, or I would have a lot more in my possession.

"You're lying!" he roared again then pulled me back to my bedroom, throwing me on the bed.

"Hello, look at the trailer I live in. I don't have anything!" I yelled back at him, but he ignored me and started going through my drawers, tossing clothes out. Then he moved to the closet and did the same.

"Get up," he told me when he couldn't find anything, pointing the gun at my head, and I slinked from the bed.

He lifted the mattress, and I took that as my opportunity.

I jumped up from the floor and raced down the small hallway. Searing pain hit my leg, and I collapsed to the ground as loud sounds echoed through the space. Shot. Blood.

"You stupid bitch!" he said again then grabbed my hair and pulled me toward the living room. He tossed me to the side as I inspected the wound.

There was a lot of blood, and I needed to stop it. Slowly, I took off my belt as my father tore apart my living room, finding no money.

The shot had hit me in the thigh, and as much as it fucking hurt, I was a Miller. I'd be damned if I didn't go down swinging.

I wrapped the belt around my leg, pulled it tight, and bit my lip because the pain was so intense I wanted to scream. I latched the belt and breathed heavy.

"Don't fuckin' move," he ordered then rummaged through my kitchen. All of my garage sale finds crashed to the floor, shattering. A piece of a mug slid across the floor toward me right as glass began to shatter.

I tried shifting as utensils came flying at me from every direction. I covered my head as pieces hit me. I needed to get out of here. I needed help. The door was only feet away, and I needed to get to it.

"I should fuckin' kill you then go to your bitch of a mother and do her in and that whack job she calls a mother! Fuckin' kill you all!" he ranted, stepping back in front of me, waving the gun around wildly. However, he was not really paying attention to me, more frantic in looking around at my destroyed paradise.

I scanned the floor. The only thing I could find was a fork. It wasn't much, but better than nothing. I grabbed it, putting it under my good leg.

When his focus came back to me, he grabbed me again, pulling me up. Knowing it was now or never, I tightened my grip on the fork, and with everything I had, I plunged it into his eye then tried with the other hand to get the gun.

He screamed as we tussled.

A shot rang out, and blistering pain hit my temple as I was hit across the head. Then blackness seeped in.

TWENTY-TWO

STIFF

"**G**ET TO CHELSEA'S. HER FATHER'S HERE. He shot me twice and has Chelsea." Boner's words were broken in my ear as I waved my arm to the guys, and we all hopped on our bikes.

"What's going on?" I asked.

"Heard screamin'. Got clipped twice. Losing a lot of blood." Boner sounded weak, and that was something he was not.

"Fuck. Hang on, brother."

"Try," he murmured. Then the line went dead.

We were about a half-hour from Chelsea's place and wouldn't get there in enough time. I called Spook, who answered on the second ring.

"Brother. Need you and whoever's there to get to Chelsea's. Boner's been shot, and Chelsea's screaming. Her father's there."

"Fuck!" Spook roared. "Be there in ten."

The small relief that he would be there soon did nothing for my fear and anger. I'd just found her. I couldn't let anything happen to her. Not now, not ever.

As Xander, Hooch, Dawg, and I pulled up to Chelsea's house, I saw Spook and Bosco outside, their eyes coming to mine.

I hopped off. "Where is she?"

"Not here, brother."

My eyes darted between the two. "What do you mean *not here?*" I roared, stomping to the trailer with Spook on my heels. The place was trashed, and blood coated the floor. I hoped like fuck that wasn't Chelsea's.

"Not here, but someone is … on her bed."

I darted down the hallway to see her piece of shit father with a fork stuck in his eye and two bullet holes in his brain. While I knew Chelsea had no love lost there, she wouldn't put the bullets in him. The fork was up for debate.

"Who put the bullets in him?" I asked, stepping out of the trashed room and back down to the living room.

"My first guess is Gonzo. Called him, and he didn't answer."

"Gonzo has her." My gut clenched as the anger bubbled. "Fuck!" I roared, not having any control. I picked up a lamp and threw it against the wall. It shattered into a million pieces and sadly looked more in place that way. "I knew his ass couldn't be trusted!"

Once I calmed down enough, I asked, "Boner?"

"He's at the clubhouse, getting stitched up. He lost a bit of blood, so Needles is takin' care of that, too. He should be fine. Will know more in a bit," Spook answered.

I rubbed my hands over my head. How the fuck had this gotten so fucked up? And how the fuck was I going to find my woman?

Two hours. Fucking longest two hours of my life and still going. We had ridden to the house where we'd met Javier—nothing. The warehouse we had scoped out for him—nothing. Abso-fucking-lutely nothing.

I charged into Spook's office, not giving the first fuck about knocking.

His eyes shot up to mine.

"Anything?" I asked.

"Called everyone I can think of. They're combing shit. Hoping something comes soon."

"Fuck!" I roared, turning toward the wall and punching three times consecutively. My hand went through the wood paneling and hit the cement blocks the place was built out of. It hurt, but nothing hurt worse than wondering what was happening to my woman.

"Brother," Spook spoke calmly, and I wanted to punch him for being so damn at ease.

"Do not *brother* me," I snapped. "If it were your woman—"

"It *was* my woman, Stiff. You should remember. Mine was taken by my father, cut up, and that shit sticks with me every day. Don't. Do not tell me *if it were my woman*, because I fucking know!" he bellowed.

Spook was right. He knew exactly what this felt like, and I hated that for both of us.

"Fuck. What do I do? I can't just sit here."

"Brother—"

Spook's phone rang. He held up one finger as he took the call.

"Yeah," he answered, his eyes growing wide. Then he scrambled for a piece of paper and pen. He scrolled something down then looked at the phone, muttering, "Fucker."

"What?" I asked with impatience.

"Colonel."

My body stilled at the man's name. The Colonel was Trixie's father. He was also the asshole who'd taken over the business Spook's father was in of buying and selling women to men overseas. The asshole had also threatened Trixie. He was not a well-liked man, and he was pretty freaky.

Spook held up the paper. "Location for Chelsea. Let's roll. Take the van so we're quiet."

I walked over and snatched the paper out of his hand, looking at his chicken scratch to find an address about fifteen minutes away.

"Let's go!" I ordered.

I'd thought two hours were long. They were nothing on the fifteen minutes it took to get to a ranch-style house on a cul-de-sac in one of the more affluent neighborhoods outside of Dyersburg.

Every house was cookie cutter with lawns immaculately put together. The house we were going to looked like the fucking Cleaver's lived there.

"What the fuck?" Bosco questioned from the passenger seat.

"Yeah," I answered, grabbing my gun and cocking it.

I turned behind me to look at Xander. I'd kept him out of the dirty parts of this job, but with it being my woman, I needed him.

"You ready for this?"

He pulled his gun out and checked it. "Fuck yeah. Let's go get Chelsea."

It was still light, though barely, and we couldn't exactly walk down the road with guns showing. As an alternative, Dawg pulled us right into the driveway, and as soon as we stopped, we piled out. Half of us went to the back, the other to the front door, hiding our weapons as best as possible. I didn't give a shit at this point.

Surprisingly, the front door opened at a simple knock, and a large man wearing a suit answered.

With my hand on my gun, I kept it under my cut.

"Gonzo's been waiting for you," he said calmly, and I wanted to blow the fucker's head off, but I needed to play this smart. "I know you're packin', so wait here."

The man shut the door, and we stood there, looking at each other. What the fuck?

Not a minute later, the door opened, and none other than Gonzo himself stood in the doorway. His suit was pressed and clean, and his face wore a wide smile that I wanted to rip off.

"Where is she?" I asked.

"I'm surprised you found me." He looked at Spook. "You have better connections than I thought." It was an insult, but I didn't have time for this shit. "Remember, if you shoot me"—he looked at me—"you don't get your girl, and all these nice people in the neighborhood see the bad biker gang killing an innocent, unarmed man."

My hand clenched on the gun, itching to shoot.

"This is what I want: your mother. Even trade. Then this is over." He brushed his hands together like he was dusting them off.

"Why'd you take Chelsea for this?"

He smiled. "She happened to be in the right place at the wrong time. Two birds, one stone."

"Is she hurt?"

He tsked. "If you want your woman, bring me your mother. I know you have her hidden. You have an hour and a half. Then I start pulling teeth or nails, whichever I feel at the moment." He stepped back and slammed the door shut.

I stepped forward, and Spook grabbed my shoulder.

Fuck, I didn't want to do this to Xander, but I had no fucking choice. I didn't know if Chelsea was even in the fucking house.

"What the fuck?" Hooch asked as he and the guys who'd gone around back came up.

"Any views from the windows?"

He shook his head. "Locked up tight. Was waiting to hear something."

Fucking hell.

I looked at Xander and opened my mouth to speak, but he cut me off.

"Do it, Stiff. Get her, bring her here, and do the trade."

He'd given me my out, but I saw the pained look in his eye, and I fucking hated that.

"Need someone to go get my mother and bring her here. I'm not fuckin' leavin'," I announced.

I heard Spook giving orders as I stared at the house, and I continued to stare as the van drifted away.

Xander and Spook came to stand by me, and still I stared at the house, waiting for the van to finally pull back up.

CHELSEA

THE ROOM WAS PITCH BLACK and smelled clean. The carpet felt soft under my tied up body, my arms behind my back. Whatever held them bit into my skin. My thigh throbbed, and I hoped the belt had stopped the bleeding, but I could barely move it.

I couldn't remember how I'd gotten here or who brought me. I couldn't even register the length of time I'd been here; except, I had dried blood on me.

A soft click sounded in the distance, and I turned toward it. The window to wherever I was lifted, and a huge bulk of a man climbed through.

I scrambled back, afraid to scream and unable to really move.

He stepped closer, and I willed my body to move.

"Takin' ya to Vipers," were the only words the man spoke as he reached down, lifted me as if I weighed nothing, and maneuvered me out of the window then himself. He cut my restraints, freeing my hands, and I rubbed my wrists as they felt the burn.

I tried to get up, to run and get away from this man, but he picked me back up and began to jog away from the house.

STIFF

WHEN MY CELL STARTED ringing in my cut, I pulled it out and saw it said "T Calling." Instead of taking the call, I slid the bar to ignore it. Not two seconds later, it rang again with the same display. I again hit ignore and switched the ringer to vibrate.

I stood outside, looking so fucking out of place with my brother and Spook. Neither Gonzo nor his brutes came out, opened the door, or said "boo." Other people went in and out of their houses, giving us the eye. I fucking hated it, but there was no way I was leaving my woman. No fucking way.

My phone vibrated in my pocked just as the sound of crunching gravel came in the distance. I turned to see the van we'd driven earlier. I looked at my phone, and it said again, "T Calling" again.

Stupid fucker wouldn't quit. Therefore, I slid over the bar and barked, "I'm in the fuckin' middle of something."

"Yeah, sunshine, so the fuck am I," the man chimed back. "Got your woman. We're at the park, far left corner by the picnic tables."

I whipped my head to Spook. "T has Chelsea."

How the fuck had T and his men known where to find my girl? Better yet, how the fuck had they gotten her out without Gonzo and his assholes knowing?

"You're fuckin' shittin' me," Spook growled so damn low I felt the power in it.

"No. Park."

"Fuckin' take your brother and go," Spook ordered.

I looked at the van, knowing my mother was inside, then tagged my brother, and we took off in a jog.

"On my way," I told T. "She need a doctor?" I asked, not thinking straight. Of course she needed a damn doctor.

"Uh, fuck yeah. Bullet in her leg, brother. Got fuckin' blood all over my best jeans. Ain't got enough Spot Shot to clean this one up."

I clenched the phone so tight I could hear the plastic cracking.

I turned to Xander. "Need you to call Jackson. Know he's watching the mom, but I need him here with a van now. Need you to call Needles to make sure he's still at the clubhouse."

Jackson worked in the shop with me. He wasn't an actual member yet, but he was working that way. With everyone on roundup with this shit, I needed to call who was available.

Xander nodded. He wasn't even breaking a sweat from the jog, reminding me I needed to work out more.

I thanked God for knowing the ins and outs of this fucking town. When we hit the park, I looked at the area T had told me he was located. Six damn bikes were parked not too far, with the men standing around a table. On the table was my woman, tears streaming down her face.

"Brother," T called out. "Had to hold her down. Feisty one you've got for yourself, Stiff. She thought we were gonna hurt her and tried to get away."

Chelsea's eyes widened when she saw me, and her body began to shake.

I moved quickly toward her.

"You're alright, Fire," I told her while assessing her injuries.

Her beautiful face was marred by cuts and bruises. She had a bullet hole in her thigh, blood stains covering the area, and a rag of some sort was inside the hole, also covered in blood. She had a belt tied around her thigh, surely keeping the blood from flowing freely. That was good and bad. We needed to get the blood going back into her legs and feet.

My temperature rose, but I did my best to keep it in check. I needed to take care of her and not lose my shit.

"My leg," Chelsea said then gave a pained moan.

"I know, baby." I looked at Xander. "Help."

"Right." He tucked his phone in his pocket. "J is coming, and Needles is still at the clubhouse." He then looked down at Chelsea. "Got yourself in a hell of a mess, woman. Now you know there's only room for one pain in the ass in this family, and Stiff here has that covered."

While I didn't think it was possible, Chelsea gave a very soft smile, lifting the corners of her lips.

"There's my brave girl. I'm gonna take a look," Xander practically cooed.

"Be careful and don't hurt me," Chelsea chided, and I fucking loved it. She was a hell of a fighter, and we had a shitload to talk about, but I needed to know how she was first.

Xander chuckled. "Yeah, babe. Gunshot to the leg, so can't make those promises."

Xander began to inspect her as I turned toward T.

"Where the fuck did y'all come from?"

T started laughing. "We're in town for somethin'. Heard through the grapevine, which let me tell you is the shit here in Tennessee, that your woman was in trouble. Since you assholes were standin' out front, and the dickhead inside was more concerned about you fuckers than us, I jumped in and got your girl."

Trapper was a member of the Devil's Due MC. They were nomads who solved cold cases. A band of six who refused to let the shit stay cold. Each of them had personal ties to most of the crimes.

I met Trapper and the others—Collector, X, Judge, Deacon, and Rowdy—on a charity run in Cloverville, Tennessee where Collector was from. Unlike Vipers, the Devil's Due boys didn't have titles; they rode as equals, each with their own story to tell.

"Grateful for your help."

Trapper went to speak, but Xander cut in.

"Need to get her to Needles. She lost a bit of blood. I think she's runnin' on adrenaline right now, and that's about all. It's gonna crash soon. I didn't touch the fabric and glad I didn't. There's no exit wound, so that bullet is more than likely still in her. If it is, it could be stopping the flow of blood, which is a good thing, so I'm not fuckin' with it."

"Fuck. Call J and see how far out he is."

Xander nodded, grabbing his phone.

"What can we do to help?" Trapper asked, coming to stand in front of me.

"Fuckin' shit's goin' down at that house. Gonzo wanted to trade my mother for Chelsea. When I left, they were pullin' up with her. Don't know what the fuck's goin' on, but Spook and the guys could use a hand if you would."

Trapper looked at his crew, threw up a hand, and they nodded.

"Fuck yeah, let's go."

The other men climbed on their bikes and headed away.

Belatedly, I realized I should have told them to be quiet, but then I figured they'd know what needed to be done.

Trapper slapped me on the back. "Just don't make a habit of it." He chuckled as he walked off. "I'll mail ya a bill for the jeans on Sunday," he called out without turning around.

"Thanks, man."

Fucker was bat-shit crazy, but I was thankful as shit he had been around.

I moved over to Chelsea and grabbed her hand. "Is it just your leg, Fire?"

She nodded, tears still running down her face.

I brushed her hair away from her cheeks and planted a soft kiss on her forehead. "You're gonna be just fine, babe. I'll fuckin' make it so."

She squeezed my hand right as one of our old van's from Vipers Automotive came to a stop with J sitting in the driver's seat.

"Gotta pick you up and get you help."

"Yeah." She whimpered quietly, and I didn't fucking like it.

Where was my spitfire? Where was my girl?

I lifted her, and as I walked, I said, "We've got this, Chels. No givin' out on me. You hear me?"

A spark came to her eyes. That was what I fucking wanted. She kept it the entire way to the clubhouse, too, and even up to the point when Needles knocked her out to retrieve the bullet and close up the artery it had hit. He then gave her fluids and blood while Chelsea slept and I paced the damn room.

Despite being assured she would be just fine, I didn't fucking like it. Hated it, and I wanted her to wake up.

TWENTY-THREE

CHELSEA

GROGGY. YEAH, THAT WAS THE WORD. I floated in the clouds in a dreamlike state. I could hear Stiff mumbling something but couldn't make it out. I felt a squeeze to my hand then the whispered words, "Wake up, Chels," that came from my sister Jenn.

I wanted to wake up. I tried, but my body had other ideas and blackness overtook me.

STIFF

"WOULD YOU CALM DOWN?" Needles asked, running his fingers through his hair. "I gave her a strong sedative. She'll wake up in a couple of hours. Let her rest."

I knew he was right, and I knew he was being logical, but I wanted to see her damn eyes, wanted to hear her voice. I didn't like this. Really, really didn't like this shit.

"Fuck," I ground out.

"Okay, big man," Chelsea's sister Jenn said from the chair beside her. "Let me sit with her while you go out and hit something or throw a car or whatever it is you do to calm yourself."

If I were in a laughing mood, that would have gotten at least a chuckle from me, but I wasn't and really didn't want to leave.

"Yes, young man. You go. We'll stay," Bee said from the other side of the room, holding Jannie's hand.

They were right. Besides, I needed to get information, find out what happened after I'd left Spook and the guys. I needed to move, and me pacing wasn't helping Chelsea and certainly not me.

"Fine. You call me if she wakes," I told Jenn, who grabbed her cell and held it up, wiggling it back and forth.

"You got it, big man." She gave me a soft smile.

I took off through the clubhouse, pulling out my cell and was getting ready to call Spook when the door flew open and Spook, Bosco, Hooch, Dawg, Trapper with the Devil's Due, and then my mother came in, followed by Xander.

"What the fuck?" I asked, not giving a shit who answered. I wanted some answers and now.

"Stiff," my mother started, but I had my sights on the guys as Xander led her by me while she repeatedly called out to me.

My nostrils flared. "Care to tell me what the fuck happened?"

"Need beer and Jack, and lots of that shit," Spook told Jackson who was now at the bar.

He pulled a chair away from a table and sat, the rest of the guys following suit. They didn't have smiles, but no frowns, either. Not one of the motherfuckers gave anything away.

Spook kicked out a chair to me. "Sit."

I did, but my eyes stayed glued to everyone around me.

"So ..." Spook clicked his tongue as Jackson put several bottles of beer on the table then rushed off for more. "Got your mother out of that shit."

My attention went solely to him. "Come again?"

Spook grabbed a beer, took a heavy pull, then pointed the end of it at Trapper. "That motherfucker is nuts."

Trapper laughed. "Aw, you love me."

"Fuck no." Spook turned his attention to me. "By the time these fuckers got there, we were talkin' to Gonzo. Your mother was still in the car, and Gonzo still thought he had the upper hand. That motherfucker"—he pointed at Trapper— "ended up comin' in from the inside and shooting Gonzo in the back of the head. All I did was watch him fuckin' collapse."

Trapper shrugged. "Me, Collector, and Deacon went in the window I got your woman out of. Snuck in. We went up quiet, listenin' to what was goin' down. Those assholes, again, were stupid, so fuckin' concerned about you guys they didn't check their backs. Took out four guards and one man in the living room then the asshole at the door who thought the sun rose and fell with his ass. Not."

"Javier, too?" I asked Spook who nodded. "So this shit is really over, then?"

Trapper pulled on his beer then said, "Yep, Superman ain't got shit on us. You can thank us by getting one of those hot little things you got around here to come ride my cock." He chuckled, grabbing his crotch.

I felt so damn relieved. True, I'd wanted to fuck the man up—both of them— but I was just happy the shit was over. Now, if my woman would wake the fuck up, I'd be golden.

"T, I'll call up as many as you fuckin' want."

"Fuck yeah!" Trapper said, slamming his beer onto the table.

Fuck yeah.

CHELSEA

I USED EVERY BIT OF STRENGTH I could to open my eyes, but they wouldn't cooperate. I could hear people in the room talking about me through a fog; still, I was not waking up. I was here, but I wasn't. Confusion swarmed me, and I wanted to scream that I was here and that they didn't have to worry.

I could hear crying, and I was pretty sure it was from my mother. That didn't bode well, because my mother never cried. Being a tough cookie who could hack anything, she never had to. As a result, me not waking up appeared to be a big deal.

That scared the ever-loving shit out of me.

"How's she doin'?" Stiff's voice grumbled, and I tried with everything I had to reach out to his voice and latch on to it.

Then I felt a squeeze on my hand, but I couldn't squeeze back. Nothing in my body would work, so why was my mind so engaged?

The warmth from his hand filled my body, and since it was the only thing I could get at the moment, I took it and buried this moment in deep, along with every single one of them I'd spent with him. As much as I didn't want to think about it, I had to. I might be dying. That was the only reason I could think of for why I couldn't open my eyes, talk, or squeeze my man's hand back.

The burn in my heart hit me hard. If I could have moved, the burn would have been a physical blow that put me on my ass.

What if I never saw him again? Never spoke to him? How could I tell him how important he was to me? How much he'd made me feel when I hadn't wanted to, but he'd done it all the same? How much, in such a short period of time, he'd given me hope for a future? How I was falling in love with him or had fallen? How was I going to tell him all of that?

Panic crushed me so badly I fell into darkness.

STIFF

I held on to my woman's hand tight as she lay there, breathing on her own yet not waking up. For two days, she'd been like this, lying motionlessly, and I fucking hated it.

"Needles," I growled as he checked Chelsea for the third time today. "What's going on?"

His eyes met mine, and then he pointed to some machine he'd hauled in here. "Her brain waves are good. Heart's good. Breathing good. Head was grazed by the bullet. All the labs I drew came back good. Her body is just healing, and we need to give her time for that."

"Fuck time," I muttered, going back to my girl's hand.

Needles' words didn't placate me in the least. I wouldn't live the rest of my life without Chelsea by my side. I refused to give up. I refused to let her give up. I refused to let Needles give up.

She would wake up, and then we could move on with our lives.

CHELSEA

THE FOG SLOWLY BEGAN to clear. The sounds of people in the room became so clear the fog I'd heard them through before dissipated. Stiff, my mother, Jenn—I could hear them all as clear as day.

I wiggled my hand, and for the first time in I didn't know how long, it moved. I tried my eyes, and while they opened, it felt as though someone had shoved sandpaper in them, causing me to blink rapidly, the light in the room burning them.

"Chelsea?" Stiff asked from next to me, his body a blur.

"Hey," I croaked out, my throat raw.

"Thank fucking Christ." Stiff lifted my hand and kissed the back of it.

"Am I okay?" I didn't feel okay. My leg and face hurt, which surprised me because before, when I'd been in my cloudy haze, I felt no pain.

Stiff brushed my hair back out of my face with his big hand. "Yeah, Fire. You're gonna be good."

I blinked, and my man finally came into focus.

His eyes looked tired; big, dark bags hung under them. Worry lines marred his face even more than his usual sun-created ones. He was scared.

"I'm okay," I tried reassuring him. "But I need some kind of pain meds." I wasn't a sissy, but the burn in my leg was rough, and even a few Advil would work at this point.

"Call Needles," Stiff ordered someone as I slowly turned my head.

My mother was there with her eyes shining at me while Jenn was next to her with unshed tears in her eyes. Grams wasn't around.

"I'm good," I told them.

They each came up and kissed me on the forehead, said a few words, then left so I could rest. What I didn't get was that I'd been resting for a while. I knew this because my muscles ached like I hadn't used them, and I felt a bit weak.

"How long was I out?" I asked Stiff.

"Four days."

That shocked me. I'd missed four days of my life, lying in this bed. However, I thought about it and realized I could have spent those four days in the morgue.

Then everything started rushing back to me: my father, being kidnapped, and the strange man who'd saved me.

"My father?" I asked first.

"Dead."

A pit of regret hit me, though I still hated him. He had been willing to hurt me, but that small sliver of a child inside of me had hoped he would change. That was now gone, and I wouldn't shed a tear for him. No way. Not after everything he'd done to us.

"What about the other guys? And the one who got me out of there?"

"The guys who kidnapped you are dead. Trapper, the one who went in and got you, is part of another club."

"He is? How did he know where to find me?" I asked.

"You get stronger, and we'll talk all this shit out later."

I slowly nodded, but it felt like it was being smashed by a sledgehammer, so I stopped.

"So we're all safe now?"

His eyes gleaming at me, Stiff stood above me, still holding my hand. "Yeah, Fire. You're not goin' back to your trailer. We're movin' your shit to my place, and that's where you'll stay."

Even with the thumping of my brain, I knew I didn't want to go back to that house, not after what my father had done to me there.

The images of the fork going into his eye came back to me, and my stomach roiled. I knew I was a strong woman, able to hack quite a bit, but doing that to my own father … That was something I would never get out of my head.

"You and me, Fire." He lifted my hand. "You and me." Those words were the most beautiful ones I could have heard. Yes, it was Stiff and me.

EPILOGUE

3 WEEKS LATER
CHELSEA

Ｉ F I WERE CHARLIE, I WOULD FIRE ME. I didn't want to be fired, but I'd been off from work now for three weeks, despite the fact I'd been moving around pretty good over the last few days.

Who would have thought a gunshot to the leg would suck so badly? Not me, because I'd never thought I would be shot.

I told Charlie I would be back next week. Stiff had told him I'd be back the week after that.

A month off? He'd lost his ever-loving mind. I couldn't afford that.

I hadn't been back to my trailer, but Stiff and a few of the guys had. It was utterly pitiful the amount of stuff they'd brought back that was salvageable. Clothes made up the bulk of it. Everything in the kitchen had been trashed, and my beach had been destroyed. That had deeply saddened me. Nevertheless, I couldn't go back there, because of the memories of my father.

While I hadn't seen him after I'd blacked out, Stiff had filled me in on what had happened and where his body had been found. Therefore, I wanted nothing to do with any of my sheets, blankets, pillows—anything.

That meant I had to replace most of those items and start again, which quite frankly, sucked. Even staying with Stiff, I still wanted a place of my own. He could come with me if he wanted, but I couldn't let everything that happened to me hinder what I'd worked so hard to achieve for so damn long.

He knew this because we'd talked about it. Hell, with him, we talked about everything except one thing, and it was getting to me.

That one thing was where he'd been spending the bulk of his time this past week. Yes, he'd been around, but not like usual. Instead, Xander, Hooch, and even Bosco came around to hang out with me, saying hanging out with me was like a cakewalk.

When I had asked Stiff where he'd been, he would only tell me he'd been busy. Despite the trust built between us this past month, I was losing it with him since I knew he hadn't been here doing his busy. And since having sex hadn't been on the top of my to-do list, I couldn't help wondering if he was getting it from someone else.

I wanted that trust. I wanted to feel it, but with each passing hour he was gone without explanation, it waned. I never asked any of the guys, even though I really wanted to ask Xander.

Some nights, Stiff would come home and go straight to the shower. That pit in my gut festered because my first thought was, *He's washing off another woman.* I was a lot of things, but I wasn't a woman who would be in that type of relationship. Ever. And the more I let that sink in, the more it took root.

That was why I was sitting here on the couch in the dark at eleven twenty-three at night, waiting for Stiff to get home. I needed answers, and I wasn't sitting around another minute to get them.

Unfortunately, my fire only lasted so long, and I eventually lay down on the couch at twelve forty-seven a.m. Moments later, I was out.

"Chelsea, I've gotta go," Stiff's deep voice came from beside me.

My eyes fluttered opened to see I was not, in fact, on the couch, but at some point, Stiff carried me to bed. He was dressed in worn jeans and a navy blue T-shirt that spread across his chest.

When my eyes met his, I froze, remembering why I'd stayed up. Why I was done with this. Why I was putting an end to it.

Carefully, I sat up in the bed, still in my T-shirt and shorts from the night before. "Where are you going?"

"Work."

"Where at? And don't tell me it's at the shop, because I know that's a lie."

He narrowed his eyes. "You checkin' up on me?"

"Do I need to be?" I retorted, turning fully toward him.

"No, and I don't appreciate you doin' it," he snapped back, his brows furrowing.

Feeling like this was going way worse than it needed to be, I decided to cut to the chase.

"Stiff, if you've got someone else, you need to tell me. I'm not sleeping in the same bed with you while you're with other women."

His face turned pained, like I'd struck him so hard that it had gone clear down through his bone to his soul.

My heart lurched. I'd never wanted to do that, but it was something that needed to be discussed.

"Fuckin' sucks ass that the first thing you think of is that."

That was a direct punch to the gut and heart.

"I—"

"Need you to get dressed."

I stilled.

"Gotta show you somethin'," he said.

"Where?" I asked as he rose from the bed. It was a bizarre turn of events— going from talking about him being with someone else to him wanting to take me somewhere.

"Get dressed, and I'll show ya," he replied, his body tense and eyes hard.

My heart squeezed, and tears pricked behind my eyes. Was this going to be the end of us? I didn't want that. More than anything in this world, even having my own place, I didn't want that. I'd fallen head over heels in love with the big lug.

Slowly, I got dressed, and Stiff took me out to his Jeep. We climbed in, and then he drove.

"Stiff, I'm sorry," I told him after a while.

He turned to me. "Just fuckin' kills me that me bein' with someone else is the first thing that comes into that thick head of yours. Don't want anyone else, Chels. Only fuckin' want you." He reached over and took my hand, squeezing it.

I was unable to stop the tears from leaving my eyes. I felt every word of that deep. So damn deep.

I said nothing else, looking out the window, but Stiff wasn't done.

"Know Bee had assumptions on how I got my name, and from your reaction, I'm gettin' you think that, too. So let me clue you in on how I got the name Stiff." He squeezed my hand, and I turned to focus on him. "Learned quick in life that if I didn't stand up for my brother and myself, we wouldn't make it. Therefore, my spine got stiff. I didn't let shit get to me or bend me to its will. I fought to keep it straight, and I did." He let out a huff of air. "Not gonna lie to you and tell you I haven't had women, because I have, but not once since you came to the clubhouse has my dick been anywhere except inside you."

"I was an ass. Sorry," I whispered. "Then where have you been every night? I haven't gone to bed with you in days, Stiff. What else was I supposed to think?"

"What you do is trust that your man is takin' care of you. Have I ever let you down?" he asked.

"No." And he hadn't, not once. "Trust is hard for me and ... I'm sorry." Damn, I was now repeating myself. Shit.

"I get you, and I know it is. You get this. I'm pissed, but I'm lettin' it go. I'm lettin' it go because I've been hidin' somethin' from ya."

My heart fell to the floor of the Jeep, rolled under the tires, and was getting pummeled with each turn of the tires. While I knew he had been, after his big talk about not having another woman, I didn't want to think about what he had been hiding. Fear gripped me since I didn't know what it could be or why he would.

"You'll see in a minute," he said as I took in the surroundings.

Trees, lots of trees, and I remembered coming down this way one of the times I had been on the back of his bike. The one time he had taken me to—

That was when I saw the open clearing as Stiff drove down the road. Cars, trucks, and bikes were spread throughout the space, all of which I knew and knew well.

"The cabin," I whispered, my eyes going round.

It no longer looked dilapidated. No, the windows had been painted and new screens attached. The siding had been replaced with new wood, only making it look so much stronger. And the porch had been completely redone with new beams and posts.

As the Jeep came to a stop, my eyes shot over to Stiff as he put it in park.

"What's going on?" I whispered.

He turned fully toward me, resting his beefy arm on the steering wheel. "Know you wanted a place of your own. Know you wanted to buy it. Know you wanted to be by the beach and water. It's not the ocean, but you liked it here. I liked it here with you. So this is for us, a place for us to call home."

Tears welled in my eyes. "This is where you've been every night? Working?"

He reached over and took my hand. "Yeah, Fire. Me, the brothers, your mom, and Grams. Boner dragged his ass out, and even Charlie came by. Been tryin' to get it finished before you went back to work. Wanted us to have a home, start something permanent. Not you stayin' with me because you can't be at your place anymore. No, here will be ours."

Boner came? He'd taken two bullets for me and had to have surgery, but pulled through.

I let the tears fall freely.

"I love you," I whispered softly. "Not just for this, but for you being you. Being Stiff. Not letting me go once you got ahold."

He reached over and pulled me to him, bringing his lips close to mine. "Never lettin' go, babe."

"The moments," I uttered softly.

"Moments?" he questioned.

"Grams always said for me to cherish the moments. You've given me so many, and I keep them locked in my heart."

His lips came to mine in a soft kiss, and as he pulled away, he looked into my eyes. "Love you, Fire."

Yeah, this was better than the beach. Better than the plans I'd laid out for myself. Better than anything I'd dreamed about. Stiff made all of that come true for me.

ONE MONTH LATER
STIFF

"THE WHISKY WASN'T ENOUGH," I told my brother when we pulled up and parked in front of the jewelry shop. I'd only had one shot because I was driving, and it wasn't hacking it.

Xander chuckled, taking off his helmet. "After we do this, I'll get ya a bottle." He hopped of his bike as I did. Then he hesitated before going into the store, turning back to me. "She's not gonna get cleaned up, is she?"

We'd had our mother locked up for what felt like forever. She had been so far gone Needles had been forced to give her certain drugs to help her come down off them. We'd thought she was doing better and let her out of her room. And I didn't know how, but she must have had a stash in her purse that I hadn't found, because she was found on the floor of the bathroom, high as a kite. Then the processes of bringing her back down had started all over again.

"We're gonna have to decide whether to put her in a hospital or let her loose. With Gonzo gone, the only threat she has is to herself," I told him.

He looked down at his boots. "Fuckin' hate this."

"Me, too, brother. Me, too."

I'd sheltered Xander for so long, but I needed to let that go and let him help me. It killed me since that wasn't my instinct. However, if I wanted him to be the man he was in this club, I needed to cut those strings and let him live.

"Gotta let her go," Xander said decisively.

My brows rose in shock. "Really?"

"Yeah, she is who she is, Stiff. Can't change that. What I can do is go in there"— he pointed to the building—"get a ring for my girl, marry her, and fuck her all the time."

"Like you don't do that already," I teased.

"Fuck yeah, but it'll look better with my ring on her hand."

"Yeah, brother. Let's get this shit done so I can get drunk and back to my woman."

Xander came up, wrapped one arm around my shoulder, and slapped me on the back. "Love you, brother."

"Love you, too."

THE END

NOTE FROM THE AUTHOR:

Thank you so much for reading *Conquering*. I loved writing Stiff and Chelsea's story. I hope you enjoyed reading it, as well.

Sorry, ladies, but Stiff has been claimed. Yes. When I wrote *Challenged*, author Chelsea Camaron claimed him before the ink was dry on the paper. Being the wonderful person I am, I gave Stiff to her. She *might* share, but I wouldn't count too highly on it. In return, though, through a lot of persuasion, she gave me my man Trapper. You can read more about him in the book: *In the Red: Devil's Due MC Book One*. You can read it, but remember, T is *mine*. I'm an only child, and sharing is hard.

I would love for you to leave a review on whichever channel you purchased your book on! Reviews help us authors tremendously, even just a couple of words.

Thank you for reading and remember to live in the moment.

—Ryan

Surprise BONUS

RYAN MICHELE
COURAGEOUS
VIPERS CREED MC MILITARY NOVELLA

PROLOGUE

GABRIELLA

Hey, baby,

I'm lying in bed as I write you, thinking of nothing but you. I never knew how long seven months were until now. With each month that ticks by, I keep hoping I'll be able to hear from you. I know you're doing great things, and I hope you are getting these letters. I'm so proud of you yet miss you, love you, and can't wait to hold you in my arms.

Love always and forever,

Gabriella

XANDER

SHOTS FLEW OVER MY HEAD so close the whizzing of the bullets stung my ears.

Bombs exploded all around, making the desert an enormous dust cloud. The air was so dense it got into your eyes, making them rough as sandpaper. I needed to clean them out, but I didn't have time.

Death never had a timeframe. It crept into every nook and cranny, just waiting for the perfect time to take you.

I pushed off the building, looking around the corner into more film. Blinking rapidly to unclog some of the haze, I saw the enemy wasn't in sight. Then, using hand signals, I motioned to my Marine brothers, giving them the go sign. We each followed into step, our weapons at the ready and bodies humming with alertness.

We needed to get out of here, get to the safe location. As a RECON Marine, our mission to infiltrate a well-known enemy camp had been a bust. They'd started shooting at us as soon as we'd gotten into formation, which meant something or someone had tipped them off. Now, we needed to survive this mess.

Shots hit the dirt next to my feet. I jumped, moving to the right, the opposite way, and lifting my gun. Seeing the enemy, I aimed and fired, taking him out with one shot. My brothers then began their descent, taking out a row of attackers as we moved back.

"Fuck!" Carrington exclaimed as he fell to his knees, blood rushing out of his leg.

Dustfield, the team medic, kneeled down next to him, pulling out a strip of fabric and tying off Carrington's leg. It would be the best he could do until we got to safety. After he was done, Dustfield helped Carrington to his feet while the rest of our team, including myself, gave them cover.

We moved quickly, shots ringing in every direction. Some were from us, some from them. The sound was almost like music if you found the screams of dying men melodic.

Head in the game.

I reached for the comm. button on my shoulder. "Team Whiskey Foxtrot Lima. We need a bird."

The crackle came through our ear pieces immediately. "Roger that, Whiskey Foxtrot Lima. ETA: eight minutes till Kilo Echo Charlie touches ground."

We continued to move backward to get to the location the chopper was set to meet us, shooting for our lives.

Minutes that felt like hours later, a chopper could be heard in the distance— our ticket out of this dusty hell hole. We rushed toward the steady thump of the blades, somehow avoiding the bullets fired by the insurgents.

Seeing the helicopter, I wanted to feel joy and relief, but that would never come when you were in a war zone. I used the term *safe* very loosely. Nowhere out here was ever truly safe.

The whirl of the blades made the dust even worse, like a tornado trying to knock us down. We fought against the gusts while providing cover, the gunner on the chopper doing the same.

"Carrington," was yelled, telling me he'd made it on.

"Dustfield."

Then each name of the others was screamed through the noise as they each got on the chopper. Searing pain struck my shoulder, but I didn't lose my stance, continuing to protect my brothers with my life.

"Fuck! Collins's shot!" one of the men shouted as I kept my gun trained and shooting.

As the grenade came rolling toward me, I ordered, "Move! Fire in the hole!"

Just as I went to jump in the chopper, another bullet pierced the same shoulder, knocking me back just a bit and causing me to lose my footing.

One of my teammates grabbed me as the chopper went up, and everything exploded.

ONE

GABRIELLA

MY KNEES QUAKED AS MY STOMACH twisted in so many knots I swore I would puke at any moment. I even ran to the bathroom a few times, thinking the bile would come up and be expelled. So far, I'd been lucky with just the churning and nothing making an appearance.

I'd arrived at the airport early, afraid that I would somehow miss him coming off of the plane, that he would disappear for another twelve months, during which I would not get to have him in my arms. He was only supposed to be gone for seven, but then he was hurt and had to recover. I couldn't do it another day. I would have done it for him, but part of me was dying inside from not being with him.

I tried my damnedest to stay strong while he'd been deployed, but there had been so many nights I cried myself to sleep. His safety became every prayer at night and every thought during the day. I made deals with God, the saints, and the apostles, hoping each word would go to whoever would bring Xander back to me.

I learned how to cope while he was gone, mostly staying busy. School kept me on my game, giving me structure and routine. Add in my job, and there wasn't much time to think. For me, that was good. I'd even became handy, if you could believe it. I'd learned how to fix the toilet that kept running and never stopped. I made it stop. It took me several YouTube videos, but I finally did it.

Waiting became my life: waiting for a letter from him, waiting for a phone call, waiting for an email, waiting for any word at all. When I finally did hear something, it wasn't from him. No, Xander's brother, Stiff, called, telling me that he had been shot. The call should have been one of relief; instead, it became the most dreaded moment of my life. I kind of let loose on Stiff, but I was losing my shit. A woman could only be strong for so long.

The man I'd loved since high school—who I'd stood behind when he'd joined the Marines, who I'd kept vigil for when he'd had to go away for short periods—had been shot during this last long deployment. The worst part was I couldn't visit him. They took Xander to a hospital in Germany then brought him back to the states to Walter Reed Medical Center in Bethesda for recovery and to serve out the rest of his time in the Marines. I thought I could visit him once he came to the States, but instead, I talked to him over the phone.

Time stopped when I heard his voice for the first time in months. After so much worry, I tried my best not to cry. I knew he didn't need that weight on his shoulders. But it was hard, and I broke, anyway. His voice was the best sound in the world. Just hearing him made so many things right in my world.

I wished it had been perfect, but something inside of Xander changed while he'd been deployed. He was different when we talked. The laugher didn't come as easily as it once had. Neither did his jokes. A few times, he even barked at me like he gave orders to his men.

It hurt because he'd always been good about separating our life from the military. I sucked it up, however. I knew he'd been through a lot. I mean, hell, he'd been shot. That right there was huge. Therefore, I could handle a little attitude. For him, I would. I'd do just about anything.

"Hey, Gabby." A deep voice came from my right, and I jumped.

Turning, I saw Stiff standing tall, intimidating, and covered in leather. Stiff road with a local biker club called the Vipers Creed. I'd spoken to him a few times since Xander left, but we weren't close. We didn't hate each other or anything, but

I wouldn't say we were friends, either. To be honest, he scared the ever loving shit out of me with his bald head and magnetic looks. Not just that, though. The overall power that radiated off him could bring anyone to their knees. Even as we stood in the airport, people stopped and stared at him, openly gawking. I couldn't blame them. Stiff was a force to be reckoned with.

Stiff brought his arms around me, pulling me to his body in a tight hug, which I reciprocated.

"Hey, Stiff," I replied quietly as he pulled away, eyeing me.

"No more tears. Our boy's back."

I swiped at my face, not wanting another tear. He was right, and I needed to get my shit together.

"Right. Is your mom coming?"

Stiff shrugged. "Probably not. She's got a new piece, and even though her kid's been at war, she more than likely can't tear herself off his cock long enough to get here."

I choked on a laugh as a woman with gray hair and a cane openly stared at Stiff, her mouth dropping to the floor at his language.

Instead of responding to it, Stiff said, "Hello, ma'am," in the sweetest voice imaginable coming from this huge man.

The woman shook her head and walked off.

"You sure do have a way with the ladies," I muttered, feeling the joy come back into my life for the first time in twelve months.

Stiff had a lot of Xander's joking mannerisms. With him being older, I assumed Xander got it from him because I knew neither of them had a father growing up.

Stiff winked. "You have no idea." He looked around. "Why are you here and not up there?" He pointed to the area where passengers were sitting and waiting for planes.

"Because of stupid laws. With all the shit that Xander was fighting for over there, *we* now have to wait over here to see him. Apparently, it is a security risk for us to be up there, and we have to have a ticket." While grateful that I'd see my man today, I wanted to be right there when he got off the plane with my arms open for him to run into. Damn laws.

212 | RYAN MICHELE

"All you need is a ticket?" Stiff asked, and I nodded. "Come on." He pulled me to the ticket counter off to the right of the exit.

"Need two tickets," Stiff said, reaching into his back pocket and pulling out his wallet.

"Where to, sir?" the overly bubbly airline worker asked, eyeing Stiff with great appreciation.

I rolled my eyes.

"Don't give a fuck, just need to get up there," he told her, pointing to the seating area.

The woman's smile faded, and she went on alert. "Why do you need to do that?" she asked, looking over to another agent who wasn't paying attention. Great ... She probably thought we were going to blow up the place or something.

I stepped in. "Ma'am, my boyfriend is coming home. He's a Marine and was hurt overseas. We just want to get up there to meet him off the plane."

Her demeanor instantly changed at my words, going from alert to almost soft.

"Do you have a copy of his orders?" she asked with a smile now gracing her face.

It was my turn for my stomach to fall. "No, I—"

"Hang on," Stiff cut me off, reaching inside his leather vest then pulling out a manila envelope. "This is a bunch of shit I got while he was gone. I was gonna give it to him." He opened up the envelope and began rifling through some papers. Then I pulled one out and handed it to the agent. She smiled wide.

"I just need your IDs, and you're ready to go."

"Just like that?" Stiff questioned.

"Yes, sir. A new law was passed that, as long as you give the airline the orders, family may go up and greet their service member upon arrival." Her smile never faltered.

We were given a piece of paper to hand the guard at the gate. My cheeks hurt from smiling. This was perfect.

"Let's go see my brother," Stiff said, his smile making his face look not so scary.

Excited—no, ecstatic was more like it—we went through security where Stiff had to get a pat down and came out clean. I couldn't lie and say I didn't hold my breath the whole time, because I did. Thank God he'd left whatever he carried in that holster at home.

I bounced from foot to foot, unable to keep myself still as we waited outside his gate. We had fifteen minutes. While I had waited about a year, I swore these last fifteen minutes were going to kill me.

"Calm the fuck down," Stiff said, reclining in the black plastic chair, cool and calm as could be. How could he not be wound up with excitement? This was huge, and there he sat, stoic.

"No," I answered, continuing my pacing in front of the window. Every emotion I'd ever felt flowed through my veins in a continuous loop. My hands sweat and heart thumped wildly.

When the plane touched down, my stomach dropped. When I waited and waited for him to come off the ramp, I panicked. A woman with a small child came into the airport, and my anxiety ratcheted up. Where was he?

Then Xander stepped off the ramp and into the airport, taking my breath away. Standing so tall, he had his hair cut sharply against his head, his facial bone structure a bit more pronounced. His piercing blue eyes scanned then locked on me.

Tears welled. I couldn't hold back. I tried, but there was no use. I lurched myself at him, wrapping my arms around him and breathing him in.

He dropped whatever was in his hands and put his arms around me, kissing the top of my head as I let the tears flow. He was here … in my arms, holding me. Finally.

TWO

XANDER

INHALED MY GIRL, LOVING THE FEEL of her in my arms. Damn, I'd missed her. Her body shook as she cried, and I held her tighter. Seeing my brother out of the corner of my eye, I lifted my chin to his smile. He would wait.

There wasn't one single night, day, or afternoon that I didn't think of my Gabby: what she was doing, how she was getting along without me around, how her job was, her life, her anything. I'd missed so damn much, but I had a job to do.

While I didn't complete the mission I was injured in, my brothers went back and got it done. Fuckers were taken out and the entire structure blown. While I hated that hell hole, I wanted to be back with my team, fighting for justice. Nevertheless, the doctors said I couldn't fight.

I spent months in rehab and had surgery before that. Those assholes put two bullets in me, shattering part of my shoulder that needed to be rebuilt.

Not being in the action didn't sit right. Sitting, feeling pain, and going through therapy sucked. Doing it without my girl made it worse.

I knew I was lucky. Some guys there lost limbs. One lost both his legs. Another had part of his face burned from an explosion. I had it good compared to them, but my girl had always seen me as her hero. I couldn't let her see me in so much pain, broken and weak. Therefore, I told her she couldn't come to visit, which wasn't entirely true. There were visiting times, but I couldn't let my girl see me like that.

Did it make me a coward in some ways? Yes. Was it selfish as fuck? Yes. Regardless, it was what I needed to do.

Now, I got to hold my girl. It didn't matter how I arrived here; it just mattered that she was in my arms.

"Shh …" I consoled when her tiny body shook harder. "I've got you, Gabby."

She looked up at her name, her eyes rung with tears. "I missed you," she said quietly.

I bent, sealing my lips to hers, missing the taste of her. She didn't hesitate to kiss me back, and not until the applause came from the room did I pull away from her, searching the space. The noise jolted me into alert.

Hundreds of people stared at us, clapping their hands in recognition. I had on civilian clothes, but with one look at my carry-on, they must have put two and two together. Shit.

I nodded, saying "Thank you." Overwhelming didn't cut it; I never expected a thank you from civilians.

Unfortunately, as my eyes cased all the people, my body went on full military alert. Over in that hell hole, we never liked crowds, were warned away from them because of the possible danger there. Even being on American soil where it was supposed to be safe, I couldn't turn that off. Therefore, I scanned, looking for potential threats. I'd be damned if I let anything happened to Gabby.

"Alright, get your tongue out of your girl and give your brother a hug," Stiff said, coming up to my side.

I gave Gabby a brief touch of my lips. "Give me a sec."

She nodded, wiping her face and nose.

Stiff opened his arms wide, and I went directly into them. Stiff was the only family I really had. Sure, we had a mother, but she was always too self-absorbed to pay much attention to us kids. As the oldest, Stiff took on the father role, being the man I could depend on for anything. He made sure we had food, clothes, even a fucking roof over our heads when our mother was evicted, which was often. Stiff had always been my rock.

"Brother, I'm so fucking happy you're home," Stiff said in my ear as he clapped my back, thumping it hard.

I reciprocated, "Happy to be back home. Damn happy."

"So fucking proud of you." He pulled away, sizing me up. "And I think you've fucking grown. I can still take you, though."

For the first time in what felt like forever, I laughed. "Nah, I'm quicker," I chided, feeling a bit lighter.

"Fuck no. I'll wipe the floor with you," he challenged back, slapping my shoulder. I was happy it was my healthy shoulder, because his strength was evident.

"Never," I threw back, getting a smile from him.

Looking around the space, I was thankful everyone had disbursed and the crowd was down to nothing.

I turned back to my girl. "Can we get the hell out of here?"

Her smile graced her beautiful face. Even rosy from crying, she was the most beautiful woman I'd ever seen in my life. Her dark hair fell to her shoulders, framing her face. The blue eyes I missed for so damn long pulled me in. Damn, I loved this woman.

"Yes," she said as I bent down and grabbed my bag.

As my brother put his arm around my shoulder, I felt his pride down to my bones. "Party tomorrow night at the club. Figured you'd be busy tonight." He released me.

"Fuck yeah." My hand needed a damn break, and I needed to be inside Gabby. All fucking night long.

I grabbed my duffle and stepped out into the Tennessee air, inhaling deeply. I'd missed the smell of home. Trees, lots of trees. I fucking loved trees. I could go a long damn time without seeing sand again ... if ever.

Stiff insisted on carrying my bag, and it wasn't worth fighting over. Besides, I got to hold my girl's hand as she led the way to her car.

Outside, I stopped dead, shooting my head over to Stiff, who wore a huge, shit-eating grin.

Motorcycles lined the lane of the parking lot where Gabby led us. The United States flag and Marine flag were prominently displayed on the backs of two of them.

I looked at the leader, Spook. He'd been one of my brother's best friends for what seemed like forever. He gave me a salute, as did Bosco, Boner, Dawg, Hooch, and several of the other guys. *Fucking hell.*

"Thought you needed an escort home," Stiff told me.

"You prick. You want me to fucking do something stupid like fucking cry so you can hold it over me for years to come. Ain't. Fucking. Happening." Even if it felt damn good inside that his brothers in Vipers Creed were honoring me in their way, I would never shed a tear. That was just pure stubbornness. It didn't have anything to do with macho bullshit. It had to do with my brother never letting me live it down. And he'd be up my ass all the time about it. No thanks.

I lifted Gabby's hand and kissed it. She had fresh tears. The damn woman was going to float away at this rate.

We stopped at a Chevy Impala, and Gabby remoted the locks open with a beep. I missed the old truck we had, but it had broken down, and she'd needed something reliable.

"Love it, baby."

She shrugged. "It gets me from here to there." She opened the trunk, and we loaded up.

"We're going to follow you to your place then veer off. You and me, we catch up tomorrow night at the club. Of course, your girl can come," Stiff said.

"Good thing, 'cause I'm not sure she's going to be out of my sight."

He lifted his chin. "Make good use of your time." He chuckled.

"Unlike you, I know what to do with my dick," I retorted.

"You little shit."

"Okay, as much as I love seeing you boys go at each other, can I please take my man home?" Gabby said from beside me.

I pulled her in close and kissed the top of her head.

"You get this out, but you've got it comin' to ya," Stiff said as he moved to his bike.

I gave the guys a salute then climbed in the passenger seat. I knew the address of where Gabby moved to, but I'd never been there, and I was on restriction from driving. I understood driving here would be different than overseas, but I could have handled it. Then again, I wouldn't dismiss a direct order, either. It was only for a week, anyway.

As we rode through town, every once in a while, the guys behind us would start blaring their horns and revving their engines, drawing attention from the people on the streets. It was strange, yet it was the best fucking welcome home.

The guys rode with Spook in the lead then staggered two by two. I tagged my brother right away.

We pulled up to a small ranch-style house with tan siding. Little bushes of flowers and plants lined it with a huge oak tree out front. Gabby pulled up to the garage as I turned and watched the guys drive by, waving to each. Then I looked back at the house.

We lived in an apartment when I first joined the Marines. Gabby stayed there for quite some time, but she wanted to move to a house closer to base. The thought was we'd stay near base in case I was called to duty. Uncle Sam had another idea and medically discharged me.

"You did good, Gabby." I loved it when I put that broad smile on that face. It was strange in a way. She was so familiar yet different. More woman than the shy kid I had fallen for back in high school.

"I was so nervous you wouldn't like it. I can't wait—"

"Baby, you can show me every damn thing in this place after I fuck you. A lot. So maybe in a couple of days or a week, we'll come out of the bedroom."

She laughed and bit her lip. I missed that shit so damn much. "Alright big man. Gonna show me what I've been missing?"

"Fuck yes. House. Now." My granite cock urged me out of the car and searched out Gabby.

Fuck, she looked good. She'd always had a killer body, but these past two years, she'd really filled out. Tits and ass. Fuck yes. Her wide hips turned me on so damn much. Fuck, I needed to be in her.

She raced up to the front door, fiddling with her keys then opening it. I kicked the door shut, locked it, and then prowled toward my girl. I slammed my lips to hers as she jumped up and wrapped both her arms and legs around me.

"Bedroom," I mumbled, feeling the pain in my shoulder but ignoring it. It came and went, and I dealt. Out on missions, I went days without feeling anything because my life depended on it. I could go longer for Gabby.

She ripped away quickly. "Down the hall, second door on the right."

She didn't have to tell me twice; I was already striding that way, paying zero attention to anything else. I didn't give a shit what the walls looked like, carpet, furniture—nothing. All I gave a shit about was being in my woman.

I fumbled just a touch, not realizing the door wasn't fully open, then found the bed immediately.

I pulled away. "Baby, this has to be hard and fast. I'm not gonna last long. But then I'll take you slow all night long."

"God, yes please."

"Clothes off."

She scurried, ripping her clothes from her body, and while I wanted to love every inch of her voluptuousness, I was about ready to burst and wanted it to be inside her heat.

THREE

XANDER

I DOVE HEAD FIRST BETWEEN MY girl's legs, gripping her thighs and placing my hands under her ass. Her taste exploded on my tongue as she screamed out. I couldn't do gentle. No, I couldn't do anything but suck, nibble, and lick in rapid successions. Knowing I'd come as soon as I was inside her, I needed to get her off just once before I plowed deep.

Her legs trembled in my hands as her moans filled the room. Damn, I loved that, had missed it. Those sounds helped me jack off more nights than I cared to remember. I loved serving my country yet fucking hated being away from Gabby.

Gabby's hips bucked violently as a cry tore from her lips, her pussy clenching as she rode out her orgasm. Yep, I'd missed this fucking shit.

I rose and impaled myself into her hot heat while she squirmed under me, adjusting. I trusted my girl, just as she trusted me. I'd seen many men fall off and take a woman here or there. Not me. My dick stayed in my pants or my hand. I wasn't saying I hadn't been fucking tempted, because several occasions I was. A lot. More than I would ever tell Gabby. But no way in fuck I'd do that to her.

We'd given each other our word, and my word was and always would be my bond. After seeing the way my mother went from man to man, I admitted I was apprehensive at first, but Gabby had proved to be nothing like my mother. I knew it the moment I met her. That was what attracted me to her.

Her warm heat surrounded me, still pulsing from her orgasm, putting a strangle hold on my cock.

"Baby, I'm not going to last."

She smiled up at me. "Do it, X." Fuck, I'd missed her calling me that, too.

I listened, planting myself as deep as possible and holding myself there for a beat while she surrounded me. Then I let it all go, my hips moving to their own drum. It built, and my balls drew up. A few more thrusts, and I came inside of my girl.

I opened my eyes to see my woman focused on me. Those beautiful, deep chocolate eyes sucked me in.

"Fucking love you, babe," I said, staring down at her.

"Love you, too." When a tear rolled down the side of her face, I swiped it with my thumb.

"No more tears, baby. I'm here."

More tears rolled. "It's been too long. I can't do that again, Xander. Please don't make me do that again."

"I'm out, babe. Not going back." I had mixed feelings on it. On one hand, I didn't want to be medically discharged, but on the other, I was done and needed to be with Gabby. She would always be my rock.

She brought her arms around me and pulled me to her body, wrapping her legs around me. "Thank God."

I lay there, smashing Gabby into the bed. Nope, I wasn't going anywhere.

I rolled to my side, still lodged inside my girl as I pulled her with me, her arms not leaving my body. She'd told me in letters and email about her time since I'd been deployed. She hadn't had it easy with going to school and working. I was so fucking proud of her for pulling it all together. She was stronger than she thought, and I admired that.

I never knew missing someone would cut so much. Phone calls and emails just didn't do it. I'd known it would be hard, but to actually experience it first hand was something I could go another lifetime without. Not seeing Gabby every day, not being able to touch her wasn't something I'd ever put her or myself through again. I couldn't.

Gabby wiggled, and my cock stirred to life.

"Keep that up, and I'm going to fuck you again."

She smiled up at me wickedly. "Oh, yeah?"

I pressed my half-erect cock farther into her tight channel. "Fuck yeah."

She kissed me, and I took everything she gave. I loved how fierce she was for me, how she always craved me. Even before I left, our sex life had been fantastic. I mean, what man wouldn't love getting it regularly whenever he wanted with no complaints? Not any man I knew.

She pulled away. "I need to clean up."

I gave her a quick peck. "Yeah. You're still on birth control, right?"

Her devilish smirk stirred my dick. "Yeah, babe. We're not ready for kids yet."

She lifted herself off me, and I watched her sexy-as-fuck ass walk toward a door. The light flicked on, and I could see it was the bathroom. Nice.

Gabby emailed me pictures of this place, but I didn't have a lot of time to look at them. Fuck, while overseas, I hadn't had time for shit except staying alive and keeping my men alive.

Looking at pictures of a house I might never see in person hadn't been top on the list; telling her I was alive and that I loved her was. Priorities were one of the main things I'd learned as a Marine. Sure, I got it from my brother, too, but in the Corps, it was drilled into you. It became your survival.

Gabby was my top priority now. Now and forever.

She strode back in, her tits jiggling with each step as her hips swayed from side to side. Fuck, she was sexy. She carried a wet wash cloth.

"You gonna clean me up?" I asked.

She knelt on the bed, crawling toward me. Damn, even that one little movement was sexy as hell. "Yeah, baby. Lie back."

I rolled to my back as she straddled my thighs. The warm cloth touched my cock as she glided it up and down. She said she was cleaning me, but she was really just pumping me. My half-erect cock wasn't half anymore.

She took over with her hand as she wiped around my groin with the cloth. I placed my hands behind my head, letting her work. I fucking loved this shit.

She jacked me as she cleaned then tossed the rag across the room, and it made a splat noise in the distance. She never stopped moving her hand as she positioned herself between my thighs. She cast her eyes on me as she engulfed my dick in her mouth. It jumped from her heat.

"Oh, baby, that's so fucking good." I moved my hands to her hair, threading them through her soft tresses then pulled. "Take all of me," I demanded, giving her head a push.

She pulled, resisting, but not for long. My cock touched the back of her throat, and as much as I wanted to stay there, at her gag, I pulled out, giving her air.

"Fuck yes, baby," I groaned out as she licked the head, circling it then gliding her tongue along the slit.

She pulled away, her eyes turned fiery hot. "I missed your cock."

"Oh, I get it. Missed my cock, not me," I teased.

Gabby's face turned serious. "I missed every damn thing about you, Xander. Never believe I didn't."

"Oh, baby, I'm just playin'. I know you did. I missed you like hell every damn minute." To that, I got a smile and my dick back down Gabby's throat. Words escaped me as she sucked hard, her cheeks going in at the sides. *Fuck yeah.*

Removing my hands from her hair, I lay back, enjoying the view and the feeling of my woman finally giving me head. It was so damn much better than my spit-covered hand.

She played with my balls, rolling them with her hands, then pressed on my taint. Fire erupted up my spine, and my balls drew up.

"I'm coming," I said on a gasp as I blew in her mouth, and Gabby sucked hard, wringing every last drop from my body.

I heaved in deep breaths, Gabby seeming to have taken those with my come. She licked me clean, not one drop of my seed escaping her lips. *Fuck yes.*

She then kissed the head before crawling up beside me. I wrapped my arms around her, pulling her securely to me.

We lay there, calm, sated, and fell fast asleep.

FOUR

GABRIELLA

MUSIC PUMPED THROUGH THE speakers while women and men danced on a makeshift dance floor. We'd come to the clubhouse at Vipers Creed just as Stiff had asked. He'd called earlier in the day, making sure Xander was coming.

I didn't think Stiff cared much if I came or not, but Xander wouldn't come unless I did. We'd come to the clubhouse a couple of times before he'd left for the Marines, and I hadn't minded it. What I did mind were the women who'd tried to hit on my man, and they were plentiful.

Everywhere we'd turned, there were women barely dressed, ready to get down on their knees for Xander. This time was no different.

Even going to the bathroom was a challenge, because when I came back, a woman was close to him, trying to get his attention. While my guy didn't take to the advances, I didn't like it. It pissed me off beyond what was reasonable. I had enough gumption to rip her stringy ass hair out of her head and knee her in the nose.

I trusted Xander more than anyone in my life. I knew he wouldn't go for it, but I still didn't like women around him. And I knew I wasn't thinking rationally, but I'd just gotten him home. I didn't need some skank throwing herself at him.

As we sat by the bar, Xander and his brother laughed and joked, reminding me of times before Xander left, when life was so different.

After graduating high school, Xander and I moved in together in a small apartment. It wasn't much, but we loved the place. It was where we made some of the toughest decisions of our lives. And it was ours.

When Xander made the decision to go into the Marines, I was proud yet scared to death. I stayed scared through basic, through deployment, through him getting shot ... until I had him in my arms. After our years, I just now felt a little of the pressure leave, though it was still there. Someone couldn't feel that fear for years and then just have it vanish in a flash.

Having him beside me made it better.

"Hey" A very pretty brunette sat next to me. She had on tight jeans with tears in them and a black Harley V-neck shirt. She was beautiful but didn't look or come across like the other woman who were vying for Xander's attention.

"Hi." Unease crept across my skin like little spiders.

"I'm Trix. The guys call me Trixie. I'm Spook's ol' lady."

My eyes alit. Spook was the president of the Vipers Creed, and the last time I'd been here, he hadn't had a girl. He sure picked a pretty one.

"Nice to meet you. I'm Gabriella, but most people call me Gabby."

She smiled wide. "Spook told me about Xander. Glad to have him home?"

I returned her smile, happy. "Yes, so very happy to have him home."

Trix narrowed her eyes toward beside me, and I turned. Another woman, this time a short-haired brunette with blonde streaks and a rack that was totally bought, came up to Xander's side. The opposite side of where I was sitting. Dammit.

"No," I barked out, and Xander jumped next to me, his eyes swinging from me to the woman next to him then back. My eyes stayed on the woman, glaring. I was over this shit. "He's taken," I said as Xander put his hand over mine on the table and gave me a squeeze.

"Babe," he said, drawing my attention away from the woman.

"Yeah?"

"All good, baby." He leaned into my ear. "The only girl on my cock tonight is you."

My blood warmed—not from anger, but from lust. Hell yes, I would be.

"Damn, man, don't remember Gabby being so feisty," Stiff stated, taking a pull from his beer, laughter in his voice.

Xander squeezed my hand. "Some things have changed a bit."

Damn right. I wasn't the awkward teen with two dead parents anymore. Well, I still had the dead parents, but after having Xander gone and needing to rely on myself to get things done, I'd grown up. I just hoped I hadn't grown into a person Xander no longer wanted.

I had to admit it was a huge fear of mine. He'd been gone a long damn time. What if we didn't fit anymore? Sex, of course, was off the charts. He took me twice more during the night. It had always been explosive, but in life, I just hoped we would be able to make everything work. I loved him and would do anything to make it so.

"Sounds like Gabby and my Trixie will get along just fine." Spook, a very handsome man with dark hair and killer looks, sat next to Trixie. "My girl here has a fire. Gotta love the women with it."

Xander released my hand and draped his arm around my back, pulling me into his strong body. Just this simple little touch that many took for granted every day filled my heart with so much joy. I would never get tired of this. Ever.

I leaned my head into him.

"Let's not let them get too close. They're liable to start an uproar," Stiff said as Xander squeezed me.

Looking over at Trix, I saw a wide grin spread across her face. Involuntarily, I did the same.

"So, little brother, whatcha gonna do now that you're out?" Stiff asked, and I felt Xander stiffen.

We hadn't talked about this—the *what to do after your back* stuff. We were in such a frenzy with him shot, recovery, rehab, and him coming home that we hadn't discussed it. Now it loomed over us.

In a few days, I would go back to work, but what would Xander do? He wasn't the type of man to sit around and do nothing. He'd always been an action man.

Throughout school, he'd always had a job, always busy. I had no doubt he would do something, but what, I had no idea.

"No clue, brother. Right now, I'm gonna spend time with my woman. That's all that matters." He kissed the top of my hair, and warmth flowed through me.

Damn, I loved this man.

"RIGHT THERE," I GASPED OUT as Xander worked my overstimulated pussy with his lips, tongue, and fingers.

He'd kept me on edge for what felt like hours, but maybe only thirty minutes. Xander's stamina had come back in full force. With that, he'd decided to torture me every single time he got his hands on me over the last four days. And I loved every damn minute of it … except right now, when my body was ready to explode and he wouldn't give me what I needed.

I arched my back and wiggled my hips, trying to get his tongue just a little higher. A beefy arm came across my hips, and I felt Xander shake with laughter, which I didn't find the least bit funny at the moment.

"Dammit," I growled, lifting my head to look down at him.

He lifted his eyes to mine, the side of his lip tipped as he continued his assault on me.

I lowered my hips to the soft bed, but the ache inside me grew.

Suddenly, suction came to my clit as Xander rubbed his fingers on that magic spot inside my core. I closed my eyes as lights spasmodically sparked behind my lids, my body arched, and everything around me was silenced as the orgasm overtook me.

Coming down, I wasn't prepared for Xander to pick me up and fling me like I weighed nothing on top of him so I straddled his legs. He held my torso until I became steady.

"Ride me, baby," he ordered as I bit my lip.

Damn, he looked so damn sexy lying on the bed, his eyes only for me, wanting me, craving me. I loved this man with everything I had inside of me.

I did as I was told, placing him inside me and falling down to his hips. He filled me, stretching me deliciously.

I had a vibrator I used while he was gone, but it was nothing like this. Nothing would ever be like this.

While I moved up and down, using my knees, he held my hips, digging into my flesh.

"Harder," he called out.

I let everything loose, rocking up and down as fast as I could, getting the friction we needed.

"I'm gonna come," I whispered as he joined his hips in the movements, sending me flying over the edge. Xander pumped four more times, seating himself inside me so damn far and then releasing into my body.

I fell onto him, my head on his chest, the rise and fall of his breaths mimicking mine. This was what I'd missed: this connection, this time. Yes, the sex was unbelievable; it always had been. But this right here, his arms wrapped around my body, him still inside of me after screwing my brains out … This was what I loved about my man.

FIVE

XANDER

GABBY WENT TO WORK TODAY. I was so damn proud of her for going to school and getting her degree as a nurse. She worked at a local office and told me repeatedly that she loved it. I didn't know how in the hell she survived me being gone, her by herself, but she had.

Her parents died when she was in her teens, and she moved in with her grandmother. Her parents left her the money to go to school. She wanted to use the money for us to start our lives, but it was something I put my foot down on. She had always dreamed of becoming a nurse, and she had the means to do it. She was so damn smart and needed to use it. So, after several fights, I won. She went to school; I went off to the Marines.

Now, as I sat here on the couch, flipping through the television, I had to figure out what in the hell I was going to do with my life. I'd spent the last four years killing bad people, avoiding bombs, and protecting my team. Everything had changed now, and I wasn't sure what I should do.

I had several options. I'd always been good with my hands. I could fix pretty much anything, and with my experience in the field, I was able to work on engines, as well. I could go to school when the semester started again, whenever the hell that was, but I had no idea what I wanted to do. Therefore, I sat and watched mindless television, none of which I remembered.

On show four, I felt so damn antsy I had to get up. I looked out the window, seeing the green yard. I hadn't mowed in so damn long, so I went out to the garage and took my time in the yard, mowing, weeding, and watering some of Gabby's plants. Well, I guessed they were my plants now, too.

Gabby had done a good job when picking this place out. The apartment we were in before was small, while this place had a huge yard and even felt like a home. She did the girly shit inside, but it wasn't over the top; it was understated and relaxing.

Too bad I wasn't meant for relaxing.

I'd only been out a week, but it seemed like longer. I had been riding the high of coming home, feeling the euphoria of having Gabby in my arms and seeing my brother. Today, everything crashed.

With Gabby gone and me alone, memories were hitting me from all angles. It was so fucking strange how life could go on while I'd been gone. I didn't want to resent it, but in a way, I felt it like a punch to the gut. While I fought and tried not to get killed, everything here went on like I was vapor. I fucking hated that.

I knew Gabby would choose a safe neighborhood, yet I couldn't help looking around every few seconds while outside, only turning my back during short periods when I had to. Earlier, when a car drove by and backfired, the sound had put me at attention and made me duck behind the house for cover. Simple things civilians wouldn't see as issues, I couldn't help seeing as the opposite.

After realizing it was a car instead of a bomb or sniper, it took me a bit to cool my shit. I did, but I still didn't like that feeling whatsoever.

I hadn't felt "safe" in years, always on guard, never sleeping with both eyes shut. Hell, this past week I'd slept better than I had in four years.

Not having Gabby with me, I felt more on edge.

When Gabby pulled into the driveway, I felt relieved, almost like I could breathe again. She was here, and I could protect her.

"How was your day?" she asked with a huge smile on her face as she wrapped her arms around me tight, giving me a kiss. It wasn't enough, so I dove deeper. Damn, I loved kissing her. All the uncertainty I felt earlier washed away, and physically, I could feel myself relax.

I pulled away slowly, giving her another nip before answering, "Worked outside."

She smiled wider. "I saw that. Thanks. It's nice having someone to help out."

I knew in my gut she was teasing, but it hit me hard. I hadn't been here for her for so damn long. She'd had to do everything on her own. I wanted to take all the burdens from her that she'd felt and make everything right.

"I'll do more of it."

"Hey." She knit her brows as she focused on my eyes. "You have nothing to worry about. You were doing your job, just like I was here. Now we do it together."

I said nothing because what could I say? Instead, I kissed her, needing that comfort. She reciprocated, and I reveled in it.

"Let me change, and then I'll make some supper," she said, pulling away.

My cock had other ideas. After being buried inside of Gabby for a week, he was needing some attention.

"Nope."

She gasped as I turned her around, pressing her stomach to the back of the couch.

"Need to fuck you."

"I …" she started, but I didn't let her finish.

I pulled her scrubs down to her knees along with her underwear, undid my jeans, and found her heat. I groaned as she did. She couldn't spread her legs very far, which only added to the tightness around my dick.

Hard and fast, I took her with abandon. The couch moved with each thrust as I dug my fingertips into her hips over and over and over.

She screamed out her release, and I followed suit, only groaning, instead.

After coming down, I pulled out and pulled up her clothes, adjusting them, and then did mine. She rose, and I kissed her shoulder.

"I needed that, baby."

She turned in my arms. "Me, too. Missed you today."

"You, too." I kissed her again. "Now feed me."

She laughed, one of the most beautiful sounds I'd heard. I should tape that shit. Then I remembered I didn't have to go back, so I could hear it whenever I wanted. *Nice.*

Gabby cooked homemade chicken and noodles. Damn, this past week, she'd spoiled the shit out of me, cooking all my favorites, saying *"It sucked just cooking for one."* She'd always had a knack for cooking and was damn good at it.

The doorbell rang, and I bolted from the seat, the chair falling to the ground in a clatter. My heart raced as I turned toward the door. Everything inside me went on full alert. The sounds of the house came front and center: the sink faucet dripping, the air conditioning kicking on, the small taps outside the door like whomever was there was impatient.

Gabby rose, and my head swung to her. "Stay."

Her eyes widened at my cold tone, but I didn't have time to deal with it. I needed to figure out whom the threat was and not let them hurt my woman.

I moved swiftly to the door, looking through the peephole. My mother stood on the other side.

My alertness mixed with anger. I'd been home a fucking week with no phone call, nothing, and now she finally got off the dick she'd been on and came to see her son she hadn't seen in years. Not to mention, she showed up unexpectedly. Fuck this.

I swung the door open.

"What the fuck are you doing here?" I barked, and my mother's eyes widened.

SIX

GABRIELLA

MY HEART STOPPED AT THE ABRUPT TONE in Xander's words. Sure, his mother hadn't been around much since I'd known him, but he'd never had this anger toward her. He'd let whatever was going on inside of him roll off his back when dealing with her. This man, though, wasn't going to let anything roll.

Cheryl tensed, her eyes shooting toward me, asking *"What the hell?"*

I had no answer for her, so I shrugged.

"Xander, I came to see you." Her voice came out shaky.

"I've been home for a fucking week, Mother. Now you come by, unannounced, and what? You want me to put on a happy face because you took the time to pry yourself off whatever poor schmuck you're in bed with to come to see your kid? No." Xander placed his arm on the doorframe, blocking the path inside.

I moved, coming up behind him.

"I told you to stay over there," he barked, this time directed at me.

My stomach fell to my knees. Why on earth was he talking to me like that? What had I done?

I took a step back, unable to formulate words.

Xander didn't care for the silence and turned back toward his mother.

"Last time I'll ask, why the fuck are you here?"

"I …" Cheryl started then stopped and pulled in a breath. "I wanted to see how you were, make sure you were okay."

"I'm alive; that's all you need to know."

Cheryl crossed her arms over her body. "Xander, what's gotten into you?"

I wanted to yell at her to shut up. Didn't she see that her boy was close to snapping? That, for some reason, she was triggering something inside of him just from being here? Couldn't she see this was a really, really bad idea?

"*Into me?*" he growled back, and the hair on the back of my neck rose from the determination and intent in his voice. "How many times did you write me while I was gone?" He didn't wait for her to answer, just continued, "Call? Answer the fucking phone when I called?" He shook his head.

"I—"

"No, I took the fucking time to call you from halfway around the damn world, and you didn't have the time to answer. I wrote you fucking letters that never got responded to."

I didn't know any of this, but as he laid it all out, my stomach churned for my man.

"Fuck, emails, Mother! Not one damn response. So, *no!* I don't give a fuck that you're here. I don't give a fuck that you want to see me. I don't give a fuck that you took time out of your life to drag your sorry ass here. I don't give a flying fuck anymore."

The last part was so loud I was sure the neighbors heard, but I felt powerless to stop it. Instead, I stood there, watching the train wreck.

"You do not talk to me like that, Xander Collins. I'm your mother!" Cheryl screamed in outrage, not wanting to be outdone by her son.

"My mother? A mother gives a shit about her kids. You don't. Leave," he growled menacingly.

"You don't want to see me?" She looked almost hurt, but her words were more of shock.

"No. You don't need to come back, either." Xander didn't wait for his mother to respond before he slammed the door closed and prowled down the hall, waves of anger penetrating the air as he moved.

When the door down the hallway slammed shut, shaking the pictures on the wall, I jumped.

I felt the tears well up, but I pushed them down. I wouldn't cry. He was home, something I'd wanted for so damn long. Him angry, I could handle. I would handle it.

Coming unstuck from my spot, I moved to the kitchen and began cleaning. My mind raced, but keeping my hands busy helped.

I HEARD HIM BEFORE I saw him. I sat on the couch, watching some mindless reality show, not catching a damn word anyone said. He'd been in the bathroom for a long time. The shower water had clicked on, and I'd heard nothing from him. Even when it clicked off, he hadn't come out. Something inside me told me to let it be. Whatever happened to be going on in his head, he needed to work out. I couldn't be there to fix it, even if I so desperately wanted to.

Instead, I sat on the couch, waiting. Wondering. Worrying. Thinking. Hoping.

He sat next to me, and I dug deep inside of me, kind of afraid of what I'd see next to me. When I turned to him, he was staring at the television. He must have felt my movements because he turned to me.

His eyes held a sadness I wasn't accustomed to seeing in him. It physically pained me to see him hurt, like a punch to the gut. He'd already endured so much in this life; he didn't need more. I also couldn't say it didn't scare me. The anger—hell, full outrage he felt toward his mother and how he'd let it rip.

He reached for my hand and kissed the top of it. "Sorry, babe." He shook his head like he was trying to clear something from his brain. "I can't be around her. She pisses me off to a point that I blow."

I bit my lip. I wanted to say, "*You weren't like that before,*" but refrained. Instead,

I just listened.

"She hasn't been there for Stiff and me since we were born. Now she doesn't exist to me."

I shivered, unable to hide it.

He squeezed my hand. "I bet you anything she needed money or a place to stay. There's no way she came here out of the goodness of her heart. She doesn't have that."

I couldn't disagree with the statement. I'd seen it first hand when we'd started dating in high school and then every other time I'd seen her after that. She never had the interests of her kids before hers.

"But I'm not sure why I blew up the way I did." He pulled away from me and laid his head on the back of the couch, moving his hand to the top of his head. "I just don't know why," he said again.

I had no answers for him but said, "We'll figure it out."

He turned back to me. "I'm sorry I yelled at you. I do know where that came from." He sat up then pulled me into his body so I sat on his lap, my head resting on his shoulder. "I had a whole team I was in charge of. I was their life or death. I protected them with everything I had."

I suddenly felt queasy because I knew he'd taken bullets for those men, almost leaving me.

"Now I'm not in that world anymore, and it's going to take me some time to get my head around that."

"Do you think you need to talk to someone?" I suggested hesitantly.

He blew out deeply, his chest collapsing. "Nah, I'll be fine."

My body was thrown off the bed, my eyes shooting to alert. Xander's heavy body was on top of mine, his breathing coming hard and fast as he reached around the floor, trying to find something.

My back ached from the fall. It felt like a shoe was digging into my back.

"Xander," I said, tapping his arm. "Get up."

He said nothing, just continued to look for whatever he was grasping for.

"Xander!" I yelled more loudly.

He again said nothing. Whatever was in my back dug in farther with each of his frantic movements.

"Xander!" This time, I screamed as fear hit me that he wasn't going to get off me.

I began hitting him in earnest, trying to get his attention.

His head snapped to mine, and a cold shiver went down my spine. His eyes were open, but they were void, vacant, empty. The life that was Xander ceased to exist.

Fear like no other spiraled as I tried to get up again.

I squirmed hard, trying to get loose, as he trapped my wrists above my head. I lied. This was when the fear really hit.

I started screaming, "Xander! Stop it! Let me go now!" I said the words over and over as I tried to get away. He was strong, though, keeping me pinned to the floor.

I bucked my hips then pulled my arm hard, getting it free. I slapped Xander hard across the face, needing him to snap out of whatever this was. His face didn't move from the hit, and the empty eyes staring at me grew intense. How could empty eyes grow intense?

"Xander! It's me, Gabby! Get off!"

Somehow, at my name, he blinked. It was like a light dawned in him, and he released me quickly, getting off me and moving to the other side of the room. He fell onto the floor, his back to the wall and a shocked, stunned look on his face.

I sat up and rubbed my wrists, not quite sure of what had just happened, afraid of saying anything.

Pulling myself together, I moved to the bed and sat on the edge. Xander remained where he was, his head in his hands.

What was I supposed to say or do? I had no clue. I didn't know what any of this meant. For two weeks, we'd had some seriously weird crap happening, and it needed to stop. That first week he was home had gone fine. This last one had been a rollercoaster ride, some up and some down. The down scared the hell out of me when Xander would lose his temper in a flash or when his mood would abruptly change. This happened regularly and seemed to be getting more frequent instead of less.

I took him to the grocery store, and his attentiveness to the surroundings took me aback. He eyed every single person like they were going to hurt either him or me at any moment. His body was wound so tight I feared he may have a heart attack or something. After that first time, I vowed to make the trips myself.

My coworkers got me a bouquet of balloons with a 'welcome home' banner on them for Xander. I was excited to come home with them. He seemed fine with them … until one of them popped. His reaction scared the shit out of me, his eyes turning so damn cold. The balloons made a hasty exit.

The almost car accident was the worst.

I shook my head, clearing out those thoughts.

"Xander," I said softly, and he lifted his head to look at me, shame pouring out of his eyes. "I'm fine," I reassured him, but he shook his head. I sucked in deep and moved to the floor in front of him, crossing my legs. "Baby, this isn't getting better. I think you need to talk to someone."

"Who? So some shrink can tell me how fucked up my head is?"

I winced at his tone but kept going. "Maybe. I don't have the answers, but I've been looking into—"

He jackknifed off the floor and began pacing. "You've been looking into what, Gabby?" he said in an accusing tone.

I rose and sat back on the bed, watching his movements as he moved back and forth. He walked like a caged animal, ready to pounce at any time. I knew I needed to tread carefully. Even with my training as a nurse, it was difficult.

"At the VA, they have people there you can talk to who are going through the same things you are. Who can help," I tried.

"Yeah, right. This shit…" He reached behind his head and rubbed his neck as his movements continued. "It's in my head, Gabby. I don't know what it is, but I can't stop it."

"I know," I whispered. "But Xander, it's starting to scare me."

He stopped his movements, his eyes coming to mine, the pain seeping back. I needed to get this out, so I powered on.

"First, your mother then checking around the house in the middle of the night to make sure it was safe and the constant phone calls to make sure that I'm okay while I'm at work. Add in the almost car wreck we were in."

"That wasn't my fault. That dick was trying to run us off the road."

"No, Xander. He had his signal light on and was moving in front of us on the highway. It wasn't anything malicious. It's how people lane change, baby, and you took it all wrong, almost getting us both hurt." It was scary to nearly miss the cement wall partition because Xander got so pissed when the guy got in front of us.

"I …" He looked at the ground. "I don't know. It seemed like he was going to ram into us."

"He wasn't, Xander. He was close to us, yes. I'll give you that, but he was just changing lanes."

"You hate me, don't you?" he asked softly.

"No." I rushed to him. "I love you. I just don't know how to help you or what you need."

"You, baby. All I need is you." He pulled me into his arms, and I wrapped mine around him.

"We need to figure out what's going on, Xander," I told him, but something told me I would need reinforcements.

XANDER KISSED ME HARD. "Love you," he told me, a smile playing on his lips.

This was the Xander I loved. Truth be told, I loved every part of him, even the ones that scared me.

"Love you, too. Are you going to apply today?" I asked with hopefulness.

He'd been going back and forth about what he wanted to do, but he still hadn't decided. First, he wanted to get a job as a laborer. Then, he wanted to go back to school. Then, he wanted to find something working on equipment. He didn't really know what he wanted, but him cooped up in this house wasn't working for him.

He shrugged. "We'll see what the day brings."

I said nothing, even though I wanted to ask him, "*How many times does the lawn need to be mowed?*" or "*Do you really need to weed around the flower beds again?*" There was no use in this, and I didn't want to fight with him.

"Have a good day." I smiled, leaving my man standing at the door.

I jumped in my car, turned the ignition, and bolted out of the driveway. With our home in the distance, I grabbed my cell.

"Yeah?" he answered on the second ring.

"It's Gabby. Stiff, we need to talk."

SEVEN

XANDER

THE ROAR OF A MOTORCYCLE'S PIPES could be heard in the distance, and I turned toward them. Stiff swung into my driveway, parking his bike and getting off. I rose from the dirt, brushing my hands off on my jeans.

"Brother," I welcomed as Stiff pulled me into a quick hug then released me.

"How the fuck you been?" he asked.

I wasn't quite sure how to answer that, so I went with, "Fine."

"Bullshit. You got any beer?"

I nodded toward the door, and then we walked inside where I grabbed two beers. We then headed to the backyard, sitting at the small patio set.

"What?" I asked. Stiff had never been one to beat around the bush about anything. Better to have him get it out and done.

"I know there's shit goin' on with ya. We gotta work that shit out."

I quirked my brow questioningly.

"Talked to Gabby earlier."

My stomach fell. Fuck me. Gabby called my brother? Fuck, I knew I had some shit in my head, but fuck ... to call my brother?

"She's worried about ya."

"Fucking hell." I took a large pull from my beer and then stood up, a sense of betrayal hitting me in the gut as anger burned. "You're shitting me, right?" I ground out, not letting Stiff finish. "I fucking don't believe it."

"Sit your ass down." Stiff said, and I glared.

"I will not sit the fuck down! She should not have gone behind my fucking back!" I roared as Stiff rose.

"Brother," he warned, but I didn't listen.

"I mean, who the fuck does she think she is, spreading my shit to other people? That doesn't fucking fly with me," I spouted off, seriously enraged.

"Brother!" Stiff said again, walking closer to me. "Calm the fuck down."

My blood only pumped harder. "Fuck off," I told him.

"You stupid motherfucker, listen to me." It was Stiff's turn to pull out his anger.

I said nothing, merely stayed rooted to the spot, too angry to let this slide.

"Gabby fucking loves your sorry ass. She's fucking scared and didn't know where else to turn. She fucking cares about you, asshole. Don't be pissed at her for that. She didn't betray shit, because if she wouldn't have told me, I'd have been on your ass harder than I am now. So stop whatever bullshit you have rolling round in that head of yours, sit the fuck down, and let's get this shit figured out."

Out of everything Stiff just said, the one thing that stood out to me was *she's scared*. My Gabby was scared? Fuck, I never wanted her to feel that way. Fucking ever. And I had a way to stop that shit, to take that fear away from her.

I sucked in a deep breath, compartmentalizing all my emotions as I nodded to Stiff.

"Good. Sit," he said.

Releasing my fists that I hadn't known were clenched so damn hard my knuckles were white, I sat.

"Don't know why she talked you," I grumbled.

"Didn't I just tell you why? Now shut the fuck up and listen," Stiff said immediately. "Talked to some guys I know. They have a group you can go to talk this shit out. I trust 'em. The guy I talked to belongs to another club, but he's a good man and wouldn't steer me wrong."

"I don't—"

"Stop it. We're sortin' you out. You've got a shit ton of life to lead, and you're gonna do it."

"Stiff, I'm not fucking talking to some random people."

Stiff leaned in close, but I didn't flinch away. "Yeah, you fuckin' are. If I've gotta duct tape your ass to the back of my bike and haul you there my damn self, I fuckin' will."

I rubbed my hand over my face. "How in the fuck can I talk about shit when I don't know what hell is wrong with me?"

"You talk because that woman you got fuckin' loves ya. You talk because you have a brother who loves ya, too. You talk because we want you around and not digging yourself into some place that you can't get out of." Stiff laid it out in true Stiff fashion. "Somethin' else."

"You gonna cure world hunger now?" I joked, trying to ease the tension inside of me, but it didn't work.

"Funny, asshole. No. Want you to come work at the shop. Spook's gonna hire you on as a mechanic. Know you know your shit and will be good at it."

"He wants to give me a job?"

"Fuck yeah. And there's somethin' else I want ya to think about."

I felt like a lead elephant weighed on my shoulders, and he was piling more shit on top.

"Want you to prospect for the club. You know the brothers—fuck, grew up with 'em."

I shook my head. I'd never had any inclination to join. Not only that, but being a Marine, I wasn't allowed to have ties to a *gang*. My brother was the closest I needed to get.

"Stop that shit and listen," Stiff ordered, which I didn't like, but he was my brother and the only one on the fucking planet I'd allow to do it.

"Go ahead."

"We're all we've got. Mom's a cunt and good for nothin'. Vipers, we're a fuckin' family, Xander. May not be blood, but it's fuckin' better than that. We choose who we have in our family. Hand pick those fuckers and only pick the best men for it."

I thought for a beat. "That why you joined? 'Cause you needed a family?"

He took a pull from his beer and swallowed. "Partly. Another part, I don't give a shit about society's rules, the proper bullshit that most people follow. In the club, I can be me. Now I am me … no fuckin' hesitation. I didn't have a way; my bothers helped me find it."

"I don't know." I shook my head.

"I'm not fuckin' around, Xander. You're doin' this shit. I'm not gonna sit back and watch you spiral down. Fuck that. I got the means to help your ass, so I'm fuckin' doing it."

"Fuck, why ya gotta get all mushy and shit," I said to ease my brother. It felt as if he were on edge, ready to implode. It wasn't something I'd wanted. Hell, none of this was something I'd anticipated.

"Shut it. You still got your old bike?"

I shook my head. "Sold it."

"No worries. We'll set you up."

"Stiff, I don't know if the club is for me."

"Brother, I'm fuckin' holding a goddamned branch out to ya. Grab the fuck on and let's roll."

I smiled and listened to my big brother.

EPILOGUE

ONE MONTH LATER
XANDER

SPOOK, MY BROTHER, AND THE Vipers gave me a chance. Not only did I start talking, I joined as a prospect of the club. I fucking loved working in Creed's Automotive, making customized cars and bikes. And the brothers grew on me.

Stiff was right, not that I would tell him. The brothers were a family, one I was slowly becoming part of. Sure, I'd known the guys for years, but this was different. I'd always been Stiff's brother; now I was becoming *a* brother. I found a team again, something I'd had for so long before it just disappeared, leaving me behind. I wanted that back. I *needed* that back. That sense of belonging was enough to pull me in.

I started talking to the guys Stiff hooked me up with. It wasn't great at first. Fuck, who was I kidding? It still wasn't good, but it was better than before. I didn't like dredging up shit. Hearing the other guys talk about everything that hit them helped in a strange way. While I didn't really want to hear it, once I did, I realized I wasn't alone. I think that was a turning point for me.

Luckily, the flashbacks were becoming more scarce. I still had a few, but I'd take once every week to three or four times a day. It would take time, but I'd get there.

The guys even hooked Gabby up with their wives or significant others. She told me talking to them helped her to understand me better and what I was going through, which was good considering I was still trying to figure it the fuck out.

Gabby … Damn, I loved that woman. Sure, we had our ups and down, but she was it for me, and that was all that mattered.

Life was beginning to turn around, and I couldn't wait to see what the future brought. One thing I knew for a fact: it would include a ring on my woman's finger.

AUTHOR BIO

Ryan Michele found her passion in making fictional characters come to life. She loves being in an imaginative world where anything is possible and has a knack for special twists readers don't see coming.

She writes MC, Contemporary, Erotic, Paranormal, New Adult, Inspirational, and many more romances. And whether it's bikers, wolf shifters, mafia, or beyond, Ryan spends her time making sure her heroes are strong and her heroines match them at every turn.

When she isn't writing, Ryan is a mom and wife living in rural Illinois and reading by her pond in the warm sun.

STALK RYAN

Facebook: http://www.facebook.com/authorryanmichele
Twitter: http://www.twitter.com/Ryan_Michele
Website: http://www.authorryanmichele.net

OTHER TITLES BY RYAN MICHELE

In The Red
Devil's Due MC Book 1
©2016 Chelsea Camaron

The event that shook one small town to its core was never solved. The domino effect of one person's crime going unpunished is beyond measure.

He's no saint.

Dover 'Collector' Ragnes rides with only five brothers at his back. Nomads with no place to call home, they never stay in one place too long. Together, they are the Devil's Due MC, and their only purpose is to serve justice their way for unsolved crimes everywhere they go.

She's not afraid to call herself a sinner.

Emerson Flint still remembers the loss of her elementary school best friend. She is all grown up, but the memories still haunt her of the missing girl. Surrounding herself with men at the tattoo shop, she never questions her safety. Her life is her art. Her canvas is the skin of others.

However, danger is at her door.

Will Dover overcome the history he shares with Emerson in time? Will Emerson lead him to the retribution he has always sought?

Love, hate, anger, and passion collide as the time comes, and the devil demands his due.

Prologue

I HANG MY HEAD AND SIT IN SILENCE. The television blares as strangers move about our house. Some of them are trying to put together a search party, and others are here with food and attempts to comfort. I want them all to go away. I want to scream or break something. I want them all to stop looking at me like I should be beaten within an inch of my life then allowed to heal, only to get beaten again. Do I deserve that?

Hell yes, I do, and more.

There is no reprieve from the hell we are in. I would sell my soul to the Devil himself if I could turn back time. Only, I can't.

The reporter's voice breaks through all of the clamor.

"In local news tonight, a nine-year-old girl is missing, and authorities are asking for your help. Raleigh Ragnes was last seen by her seventeen-year-old brother. According to her parents, her brother was watching her afterschool when the child wandered outside and down the street on her pink and white bicycle with streamers on the handlebars.

"She was last known to have her brown hair braided with a yellow ribbon tied at the bottom. She was in a yellow shirt and a black denim dress that went to her knees. She wore white Keds with two different color laces; one is pink, and one is purple.

"There is a reward offered for any information leading to the successful return of

Raleigh to her home. Any information is appreciated and can be given by calling the local sheriff's department."

The television seems to screech on and on with other reports as if our world hasn't just crumbled. My mom's sobs only grow louder.

God, I'm an ass. Raleigh was whining all afternoon about going to Emerson's house. Those two are practically inseparable. She had made the trip numerous times to the Flint's home at the end of the cul-de-sac, so I didn't think twice about her leaving.

Gretchen was here, locked in my room with me. My hand was just making it down her pants when I yelled at Raleigh through the door to just go, not wanting the distraction. My mind was only occupied with getting into Gretchen's pants.

Only, while I was making my way to home base, my little sister never made it to her friend's house. None of us knew until dinner time arrived and my sister never came home. The phone call to Emerson's sent us all into a tailspin.

While other families watch the eleven o'clock news to simply be informed, for my family, my little sister is the news.

~ Three weeks later ~

THE TELEVISION SCREECHES once again. I thought the world had crumbled before, but now it's crushed and beyond repair. The reporter's tone is not any different than if they were giving the local weather as the words they speak crash through my ears.

"In local news tonight, the body of nine-year-old Raleigh Ragnes was found in a culvert pipe under Old Mill Road. Police are asking for anyone with any information to please come forward. The case is being treated as an open homicide."

In the matter of a month, my sister went from an innocent little girl to a case number, and in time, she will be nothing more than a file in a box. Everyone else may have called it cold and left it unsolved, but that's not who I am.

The domino effect of one person's crime going unpunished is beyond measure.

Chapter One

~Dover~

GIVING UP IS NOT AN OPTION *for me … It never has been.*

"There's a time and a place to die, brother," I say, scooping Trapper's drunk ass up off the dirty floor of the bar with both my hands under his armpits. "This ain't it."

It's a hole in the wall joint, the kind we find in small towns everywhere. It's a step above a shack on the outside, and the inside isn't much better: one open room, linoleum floor from the eighties. The bar runs the length of the space with a pair of saloon-style swinging doors closing off the stock room. We have gotten shit-faced in nicer, and we have spent more than our fair share of time in worse.

At the end of a long ride, a cold beer is a cold beer. Really, it doesn't matter to us where it's served as long as it has been on ice and is in a bottle.

"I'm nowhere near dying," he slurs, winking at the girl he has had on his lap for the last hour. She's another no name come guzzler in a slew of many we find throughout every city, town, and stop we make. "In fact, I'm not far from showing sweet thing here a little piece of heaven."

"Trapper." Judge, the calmest of us all, gets in his face. "She rode herself to oblivion until you fell off the stool. She's done got hers, man. Time to get you outta here so you can have some quality time huggin' Johnny tonight."

We all laugh as Trapper tries to shake me off. "Fuck all y'all. That pussy is mine tonight."

"Shithead, sober up. She's off to the bathroom to snort another line, and she won't be coming back for another ride on your thigh. Time to go, brother," Rowdy says sternly.

Trapper turns to the redheaded, six-foot, six-inch man of muscle and gives him a shit-eating grin. "Aw, Rowdy, are you gonna be my sober sister tonight?"

I wrap my arm around Trapper, pulling him into a tight hold. "Shut your mouth now!"

He holds up his hands in surrender, and we make our way out of the bar.

Another night, another dive. Tomorrow is a new day and a new ride.

Currently, we are in Leed, Alabama for a stop off. The green of the trees, the rough patches of the road—it all does nothing to bring any of us out of the haunting darkness we each carry.

We're nomads—no place to call home, and that's how we like it. The six of us have been a club of our own creation for almost two years now. We all have a story to tell. We all have a reason we do what we do. None of us are noble or honorable. We strike in the most unlikely of places and times, all based on our own brand of rules and systems.

Fuck the government. Fuck their laws. And damn sure fuck the judicial system.

Once your name is tainted, no matter how good you are, you will never be clean in the eyes of society. I'm walking, talking, can't sleep at night proof of it. Well, good fucking deal. I have learned society's version of clean is everything I don't ever want to be.

The scum that blends into our communities and with our children, the cons that can run a game, they think they are untouchable. The number of crimes outnumber the crime fighters. The lines between law abiding and law breaking blur every day inside every precinct. I know, because I carried the badge and thought I could be a change in the world. Then I found out everything is just as corrupt for the people upholding the law as those breaking it.

Day in and day out, watching cops run free who deserve to be behind bars more than the criminals they put away takes its toll. Everyone has a line in the sand, and once they cross it, they don't turn back. I found mine, and I found the brotherhood in the Devil's Due MC. Six guys who have all seen our own fair share of corruption in the justice system. Six guys who don't give a fuck about the consequences.

Well, that's where me and my boys ride in. No one's above the devil getting his due. We are happy to serve up our own kind of punishments that most certainly fit the crimes committed, and we don't bother with the current legal system's view of justice served.

We're wayward souls, damaged men, who have nothing more than vengeance on our minds.

"Fucking bitch, she got my pants wet," Trapper says, just realizing she really did get off on his thigh and left him behind. "You see this shit?" He points at his leg.

Trapper mad is good. He will become focused rather than let the alcohol keep him in a haze. He could use some time to dry up. He's sharp. His attention to detail saves our asses in city after city. However, things get too close to home when we ride to the deep south like this, and he can't shake the ghosts in the closets of his mind. At five-foot-ten and a rock solid one eighty-five, he's a force of controlled power. He uses his brain more than his brawn, but he won't back down in a brawl, either.

We help him get outside the dive bar we spent the last two hours inside, tossing beer back and playing pool. Outside, the fresh winter air hits him, and he shakes his head.

"It's not that cold," X says, slapping Trapper in the face. "Sober up, sucka."

Trapper smiles as he starts to ready his mind. As drunk as he is, he knows he has to have his head on straight to ride.

"Flank him on either side, but stay behind in case he lays her down. We only have four miles back to the hotel," I order, swinging my leg over my Harley Softail Slim and cranking it. The rumble soothes all that stays wound tight inside me. The vibration reminds me of the power under me.

Blowing out a breath, I tap the gas tank. "Ride for Raleigh," I whisper and point to the night sky. *Never forget,* I remind myself before I move to ride. My hands on the bars, twisting the throttle, I let the bike move me and lift my feet to rest on the pegs. As each of my brother's mount, I pull out, knowing they will hit the throttle and catch me, so I relax as the road passes under me.

We ride as six with no ties to anyone or anything from one city to the next. We have a bond. We are the only family for each other, and we keep it that way. No attachments, no commitments, and that means no casualties.

We are here by choice. Any man can leave the club and our life behind at any time. I trust these men with my life and with my death. When my time is called, they will move on with the missions as they come.

We don't often let one another drink and drive, but coming south, Trapper needed to cut loose for a bit. He may be drunk, yet once the wind hits his face, he will be solid. He always is.

At the no-tell motel we are crashing at, X takes Trapper with him to one of the three shit-ass rooms we booked while Judge and Rowdy go to the other. The place has seen better days, probably thirty years ago. It's a place to shit, shower, and maybe, if I can keep the nightmares away, sleep. I have never needed anything fancy, and tonight is no different.

I give them a half salute as they close their doors and lock down for the night.

Deacon heads on into our room. Always a man of few words and interaction, he doesn't look back or give me any indication that he cares if I follow or stay behind.

I give myself the same moment I take every night and stand out under the stars to smoke.

I look up. Immediately, I can hear her tiny voice in my mind, making up constellations all her own. Raleigh was once a rambunctious little girl. She was afraid of nothing. She loved the night sky and wishing upon all the stars.

Another city, another life, I wish it was another time, but one thing I know is that there is no turning back time. If I could, I would. Not just for me, but for all five of us.

I light my cigarette and take a deep drag. Inhaling, I hold it in my lungs before I blow out. The burn, the taste, and the touch of it to my lips don't ease the thoughts in my mind. Another night is upon us, and it's yet another night Raleigh will never come home.

The receptionist steps out beside me. She isn't the one who was here when we checked in earlier. When she smiles up at me, I can tell she has been waiting on us. Guess the trailer trash from day shift chatted up her replacement. Well, at least this one has nice teeth. Day shift definitely doesn't have dental on her benefit plan here.

"Go back inside," I bark, not really in the mood for company.

"I'm entitled to a break," she challenges with a southern drawl.

"If you want a night with a biker, I'm not the one," I try to warn her off.

"Harley, leather, cigarettes, and sexy—yeah, I think you're the one … for tonight, that is." She comes over and reaches out for the edges of my cut.

I grab her wrists. "You don't touch my cut."

She bites her bottom lip with a sly smile. "Oh, rules. I can play by the rules, big daddy."

I drop her hands and walk in a circle around her before standing in front of her then backing her to the wall. I take another drag of my cigarette and blow the smoke into her face. "I'm not your fucking daddy." I take another long drag. Smoke blows out with each word as I let her know. "If you wanna fuck, we'll fuck. Make no mistake, though, I'm not in the mood to chat, cuddle, or kiss. I'm a man; I'll fuck, and that's it."

She leans her head back, testing me.

"Hands against the wall," I order, and she slaps her palms against the brick behind her loudly.

Her chest rises and falls dramatically as her breathing increases. She keeps licking and biting her lips.

"You want a ride on the wild side?"

She nods, pushing her tits out at me.

"You wet for me?" I ask, and she giggles while nodding. "If you want me to get hard and stay hard, you don't fucking make a sound. That giggling shit is annoying as fuck."

Immediately, she snaps her mouth shut.

I yank her shirt up and pull her bra over her titties without unhooking it. Her nipples point out in the cold night air.

"You cold or is that for me?" I ask, flicking her nipple harshly.

"You," she whispers breathlessly.

I yank the waistband of her stretchy pants down, pulling her panties with them. Her curls glisten with her arousal under the street light.

With her pants at her ankles, I turn her around to face the wall.

"Bend over, grab your ankles. You don't speak, don't touch me, and you don't move. If you want a wild ride with a biker, I'm gonna give you one you'll never forget."

While she positions herself, I grab a condom from my wallet and unbutton my four button jeans enough to release my cock. While stroking myself a few times to get fully erect, part of me considers just walking away. However, I'm a man, and pussy is pussy. No matter what my mood, it's a place to sink into for a time.

Covering myself carefully, I spread her ass cheeks and slide myself inside her slick cunt.

The little whore is more than ready.

I close my eyes and picture a dark-haired beauty with ink covering her arms and a tight cunt made just for me. I can almost hear the gravelly voice of my dream woman as she moans my name, pushing back to take me deeper, thrust after thrust.

I roll my hips as the receptionist struggles to keep herself in position.

Raising my hand, I come down on the exposed globe of her ass cheek. "Dirty fucking girl." I spank her again. "I'm not your fucking daddy, but I'll give you what he obviously didn't." I spank her again and thrust. "Head down between your legs. Watch me fuck your pussy."

She does as instructed and watches as I continue slamming into her. Stilling, I reach down and twist her nipples as she pushes back on me.

Her moans get louder as I move, gripping her hips and pistoning in and out of her.

I slap her ass again. "I said quiet."

I push deep, my hips hitting her ass, and she shakes as her orgasm overtakes her.

"Fuck me!" she wails.

I slam in and out, in and out, faster and faster, until I explode inside the condom.

She isn't holding her ankles by the time I'm done. She's still head down, bent over with her back against the wall as her hands hang limply like the rest of her body, trembling in aftershocks.

Pulling out, I toss the condom on the ground and walk away, buttoning my pants back up.

"Collector," I hear X yell my road name from his doorway. "You ruined that one." He is smoking a cigarette. It's obvious he watched the show.

The noise has Judge coming to his door and giving me a nod of approval.

I look over my shoulder to see the bitch still hasn't moved. Her pussy is out in the air, ass up, head down, and she's still moaning. Desperate, needy, it's not my thing.

"I need a shower," I say, giving X a two finger salute before going into my own room. Deacon is already in bed and doesn't move as I go straight back to the shit-ass bathroom to clean up.

I wasn't lying. I smell like a bar, and now I smell the skank stench of easy pussy. I have needs, but I can't help wondering what it would be like to have to work for my release just once. It's not in my cards, though. Just like this town, this ride, and that broad, it's on to the next for me and my bothers of the Devil's Due MC.

Amazon

http://amzn.to/1nGPebJ

About the Author

USA Today Bestselling author Chelsea Camaron is a small town Carolina girl with a big imagination. She is a wife and mom chasing her dreams. She writes contemporary romance, erotic suspense, and psychological thrillers. She loves to write blue-collar men who have real problems with a fictional twist. From mechanics to bikers to oil riggers to smokejumpers, bar owners, and beyond, she loves a strong hero who works hard and plays harder.

Chelsea can be found on social media at:
Facebook: www.facebook.com/authorchelseacamaron
Twitter: @chelseacamaron
Email: chelseacamaron@gmail.com

Made in the USA
Middletown, DE
03 February 2017